THE BAYOU BULLETIN

Goings-On Around Town
A monthly column by
Ms. Emilie Legendre

The lazy days of summer are over, but our sleepy little town has seen its fair share of excitement. Just last week Shelby Delacroix was driving down the bayou road when someone hit her car with a load of buckshot, shattering her windshield. Although she considers the occurrence simply a matter of being in the wrong place at the wrong time, the incident has left many people wondering. Especially after the disastrous fire last month at Delacroix Stables. Is somebody holding a grudge against the Delacroix clan?

But maybe one grudge has finally been put to rest. It seems that after an absence of ten years, Madeline Belanger Delacroix has finally come back to the town that has missed her charm and sophistication since her divorce from our newest judge, the Honorable Justin Delacroix. If I hadn't seen it with my own eyes, I'd never believe our esteemed Justin would take to squiring around town a girl young enough to be his daughter. His ex is definitely in for a big surprise...if she still cares, that is.

Margot Dalton is acknowledged
as the author of this work.

ISBN 0-373-82570-6

FRENCH TWIST

This edition published by arrangement with Harlequin Books S.A.

DELTA JUSTICE

French Twist

MARGOT DALTON

Harlequin Books

TORONTO • NEW YORK • LONDON
AMSTERDAM • PARIS • SYDNEY • HAMBURG
STOCKHOLM • ATHENS • TOKYO • MILAN
MADRID • WARSAW • BUDAPEST • AUCKLAND

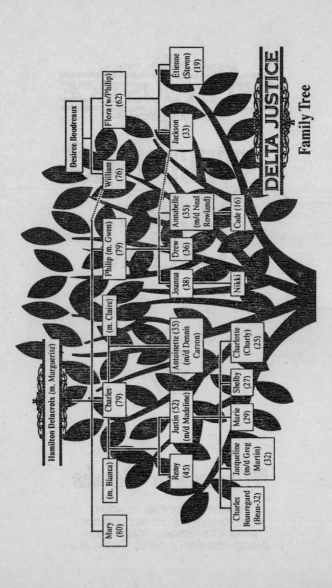

DELTA JUSTICE
Family Tree

Hamilton Delacroix (m. Marguerite)

Desiree Boudreaux

Mary (80)

(m. Bianca)

Charles (79)

(m. Claire)

Philip (m. Gwen) (79)

William (76)

Flora (w/Philip) (62)

Justin (52) (m/d Madeline)

Antoinette (35) (m/d Dennis Carron)

Remy (45)

Joanna (38)

Drew (36)

Annabelle (35) (m/d Neal Rowland)

Jackson (33)

Étienne (Steven) (19)

Charles Beauregard (Beau-32)

Jacqueline (m/d Greg Martin) (32)

Marie (29)

Shelby (27)

Charlotte (Charly) (25)

Nikki

Cade (16)

CAST OF CHARACTERS

Madeline Belanger—Ex-wife of Justin Delacroix. She's come back to Bayou Beltane for one reason—to discover who's behind the attacks on her children. She was looking for trouble, but found love instead...with her children's father.

Justin Delacroix—Newly appointed judge. Ten years ago he lost the only woman he'd ever loved. But now that he has a second chance, is he any closer to becoming the man she wants?

Shelby Delacroix—Daughter of Justin and Madeline. She's been fixing her dad up for years with no luck. How was she to guess that the only woman for Justin was her mother?

Claudia Landry—Remy's assistant and bait-shop operator. Justin taught her how to act like a lady. Unfortunately everybody in town thinks she's his woman, too.

Dear Reader,

I was so happy to be included as one of the writers in the DELTA JUSTICE series, because I love both the setting and the characters.

Louisiana is truly unique. It seems to hold the same place within the soul of America that Quebec has in the hearts and minds of Canadians like myself. Beautiful, warm and easygoing, Louisiana retains its own texture and ambience, its own history, personality and a fierce sense of pride.

And I was also fascinated by the wide-ranging and colorful Delacroix family, who are the very embodiment of southern Louisiana. Of all these interesting people, though, I couldn't help becoming intrigued by Justin Delacroix, whose personality changed and developed throughout the series in a fashion irresistible to any writer. When I finally realized Justin might have a second chance at happiness with his beloved ex-wife, Madeline, whom he hadn't seen for ten years, I was utterly hooked.

I hope you, too, enjoy this new story of life in Bayou Beltane, a world that's rich, colorful and passionate, with a uniquely *French Twist*.

Warm best wishes,

Margot Dalton

CHAPTER ONE

MADELINE WOKE ON SUNDAY morning with a craving for *pain perdu,* once upon a time a favorite breakfast treat. She lay quietly in her bed and stared at the ceiling, trying to convince herself that what she really wanted was half a grapefruit and a bagel.

After all, a woman of fifty-one didn't maintain her trim figure by gobbling fat and sugar at the breakfast table. Madeline couldn't even remember the last time she'd eaten something so sinfully self-indulgent when she was all alone.

But the distressing urge persisted. Finally she got up, slipped into a silk dressing gown and belted it around her waist, then pulled on a pair of embroidered slippers and made her way downstairs to the kitchen.

Madeline lived in a loft-style condo near the downtown core of Aspen. The place was ruinously expensive, but she'd chosen this particular building because the apartments weren't as quaint and consciously rustic as most of the accommodations in the crowded ski and holiday resort.

"If I'm going to be living in a bunkhouse," she'd commented to her daughters, "then I prefer it be a bunkhouse with crystal chandeliers and nice plaster cornices on the ceiling moldings."

Despite Madeline's jokes, the apartment was hardly a bunkhouse, nor was it luxurious enough for chandeliers and cornices.

But it was a very comfortable place, and her light, sure touch with furniture and decorating made it beautiful.

"Honestly, I don't know how you do it, Mama," Jax had commented wistfully during her most recent visit, soon after she'd announced her pregnancy. "Nothing matches, yet everything looks perfect. If anybody else tried to put Shaker-style chairs with that rosewood table, the whole effect would be ridiculous. When you do the same thing, it's breathtaking."

Madeline had laughed and hugged her daughter. "People are always so concerned about matching. I never think about such things. Look at my home, Jacqueline." She'd waved her hand at the array of colors and fabrics, of different woods and styles of furniture, of sleek modern pieces standing next to antiques. "One thing unites all of this, you know, and makes it blend together."

"And what's that, Mama?"

Madeline kissed the younger woman's tanned cheek. "The fact that every single object in this apartment is something I love."

Jax grinned and settled into a soft leather armchair, propping her stockinged feet on a little petit-point stool. "Then no wonder I feel so comfortable here, Mama," she said. "Because you're something that *I* love."

Madeline smiled, remembering. It was wonderful, almost miraculous the way cool, elusive Jax seemed to have been softened by her relationship with Matt Taggart and his children.

Madeline had met all of them in April when they flew up to Aspen for some late-spring skiing, and she'd liked Matt and his children immediately. She especially loved the way Jax seemed so warm and maternal, so at peace with herself and the rest of the family.

At one time, Jax had been furious with her mother for leaving Justin after more than twenty years of marriage. In fact, all the girls had been angry and upset in those days, Charlotte and Shelby most of all.

But everything seemed to be changing in the lives of Madeline's daughters. Now Charly had found a mate, too. Even Beau had fallen in love.

Madeline brushed at the tears that seemed frequently to overwhelm her these days. It made her sad to realize such momentous things were happening in the lives of her children, and she was more than a thousand miles away.

She forced herself to put the unhappy thoughts from her mind, wandered into the tiny kitchen and took out a loaf of day-old French bread, eggs, milk and a copper skillet. She cut the thick slices of bread into strips, dipped them in beaten egg and milk, fried them lightly in oil until they were golden and crusty, then dusted them with cinnamon and icing sugar.

Finally she put a cup of coffee, a crystal jug of maple syrup and the plateful of rich food on a tray, and carried everything to her glassed-in terrace, where she could enjoy the view while she ate.

At this hour of the morning, in the privacy of her apartment, Madeline looked much more casual than she did at work in her downtown art gallery. Her dark hair tumbled around her face, framing the wonderful bone structure, huge gray eyes and delicate skin, which had made her a beauty in her youth and had not diminished in her middle years.

She smiled wistfully as she gazed out the window. The morning was glorious, the trees a riot of autumn colors on this crisp morning in early October. Snow had fallen during the night in the mountain passes, dusting sunlit peaks with a dazzling blanket of white.

"Lovely. The most beautiful place in the world," Madeline whispered aloud.

But despite the splendor beyond her windows she found

herself suddenly overcome with a passionate, wholly irrational longing for southern Louisiana, a wave of homesickness so deep and visceral that it literally took her breath away.

She got up to pour herself another cup of coffee, struggling once again to hold back the flow of tears while she tried to determine what had triggered all this nostalgia.

Maybe it was the *pain perdu,* so powerfully evocative of breakfasts at the big house near the lake, surrounded by ancient live oaks hung with Spanish moss, and peacocks trailing their feathers arrogantly as they strutted across the grass.

Madeline could actually see her children in the kitchen, like figures from a dream world, enjoying the special Sunday morning breakfast away from the adults.

"Mama makes the best *pain perdu* in the whole county," five-year-old Marie said. Her black curls glistened in the sunlight, her face was smeared with syrup and she had a lacy white bib tied around her neck to protect her Sunday dress.

With characteristic determination, Jax and little Shelby were both eating silently, trying to devour as much of the rich treat as possible before their grandfather arrived in the doorway to announce the car was leaving for church.

"That's because Mama's from France," Beau said loftily to his younger sister as he plied the syrup jug. "And *pain perdu* is really French toast."

"But you know, darling, we didn't eat like this in Paris when I was growing up," Madeline told her son from the counter where she and Odelle were mixing more eggs and milk.

"What did you eat for breakfast when you were a little girl, Mama?" All the children loved to hear stories about Madeline's girlhood in Paris.

"Actually, *Maman* and *Papa* favored the English style

of breakfast, with things like calf's liver and lamb's kidney and kippered herrings in rows of silver chafing dishes on the sideboard.''

"Yuck!" Beau shouted.

"Bwead!" Baby Charly effectively put an end to the discussion by banging her silver teething mug on the tray of her high chair with a deafening clatter. "Want bwead!"

Madeline sipped her coffee and, lost in her memories, smiled dreamily at the rustling veil of leaves beyond the terrace.

She could almost hear their childish talk and laughter, feel the mellow sunlight in the old kitchen with its red brick floor and heavy roof beams. Those distant years with the children always seemed bathed in sunshine when she recalled them, though there must have been cold, rainy days, too.

Madeline frowned and toyed idly with the handle of her coffee cup.

The sweetest memories of all were the ones that involved Justin, times when he'd spent the occasional Sunday morning with his family, gone with them to the beach to look for shells or played football on the lawn in the mellow, rainbow-colored sunsets of the bayou.

But most of the time Justin had been off at work or playing golf with his business associates, and she'd been alone with the children....

The doorbell rang, startling her.

She went out through the kitchen to the terrace and opened the door to find a small person gazing up at her solemnly, clutching a plastic-wrapped sheaf of romaine lettuce.

"Hello, Madeline," the child said. "Daddy says thanks very much for the lettuce you loaned him. We bought some more when we went grocery shopping yesterday but he forgot to give it to you."

"Good morning, Jennifer." Madeline smiled at her visitor, took the sheaf of lettuce and drew the little girl inside the kitchen. "My goodness, don't you look pretty today."

Jennifer was seven years old, small and wiry, with a cap of dark hair cut into shiny bangs and a drift of freckles across a straight little nose. In fact, she looked so much like Shelby at the same age that Madeline started to feel wistful again.

"See, Madeline? I'm wearing my new outfit," Jennifer announced.

She twirled around in the center of the kitchen without self-consciousness, looking adorable in red tartan leggings and a fleecy white top trimmed with plaid collar and cuffs.

"That's very, very chic," Madeline said solemnly. "Tartan is fashionable this year, you know."

Jennifer rewarded her with a winsome, gap-toothed smile, then sniffed the air like a hunting dog. "Hey, what smells good?"

"I'm having *pain perdu* for breakfast," Madeline said gravely. "Would you care to join me?"

The little girl hesitated, suddenly cautious. "What is it?"

"*Pain perdu?* I think you'd probably call it French toast." Madeline dipped a slice of the bread into whipped egg white and turned the heat on under the frying pan. "See? I soak the bread in egg, fry it until each slice turns gold, and then dust it with sugar and cinnamon."

"Yummy."

Jennifer pressed closer to watch, her sleek little head resting against Madeline's arm.

"I'm real hungry," the child announced after a moment, rubbing her stomach under the fleecy top.

"Haven't you had breakfast yet?" Madeline turned the bread lightly with a spatula.

Jennifer shook her head firmly enough to set the mop of

hair swinging. "Daddy's still in bed with Kelly." She made a small grimace of distaste.

"Does Daddy know you're here?"

"I told him I was coming over," Jennifer reported. "He said I should bring the lettuce and stay for at least half an hour, but I don't know why."

Madeline concentrated on the toast and wisely said nothing.

Jennifer's father, Tate O'Sullivan, was in his early thirties and lived in one of the adjoining condos. Tate had divorced his wife, Tanya, three years earlier, when Tanya began to express more desire to be a professional skier than a full-time mother. Now Tate entertained a series of attractive young ladies at his condo, and Jennifer saw her mother only rarely, especially during the fall and winter months when Tanya was busy with her training and competition.

Tate O'Sullivan was also Madeline's business partner in a small gallery in downtown Aspen called Bare Bones, which supplied costly baubles to the rich and famous.

She and Tate had opened the gallery seven years ago, when he'd needed a place to exhibit his wildlife art and Madeline had needed something to do, as well as a way to invest part of her divorce settlement and the inheritance from her parents. Their venture had succeeded beyond their wildest dreams and was now one of the most prosperous galleries in all of Aspen, a town famous for its trendy little shops and boutiques.

They had a busy three-part operation comprised of a comfortable workroom in the back where Tate and Madeline both did professional-quality paintings, a gallery where they displayed and sold their work, and a boutique that specialized in all kinds of exotic jewelry and souvenir items.

Over the years she and Tate had become friends as well as business partners, and she was very fond of little Jennifer, who often struck her as a rather lonely and wistful child.

Madeline took a plate from a glass-fronted cabinet and set the French toast on it carefully, then carried the plate into the dining room.

"We'll eat at the table where we can see the mountains," she told Jennifer.

The little girl looked around, sighing with pleasure. "It's so pretty here."

Jennifer climbed into a chair by the table and sat up very straight. She watched covertly as Madeline smoothed a napkin over her housecoat. Then she did the same, trying to look as if she regularly dined in such formal surroundings.

Madeline hid a smile. "When my little girls used to have breakfast with us on Sunday morning," she said, "they always had a special treat."

"What?" Jennifer asked, her eyes bright.

"They each had coffee from one of my Wedgwood cups. Would you like some?"

Jennifer's mouth dropped open. "I get to drink coffee?" she breathed.

Madeline got up to take one of the lovely, delicate blue cups from the sideboard. "Just a very little," she said, "with lots of milk. You may add as much sugar as you like, and you must remember to be very, very careful of the cup."

"Okay."

Jennifer watched with anticipation while her hostess poured coffee from the silver pot and added a generous serving of milk.

The little girl stirred sugar into her pale brew, then sipped it lustily and popped a slice of French toast into her mouth.

"This is nice," she said again, while syrup dribbled down her chin.

Madeline reached forward gently to wipe the child's

mouth with a napkin. "Well, you know, I'm very grateful for the company," she said. "Because I was feeling lonely this morning."

Jennifer gave her a bright glance. "Daddy says you have a boyfriend."

"Oh, does he, now?" Madeline said with amusement. "Well, I've met a gentleman who takes me out occasionally to dinner and the symphony, but we can hardly call him a boyfriend."

"What's his name?" Jennifer asked, eating another strip of French toast and washing it down with a huge mouthful of her "coffee."

"Gerald Stapleton. He owns several businesses in Denver, and he's a very nice man."

"But not a boyfriend?"

"No, dear. Not a boyfriend."

"Daddy has lots of girlfriends," Jennifer volunteered after a moment. "Kelly is one of his girlfriends."

"I know that, *chérie.*"

"I'd rather have a daddy and a mommy than a daddy and a lot of girlfriends," Jennifer said casually, tracing the handle of the cream jug with a sticky forefinger.

Madeline considered. "I think most people would rather have it that way."

"What about your little girls?" Jennifer said. "I mean, the ones who used to drink coffee with you."

"What about them?"

"Did they live with you or their daddy?"

"They lived with both of us," Madeline said. "Their father and I didn't separate until they were almost all grown up."

"That would be better," Jennifer said after some thought.

Privately, Madeline agreed. In fact, it was one of the

reasons she'd stayed at Riverwood for all those years after her relationship with Justin grew so lonely and difficult.

She simply could never bear to drag the girls away from their friends and their life on the bayou, and she couldn't bring herself to leave them behind.

But eventually the time had come when it was impossible to do anything else....

"Why do you look so sad?" Jennifer peered up at her curiously.

"Do I look sad?" Madeline forced herself to smile at the little girl. "Well, I certainly don't mean to. I'm very happy to have your company, Jennifer. This is a great treat for me."

"I can't stay long," the child announced. "Daddy and Kelly are taking me to the football game today."

She looked at the Mickey Mouse watch on her thin wrist, a recent gift from her father. Jennifer was inordinately proud of the watch, although she couldn't tell time yet.

"Have I been here a half hour?" she asked, holding the watch up for Madeline's inspection.

Madeline leaned over to consult Mickey's hands with grave seriousness. "Almost. By the time you've helped me to clear the table, I'm sure it will be at least half an hour."

She and her small guest carried the cups and plates into the kitchen and tidied the countertop, chatting amiably. When Jennifer left, running back through drifts of fallen leaves to her own condo, Madéline stood on the terrace and watched.

She went back inside and rinsed the dishes, put away the Wedgwood cups and the silver coffee service and hung the dish towel on its rack, then began to wander restlessly around her apartment.

The sun drifted behind a bank of clouds, casting most of the rooms into shadow. For once, Madeline's pleasant apartment with its gracious furnishings was no comfort to her at all.

Still feeling chilled, she climbed the stairs to change into woolen slacks and a turtleneck, brushed her hair and dabbed on some lipstick, then went downstairs again.

At last, unable to bear the silence any longer, she picked up the phone and dialed, waiting tensely for an answer.

A woman's voice responded after several rings. "Delacroix residence, Mary speaking."

"Aunt Mary? It's Madeline. How are you?"

"Madeline! How wonderful to hear your voice. I was just thinking about you."

"Were you, dear?" Madeline asked wistfully.

Except for her children, of course, Justin's Aunt Mary seemed to be the one member of the Delacroix family that she missed the most.

Madeline pictured the older woman's tall, awkward body, her endearing bony face and gentle hands. Aunt Mary had always been her friend, even during those early years when both Madeline's family and Justin's had turned their backs in anger and left the young couple to struggle along on their own.

After the twins—Beau and Jax—were born, it was Aunt Mary who came to help, though she'd never raised a child of her own. She gave freely of her time, even ignored Justin's stiff-necked objections and spent money from her own funds to hire a nursemaid for Madeline, who was practically numb with fatigue in those days.

And finally it was Aunt Mary, with her soft-voiced stubbornness, who'd managed to effect the reconciliation with Justine's father and stepmother. She'd brought all of them together one afternoon in her own house: Charles and Claire, Remy and little Antoinette, Justin and Madeline and the twins, and told them with astonishing firmness that nobody could leave until all of them kissed and made up.

Soon after that, Justin and Madeline had moved into the big house at Riverwood with Charles and his family, and life had become so much easier.

But sometimes, even after all these years, Madeline still missed the little cottage in Bayou Beltane where they'd lived at first, before Beau and Jax were born, when she and Justin had been young and so much in love....

She put the thoughts hastily from her mind and listened to Aunt Mary, who was telling her about Uncle William's arthritis and a new herbal remedy from Desiree that gave him some relief.

"It must seem rather awkward," Madeline said shyly, "to have Desiree caring for Uncle William." She paused, feeling embarrassed. "You know, because of..."

"What do you mean, dear?" Mary asked, sounding genuinely puzzled. "Desiree's always looked after all of us."

Madeline stared at the receiver in disbelief, wondering what to say.

Aunt Mary didn't know! Her mind whirled. If Aunt Mary hadn't been told the truth about Desiree's past, it meant William didn't know, either, since the two old people had no secrets from each other.

Madeline felt baffled impatience, followed by a slow-growing outrage.

This was so typical, exactly what she'd always hated about her ex-husband's family. They had so many dark, hidden things buried away in their family history, and none of them were ever brought into the open. Secrets were the air they breathed.

After all these years away from the Delacroix, she'd almost forgotten how stifling and infuriating they could be.

"Madeline?" Mary was saying. "Is something the matter, dear?"

Nothing! Madeline wanted to shout. *Nothing's wrong at all, Aunt Mary, except that Desiree is actually Uncle Wil-*

*liam's birth mother, you know, but it seems nobody's both-
ered to tell you the truth.*

Or him, for that matter…

She couldn't do it. After all these years away, the last
thing she wanted was to involve herself in all that dark,
swirling chaos again.

"Is Uncle William feeling all right otherwise?" Madeline pictured the gentle old priest as she'd last seen him,
his face luminous with concern for others.

"It's been hard for him to adjust to retirement," Mary
said. "But he seems to be coping well. He spends even
more time in prayer than he used to, and I know it's a real
comfort to him."

"And how about you?" Madeline asked. "I miss you so
much, Aunt Mary. I'd give anything to be sitting on your
veranda right now with a nice tall glass of iced tea and a
cat in my lap."

"You should come for a visit, child. I haven't seen you
for so long."

"Yes, you have. I was out just a few months ago when
Charly was recuperating after her accident, remember?"

"Oh, that," Mary scoffed. "That was such a whirlwind
affair, you didn't even have a chance to visit with anybody."

"I know," Madeline said. "I was so worried about her."

"Well, she's fine now," Mary said. "The girl's as sassy
and full of jokes as ever, and so much in love with that
handsome young man of hers that she can hardly see
straight."

"Really?" Madeline said, with a little catch in her voice.
"You know, it seems all the—the children are falling in
love. I feel so far away."

"Maybe Charly will settle down now that she's found a
man she cares about."

"But we can't push her," Madeline said gently, recalling

her own miserable experience in marriage. "A woman must be allowed to choose her own path if she's going to find happiness."

"That wasn't how it was done in my day. When I was young, a woman had no say over what happened to her life. The men got together and decided everything."

"Oh, yes, that's what they did. And a dreadful mess they made of things, too," Madeline said with a grimace.

"Yes," Mary agreed. "A perfectly dreadful mess." She sounded so sorrowful and distant that Madeline was alarmed.

"Are you really all right, darling?" she asked. "Are you taking good care of yourself?"

"I'm trying. But the doctor said I should avoid all stress, and I swear, I truly don't know how that's possible in this family. Not when such terrible things are happening."

Madeline's hand tightened suddenly on the receiver. "What terrible things, Aunt Mary?"

There was a strained silence.

"Aunt Mary? What's going on?"

"Nobody wants you to know," Mary said reluctantly. "They don't want you to be worried when you're so far away."

"Aunt Mary, what are you talking about?" Madeline felt a rising panic. "Is this about one of my children? I want you to be honest with me."

There was a pause while Mary evidently struggled with herself, then gave in. "Has Shelby told you anything about what's been happening to her lately?"

"She…" Madeline stared blankly at the window. "No, just that she's still having problems with Travis, and I'm sure she misses him. Why, Aunt Mary? Is something going on with Shelby?"

"I don't know if I should—"

"Aunt Mary, tell me!"

"Shelby was driving on the bayou road last week when somebody hit her car with a load of buckshot. The windshield was broken all to pieces, and she almost ran off the road."

Madeline sank into a nearby chair, trembling with shock.

"Somebody shot at her?" she whispered. "Aunt Mary...what on earth is happening down there? Were the police notified? Do they know who did it?"

"Everybody thinks it was just some hunter with a bad aim. Charly says they'll shoot at a coon on the veranda railing even when Granny's sitting behind it in her rocker. She and Shelby laughed the whole thing off."

"Laughed it off," Madeline echoed faintly. "Dear Lord."

"Well, they could be right," Mary said. "It might have been an accident. Stray gunshots happen all the time around here. But how about those strange phone calls she's been getting, and that other time when somebody shot at Beau and Shelby when they were riding in the woods? It's all pretty upsetting, don't you think? Especially on top of what's just happened."

Madeline huddled in the chair, feeling faint and sick.

"What happened?" she whispered.

"The barn burned down. It was so—"

"The *barn* burned down?" Her mouth turned to dust, and her throat constricted with fear. "Were any of the...Aunt Mary, was anybody hurt?"

"Beau worked like a madman to save the horses. He has some...bad burns," Mary said with reluctance. "But," she added hastily, "he's not in the hospital or anything. Desiree's looking after him, and his hands are healing well."

"Dear God, his hands," Madeline whispered, trying not to cry. "And the others? Shelby...is she all right?"

"She wasn't hurt in the fire, if that's what you mean. But she's..." Mary's voice trailed off, then strengthened again. "I'm worried. Especially when she's been involved in..." Again she paused.

Since her heart attack, Aunt Mary's thoughts occasionally seemed rambling and disconnected. Madeline felt another sharp stab of concern. "What's Shelby gotten herself into?"

Mary sighed. "You know what a bulldog that girl has always been whenever she sinks her teeth into something."

"Oh, yes," Madeline said grimly. "Yes, I know what Shelby's like."

"I don't know what's going on, but I'm afraid she'll come to grief. Sometimes I wonder if she's begun poking into all that old family history, even though I asked her not to."

"What family history, Aunt Mary?"

Madeline strained to hear, wondering if Mary was crying. But when the old woman spoke again, she seemed more composed.

"Desiree is worried, too. She says terrible things will happen to the living if the dead are disturbed."

Madeline shivered. She'd grown up in a cosmopolitan, scholarly household, far from the ancient superstitions and dark practices of the bayou. But she'd known Desiree Boudreaux all of her adult life, and she believed in the old woman's powers.

"Does she see danger to Shelby?"

"She sees death and disaster. She says the ghosts of the past will rise up in anger if they're not left at peace."

"Oh, God..." Madeline sat in her apartment, looking at the tranquil glories of an October morning in the Colorado Rockies. But her mind and heart were in that murky swampland beyond the Delta.

"I think," she said at last, "that it's probably not ghosts threatening Shelby."

She remembered what Shelby had told her about the custody case involving Lyle Masson, his power in Louisiana and his terrible anger when the young upstart lawyer had thwarted his attempt to recover his son.

It wasn't good to make enemies of men like that.

But Shelby had always been so impetuous. Ever since childhood, she'd stood up to bullies and never thought about the consequences.

"Look, I think I'm going to come out there," Madeline said impulsively. "I want to see for myself what's going on."

"Thank God," Mary whispered. "You know, I've been feeling so alone in all this. I'm glad you're coming, Madeline."

"I don't know what I can do, though. I've certainly never been able to do much with Shelby."

"That's true, but at least you can have a look around and see if Desiree and I are just old women imagining things, or if you can sense a dark cloud hanging over the family."

"Aunt Mary, listen…" Madeline began.

"Yes, dear?"

"No parties or anything, you hear? I don't want to attend any family gatherings. I just want a chance to talk with people on my own. Is Justin…" She hesitated. "Is he around much these days?"

"He's not working at the firm anymore now that he's a judge, but he seems as busy as ever."

Madeline considered. "I suppose I'll have to meet with him," she said reluctantly. "He might know something about what's been going on with Shelby."

"Didn't you see him when you were out here last winter?"

"Not once. I stayed in New Orleans and managed to avoid everybody but the children. And that's certainly the way I'd prefer things to stay, but…'' Madeline's voice trailed off.

"You know, Desiree's worried about Justin as well,'' Mary said unexpectedly.

Madeline glanced at the telephone receiver in surprise. "Why? Is he upsetting the ghosts from the past, too?''

"Desiree says he's lost himself, and he's too much alone. She says he needs to find a path that's right for him.''

"Well, I think that's probably true for all of us, isn't it?''

"Perhaps. Will you stay with us when you come? William would love to see you.''

Madeline thought wistfully about the old Cajun-style bungalow where Mary and William lived. Shady and tranquil as it was, it was just across the footbridge from Justin's big house at Riverwood….

She shook her head. "I don't think so. I'll take a room at the hotel, and come over to visit you as soon as I arrive.''

"I can hardly wait to see you.'' Mary sounded so eager that Madeline couldn't have changed her mind if she'd wanted to.

"Now, don't tell anybody I'm coming, Aunt Mary,'' she warned again. "I plan to drop in out of the blue and try to get a feeling for what's going on.''

"Not a soul,'' Mary agreed. "Please take care, darling, and come as soon as you can.''

Madeline hung up and looked around, torn by a flood of emotions at the thought of her upcoming trip. Although she wasn't entirely sure how much credence she gave to Aunt Mary's fears over Shelby, she still felt concern for her children and a reluctant dread at the thought of returning to the bayou.

Most disturbing of all, though, was the unexpected prospect of meeting and talking with Justin again after all these years.

She'd thought she was completely over the man, grown far beyond all those old memories. But now Madeline realized that the mere thought of sitting across a table from him was almost more than she could bear to contemplate.

CHAPTER TWO

JUSTIN WAS DRESSING for the evening, wondering gloomily what he'd gotten himself into. He stood by the cheval mirror in his bedroom, scowling at his reflection as he knotted a sober gray tie.

"That's a pretty grim expression," Shelby commented, popping her head inside the door.

"Does this tie go with my shirt?" he asked.

She came in and stood next to her father, slipping her arm around him. Silently, they both studied his image in the big oval mirror.

"Don't you have something a little brighter?" she asked. "You look like a banker."

"Or a judge," he said dryly, making her chuckle.

She rummaged through the tie rack on his closet door. "Here," she said. "Try this one."

He recoiled in alarm. "I don't think so."

"Why not?"

"That pattern's far too loud, isn't it? I wouldn't want to…"

"What?"

"Send the wrong message," he said reluctantly.

"Like what?" She glared at him, clearly exasperated. "That just maybe you might be enjoying yourself a little?"

Justin tugged at the knot in his tie and pulled it off, refusing to answer.

"Here's a nice one."

He glanced at the tie she was holding and shook his head.

"There's a stain at the bottom. I keep forgetting to have it cleaned."

Shelby examined the tie more closely, then tossed it onto the bed and returned to the rack.

"Look, how about this? It's beautiful." She held up a navy tie dotted with small silver crests, peering at it curiously. "Why don't you ever wear this tie? I love it."

"Madeline gave me that on our twentieth anniversary."

"Oh." Shelby put it back hastily and selected a neutral burgundy stripe. "Here," she said with forced cheerfulness. "This one should be boring enough to suit you."

He took the tie and began to knot it while Shelby watched. "You don't look exactly happy about this," she said.

"I just don't see the point, that's all."

"The point?" She stared at him. "The point is to dress up, go out for a pleasant evening and enjoy yourself."

"But this woman is twenty years younger than I am. We have almost nothing in common, and her children make me nervous. Why is she going out with me?"

Shelby sighed and took his arm, pulling him around to face the mirror again. "Look at yourself. What do you see?"

Justin eyed his reflection. "I see a weatherbeaten, gray-haired guy in his fifties who's dating a thirty-year old."

"For one thing, Virginia Carmichael is thirty-seven, at least. And for another thing, you're not so bad-looking."

"Thanks a lot," Justin said dryly.

She grinned. "Now, don't pretend you can't see how all the girls in the office watch your every move. Especially that new typist. What's her name? The one with the—"

He waved his hand to silence his daughter, feeling intensely uncomfortable, and finished knotting the burgundy tie.

Justin couldn't bring himself to confide his real concerns

about Virginia Carmichael, especially since Shelby and Joanna had gone to such pains to get this relationship off the ground. But the truth was, he had no real feelings for the woman, and he knew he was heading into dangerous territory.

This was their third date. After tonight he had to end the relationship somehow, which would be awkward because she was a legal secretary in his office, somebody he saw every day.

Or he had to begin moving things to a more intimate level, and that prospect was equally daunting. In fact, it was probably a whole lot worse.

At one time, he thought with a sigh, life had been so simple....

Shelby heard the sigh and gave him a sharp glance. "What's the matter?"

"Nothing. I just don't know if I'm very good at dating, that's all."

"Well, you'd better start learning," she said briskly. "You don't want to be alone for the rest of your life, do you?"

He considered and shook his head. "No, sweetheart," he said gravely. "I don't believe I do."

"Then you have to be like Mama and start building a social life again."

"Your mother?" he asked, suddenly alert.

Shelby was still flipping through his rack of ties, selecting the ones that needed to be cleaned. "For goodness' sake, we should have done this long ago," she muttered. "These ties are a complete disgrace. Doesn't anybody ever tend to your dry cleaning?"

Justin chuckled at the disapproval in her tone. Shelby laughed with him, gathering an armful of ties while Justin reached for his blazer.

"Did you say," he asked casually, "that your mother is dating?"

"She mentioned somebody new when I talked to her on Sunday. He's a businessman from Denver who has a chalet in Aspen."

"A businessman?" Justin asked, following Shelby out of the room.

"I don't know much about him, except that he sounds incredibly rich and sexy," Shelby called over her shoulder as she hurried down the stairs. "Look, I have to run. Joanna's coming over to pick me up in about half an hour and we're driving over to Covington."

"Why?" he asked.

"To browse through a few of the boutiques. She's looking for an antique brass cradle. You have fun, okay? And thanks for letting me use your car today."

She paused at the foot of the stairs, waiting for him to catch up so she could kiss his cheek.

"Shelby," he said, "about your car..."

"What about it?"

"I'm still concerned."

"You are? Why?"

"What if it wasn't an accident?" Justin said reluctantly. "I know Charly thinks we're crazy to worry, but I'm not entirely convinced."

"Oh, come on, don't start that again," she said. "For goodness' sake, why would anybody want to shoot at me?"

"Maybe we should talk about that." He looked at her steadily.

Her cheeks turned pink with annoyance. "I don't want to talk about it. You're worse than Aunt Mary," she said, whirling off down the hall to her own suite of rooms in the other wing of the house.

Justin was left alone in the marble-flagged lobby, gazing after her.

Various ancestors from his grandmother's side of the family stared down at him from the walls, and all of them looked disapproving. A stern gentleman in a black waistcoat frowned at Justin, his mouth pursed in distaste.

You're purely a disgrace to all of us, he seemed to whisper. *A man in his fifties who's lost his wife, can't control his children and lives in such disarray that he can't even find a clean tie to wear.*

"Leave me alone," Justin muttered aloud. "Things are different nowadays, you know. In your day, life was a whole lot easier."

Charles strolled in from the library with an armful of books and peered curiously over the rim of his glasses. "Who're you talking to, son?"

Justin waved his arm in embarrassment. "Great-grandfather Philip Dupont. That old boy always looks like he's about to reach out of the frame and rap my knuckles."

Charles grinned. "As I recall, Grandfather Philip did his fair share of knuckle-rapping, all right. Not a very comfortable person to be around. I'm hungry," the old man added. "I think I'll ramble over to Mary's and see what they're having for dinner."

"Isn't there anything in the kitchen?"

Charles shook his head. "Odelle and Woodrow have gone to Florida to visit Odelle's cousin. Apparently there was some failure of communication and Odelle didn't know Aimee was going on holidays at the same time, so there's nobody to cook for us."

His father wandered out the big front door and across the veranda while Justin headed for the kitchen with rising impatience.

He was happy, of course, that all his daughters had found men to love, but it certainly complicated his life. Nowadays there was nobody around, and the house was too much for

Odelle to do all alone, especially since she, too, wasn't getting any younger.

When Madeline lived here...

But he could hardly bear to think about the way his household had once operated. In those days there'd always been snowy white shirts and clean rooms filled with flowers, and a staff of quiet, capable people who adored Madeline so much they'd work their hearts out to please her.

Now everything in the household operation seemed slapdash. At times the place wasn't even particularly clean, and despite Odelle's best efforts, the hired help were sometimes noisy, quarrelsome and presumptuous to the point of rudeness.

In hindsight, Justin often wondered how Madeline had managed to work such gentle magic. She'd never raised her voice, never seemed to assert herself in any way, but her home had been a place of stillness and beauty, of comfort and a deep, soothing peacefulness that he missed with every fiber of his being.

It wasn't just her housekeeping that he longed for, of course, but after years of pain he'd trained himself not to think about her sweet smile and bubbling laughter, her wit and gaiety, her beauty....

He wandered into the kitchen, where stacks of unwashed dishes filled the sinks and various accoutrements of Marie's "white magic" were scattered across the counter.

Marie had been out to Riverwood a couple of days earlier to harvest her herb garden. Drying clumps of plants hung in tangles from the roof beams, while a row of candles, partly burned in untidy puddles of wax, lined the deep windowsill.

Justin ducked underneath the herbs and crossed the room to open the refrigerator, looking inside gloomily. Some moldy potato salad obviously needed to be dealt with at once. He also spotted a withered orange, a dish of okra and something he couldn't identify at all....

He closed the door hastily, his stomach rumbling, and glanced at his watch. Maybe if he hurried there'd still be time to grab a hamburger in town before he went over to pick up Virginia.

He found his car keys on the cluttered hall table where Shelby had left them, ran down the wide curving steps and headed for the garage, feeling so miserable and out of sorts that it was all he could do not to slam the door and kick the tires.

THEIR DATE HAD BEEN a movie, followed by a snack in Rick's Café. Justin was uncomfortable and self-conscious throughout the evening, aware of his neighbors watching him as he squired Virginia awkwardly around town.

He fancied he could detect snickers of amusement, even some veiled glances of pity. A man over fifty, out on the town with his pretty young secretary. It seemed like such a cliché.

"We should have gone to the city," he said abruptly as he parked in front of Virginia's house afterward.

She glanced at him in the shadows. "Why?"

"I don't know." He frowned at his hands on the steering wheel. "It just seems kind of...adolescent, hanging around in town like this. In fact, I did the same thing when I was eighteen years old."

"With Madeline?" she asked.

He turned to look at her.

She really was an attractive woman. Virginia Carmichael had a lush figure, artfully blond hair and a great clothes sense. But for some odd reason, her good looks left Justin utterly unmoved. She could have been a doll or a picture cut from a magazine for all the warmth she inspired in him.

"Yes," he said, more curtly than he'd intended. "I remember taking Madeline to the movies here in town more than thirty years ago.''

"Then you're right." She reached for the door handle. "We should probably have gone to the city."

Justin got out and walked around to open her door, but she was too fast for him. She thrust the door open and stepped onto the curb, gathering her stylish cape around her with an impatient gesture.

Too late, he recalled that Virginia was a modern woman who didn't like having doors opened for her by a man. She considered it patronizing and sexist.

Suddenly, with dismaying clarity and a harsh stab of pain, Justin remembered what it used to be like to escort Madeline for an evening on the town.

She always looked marvelous, and despite her gentle strength she made a man feel like the kind of tough, confident fellow who could blaze his way through jungles with a machete or fight off hordes of villains to protect her.

In fact, Madeline had always appreciated the little touches of courtly politeness that Justin had been taught from boyhood, like opening doors for ladies and walking on the outside of the sidewalk.

"A true Southern gentleman," she'd once told him soberly, her wonderful eyes sparkling with humor, "must surely be the most delicious creation on God's green earth."

Now, why had that ancient memory come back to haunt him at this particular moment?

"Tell me what you're thinking about," Virginia demanded as they reached her doorstep.

Justin gathered himself together hastily. "Nothing. Thanks for a nice evening, Virginia."

"Would you like to come in?"

"I don't think so." He took a deep breath. "Virginia, I'm not sure this is..." He paused, floundering.

"You don't think this is going to work out," she said calmly, reaching out to touch his arm. "And you're probably right. But I've really enjoyed our time together, Justin. Thank you."

He felt strangely deflated, watching as she rummaged in her bag for the door key. "Virginia, I don't mean... Look, you're a lovely woman," he said, realizing that he meant it.

She smiled sadly, opening the door. "And you're a very attractive man. It's just a pity you're not free, that's all."

"What do you mean?"

"Oh, Justin." She gave him a glance that was both exasperated and sympathetic. "Thank you for a very pleasant evening."

Before he could say anything more, she vanished and he was left staring at a closed door.

Justin hesitated on the front step, battling his conflicting emotions. Ironically, now that the break had been neatly accomplished, he began to find her a little more attractive. Especially since she'd been so understanding.

The night pressed around him, murmurous and silvery with moonlight, making him feel very much alone. For a split second, he actually considered ringing the doorbell and asking if he could come in for a nightcap, after all. But he resisted the urge.

He'd accomplished his goal and extricated himself from an awkward relationship without causing any real pain or mess. It would be foolish to complicate things again just because he was lonely.

But the thought of going home to his big empty house was almost intolerable....

Justin wandered back to his car, got in and began to drive. Without fully realizing what he was doing he found himself heading down St. Claire Avenue, across the bridge and onto Magnolia Street.

He pulled over to the curb, parked his car and looked around curiously. It had been years since he'd come over here. The neighborhood still seemed quiet and reasonably well tended, though some of the gracious old houses were gone now, replaced by ugly square apartment buildings, and a few of the smaller places had begun to look vaguely run-down.

It was a working-class neighborhood, apparently populated mostly by young families. Bikes and tricycles were abandoned on some of the front lawns, glinting under the street lamps, and ghostly swing sets hung in the yards.

Justin got out and walked down the block to a little cottage that was partially obscured by a giant pecan tree. He stood with his hands in his pockets, staring at the house while the moonlight poured onto his shoulders and his hair lifted and stirred in the breeze.

The place had once been buttercup yellow with pale green shutters, but now it was painted a trendy shade of gray and the trim was lavender. Apart from the color, though, nothing much had changed.

He could see a trumpet vine climbing up the trellised veranda and onto the roof, the same vine Madeline had planted all those years ago.

Memories washed over him, leaving him breathless with pain. As if it were yesterday, he could see his young wife in her denim shorts and maternity smock, getting up from the flower bed where she'd been planting a neat row of seedlings.

"I want a vine-covered cottage," she told him gravely, "with you inside it, my darling. And that's all I want in the world."

She was nineteen and he was twenty. She held a yellow-handled trowel, and her long dark braid lay over her shoulder. She was six months pregnant with the twins, already huge. And he'd never thought it was possible to love any-body so much.

"Madeline," he whispered now, thirty-two years later. "My sweet darling…"

Tears burned in his eyes. He brushed them away, still looking hungrily at the cottage.

Until the twins were born, they'd been all alone here, abandoned by both their families but so deeply in love they didn't care about anyone else, not in those early days.

He wondered when the tensions had started and their dreams begun to fade.

Justin had never fully understood what went wrong. He'd been working so hard in those years, paralyzed by the sud-den responsibility of a wife and family, hurrying to get himself through law school so he could support them prop-erly. Most of the time he'd been away in the city, coming home on weekends to Bayou Beltane for a few precious hours in his young wife's arms.

But Madeline had changed overnight from a lover to a mother. All at once she was buried under mountains of diapers and bottles, preoccupied with teething problems and round-the-clock feedings.

When Aunt Mary hired the nursemaid for them, Made-line had been pathetically grateful, but Justin had been an-gry. In his youth and hurt pride, it seemed like a message from a disapproving family that he couldn't care for his children without their help.

In fact, the first real fight with Madeline had been a bitter argument about the nursemaid.

Now, remembering, he was appalled at his own selfish-ness, at the way he'd put his pride ahead of Madeline's welfare. His position had been wrongheaded and thought-less, but he'd never actually realized it so clearly before.

Still, she'd done her best to forgive him and be under-standing.

After the rift with his family was repaired by Aunt Mary and they moved back into Riverwood with the children, things had improved for a while between Justin and his wife. During the years when the new babies were coming along and growing up, Madeline had struggled to restore their marriage. With her gentle gaiety she'd tried to draw him out, to include him in the children's lives and be close to him again.

But during those years he'd been so engrossed in getting ahead and making a success of his career, showing everybody how well he could cope. After a long time she must simply have given up, withdrawn into her preoccupation with the children and let him go about his life.

Justin hadn't been tuned in to her feelings back then. Now, in retrospect, he fancied he could see the exact moment when she'd stopped trying. For years she must have been going through the motions, biding her time with her usual quiet thoughtfulness as she waited for the children to be old enough that she could leave without hurting them too badly.

Justin stood in the darkened street, bowed by the weight of his sorrow, the vanished opportunities of his youth and the sweet love he'd squandered for reasons he couldn't even fully understand anymore.

At last he turned away from the little cottage and trudged back to his car, feeling more deeply alone than he'd ever been in his life.

ON THE WAY HOME, he took a turn around the swamp road, watching how the moonlight glistened softly on the water and silvered the branches of the ancient cypress trees.

A solitary light burned at the little cluster of shacks where Remy's swamp-tour business was located. Justin slowed, wondering if his brother might be working late in his office. Suddenly hopeful, he cut the engine and coasted down the road toward the buildings.

Maybe he could hold his loneliness at bay for a while by having a drink with Remy, sitting back in one of the old office chairs with his feet up and reminiscing about their boyhood. Remy seemed a whole lot more mellow and approachable now that Kendall was in his life.

The thought of his taciturn, hard-edged brother finding love and happiness made Justin feel even more isolated.

But as he neared Remy's place, he realized to his disappointment that the light wasn't in the office, after all. It was the bait shack that seemed to be occupied, its door standing partly open. Justin sat for a while and looked at the light and the open door. He glanced down at his cell phone, wondering if he should call somebody or investigate on his own.

Finally he got out of the car, trod softly up the wooden walkway to the shack and peered inside.

A boy sat huddled on a chair at the back of the little room. He wore denim overalls, a tattered plaid shirt and a baseball cap pulled low on his head, and he was crying as if his heart would break.

Justin was so shocked that he stood rigid for a while, staring. He found it odd and unsettling to see a boy crying with such passion.

Finally Justin cleared his throat and moved inside, closer to the youngster. "Is there something I can do to help, son?" he said gently.

The boy threw his head up, staring wildly and clutching the arms of his chair.

Justin looked at the red, tear-streaked face and felt a painful surge of embarrassment.

It wasn't a boy in the shack at all. The sobbing youngster was Claudia Landry, Remy's young assistant and bait-shop operator.

Now that he'd seen her face, Justin also recognized the girl's thin body and ungainly, awkward look. But her messy tangle of dark hair was tucked out of sight under the cap pulled low over her eyes, which was why he hadn't recognized her.

"I'm really sorry to startle you," he said, distressed by the look of naked misery on her young face. "I saw the light on and thought maybe Remy was down here, working late."

She shook her head, gulped and rummaged briefly in the pocket of her overalls, then gave up and wiped her face on her shirtsleeve. "Remy ain't here," she muttered. "He's gone to the city for the rest of the week."

While Justin watched, she got out of the chair with a brave show of casualness, grabbed her jacket and started toward the door. "Sorry to trouble you, Mr. Delacroix. I was just doing up some work here, but I reckon I'll be leaving now."

Justin reached out to touch her arm as she passed. "What's the matter, Claudia?"

She looked down at her ragged high-top runners. "Nothing's the matter," she whispered. "I gotta go home now."

Justin had raised four daughters and he knew heartbreak when he witnessed it. Besides, he felt unhappy enough himself that he was reluctant to let the girl head out into the darkness with such a load of misery.

"Look, I heard the way you were crying," he said gently. "If there's anything I can do to help, I wish you'd let me know."

"Ain't nothing you can do to help."

Looking down at her bent head and her face shadowed by the peak of her cap, he hesitated, trying to remember the kinds of things that had once made his daughters this wretched.

For the most part it was some kind of boyfriend trouble,

but that was hard to picture in this case. Claudia didn't have any boyfriends. Justin couldn't recall if he'd even seen her dressed like a girl in all the years she'd worked for Remy. She was always out on the dock in her overalls, usually barefoot and dirty, swabbing boats and hauling pails of reeking chum.

"Why don't you give me a chance?" he suggested. "If I can't help, at least I can listen. Sometimes it helps to talk. You know, that's something I'm just starting to learn," he added, trying to keep up a line of chatter because he could tell that she was listening. "I'm learning that it eases the hurt if you can tell somebody about it. All my life I figured it was best to be strong and silent, try to bear the pain alone. But now I'm beginning to realize I was wrong."

She sniffled and turned away from him. "What pain, Mr. Delacroix?" she asked in a muffled voice. "What kinda pain you ever had?"

He looked down at her in surprise. "You think my life is perfect?"

"You got a big ol' house, a nice family and all kinds of money." She waved a dirty hand at his blazer and dress slacks. "You got nice clothes and you know how to wear them. You go to fancy places all the time with high-class people. Folks like me can only dream about the life you got."

Justin pulled an old chair around and straddled it while she sank back into the armchair with obvious reluctance. "That may be true," he said, "but all those things don't keep a person from being sad."

She rubbed at her face again, still sniffling.

Maybe it was the caressing darkness of the night, the lazy chirp of crickets and the rich smell of the swamp, the feeling they were the only two people on all the earth. Or perhaps it was the girl's obvious heartache, so intense that he was wrung with sympathy. At any rate, Justin found himself saying things to this unlikely confidante that he'd never told another living soul.

"You know, I ruined my marriage," he said. "I was cold and selfish, and because of it I lost the only woman I'll ever be able to love. Sometimes I feel so lonely I can hardly bear it."

Claudia watched him, astonished, her dark eyes wide with sympathy. Now that the tears were gone and the red blotchiness was fading from her cheeks, Justin realized to his surprise that she was really quite a pretty girl. Or she would be if she cleaned herself up a bit.

"I never knew none of that," she murmured thoughtfully. "I always see you driving around in your big ol' car, and it looks like you're on top of the world."

"Most people carry a load of trouble on their backs no matter who they are. So," he asked casually, "what's your trouble, Claudia?"

She lowered her head, wrung her hands together and dropped them boyishly between her knees. "It's... Bernard," she murmured. "Bernard Leroux."

Justin searched his memory. "That's one of the charter boat operators, isn't it? The big fellow who looks a bit like Bruce Willis?"

"He's better-looking than any man in the whole world," Claudia whispered, addressing her dirty running shoes. "He's just... Bernard's wonderful, Mr. Delacroix."

Justin began to understand. "And you like him a whole lot," he suggested. "But Bernard's not aware of the fact."

She looked up quickly. "How'd you know that?"

"I told you, I've raised four daughters," Justin said dryly.

The girl stared down at her hands again. "I don't know what to do. There's times I feel so miserable I think—I think I'm gonna die."

"You're not going to die." Justin leaned back in the

chair. "People don't die from unrequited love. It just feels that way. What you need is to take the situation in hand and do something about it."

"What can I do?"

"Well, let's see. Do you and Bernard have any kind of relationship at all? Does he know who you are?"

She shook her head. "He never even sees me, just looks right through me. To him, I'm the funny-looking kid on the boat dock. He doesn't even know I'm alive. Like, as a girl, you know?" she finished lamely, her cheeks flaming.

"I know." Justin watched her in silence, realizing that her description of Bernard's reaction was probably accurate. In fact, he'd always thought pretty much the same thing about Claudia himself.

"Bernard's been to college, owns his own boat and everything," she continued, looking at the floor again. "His family, they got lots of money. And I grew up down on the bayou with a passel of brothers and a mean ol' daddy who still drinks all the time."

"Where we come from has nothing to do with what we are, Claudia."

She gave him a brief, scornful glance. "Sure it does," she said. "To people like me, Mr. Delacroix, ain't nothing more important than where I come from. I can't be something I'm not."

"I don't believe that. I think any of us can be anything we want. That's what America's all about. If you want to be the kind of girl who'll make Bernard Leroux sit up and take notice, then all you have to do is decide that's what you're going to be."

"How?"

"Well, let's see. Maybe one of my daughters could help you to…"

He fell silent abruptly when he saw her look of panic.

"No!" she said. "Them girls of yours, they're all so…

Please, Mr. Delacroix, I'd be too scared. I don't want people finding out about this. Please don't tell nobody.''

"All right," he said briskly. "Then I guess we'll have to do it on our own."

"I wouldn't even know where to start." She lifted her hands, gesturing at her ragged clothes, then let them fall helplessly between her knees again. "I dunno how to dress, how to sit, how to talk right.... I dunno nothing about all that."

"Anything," Justin said.

She looked up in surprise.

He watched her thoughtfully, a little surprised at his own reaction.

A plan was forming in Justin's mind, a crazy enterprise that he would normally have dismissed without a thought.

But then, a lot of strange things were happening in Justin's heart and soul these days. He was like a different man, reckless and unmindful of all those careful considerations that had once governed his life.

"Anything," he repeated. "Say it like this, Claudia. I don't know anything about all that."

"I don't know noth—anything about all that," she repeated obediently.

"Good. Now, try to remember that. And don't say 'ain't.' That's probably enough to start with. Come on," he added, getting up with sudden decision. "It's late and we both have to work in the morning. Besides, we've got a date for tomorrow afternoon."

Her jaw dropped. "Beg pardon?"

"We've got some things we'll need to do together."

"Where we going?"

"We're going shopping for some clothes. Then on the weekend, we're going out to the Bayou Inn for a nice dinner."

"The Bayou Inn?" She gaped at him. "Land's sake, Mr. Delacroix, I never done nothing like that before."

He grinned. "Do you want to give that another try?"

She shook her head, looking dazed, then gave him a flicker of a smile in return. "I ain't—I have never done anything like that in all my life," she said primly.

Justin chuckled, feeling his spirits lift for the first time in weeks. "Neither have I. But I suspect we're both about to have some new experiences, Claudia."

CHAPTER THREE

ROWS OF TURQUOISE glowed richly on black velvet in the display case. The hammered-silver clasps and settings glistened brightly in the morning light as Madeline moved a few pairs of earrings to a better position.

She knelt on the carpet in front of the display, wearing a beige cashmere turtleneck, a long tan skirt with a leather belt, and copper jewelry.

Tate O'Sullivan wandered by, a paintbrush in his hand, and leaned in the arched entrance to the gallery as he watched her with a bemused expression.

"Lovely," he said at last. "I wish I could paint you, kneeling there like that. The line of your back and neck is so perfect."

Madeline glanced over her shoulder. "Tate, could you hand me the big squash blossom from that other display? I want to put it here in front."

He unlocked the cabinet she indicated, took out the lavish piece of jewelry and brought it to her, watching while she hung it carefully over a deer's antler mounted in oak.

She winced at his oil-stained fingers, then leaned forward to study the necklace. "I hope you didn't get any paint on this."

He waved his hand casually. "If I did, it'll just add to the value of the piece. An O'Sullivan original."

"Listen to the boy. Such an arrogant youngster." Madeline closed the case, locked it and got to her feet, brushing at the front of her skirt.

"Ah, Maddy, but you find my arrogance appealing, don't you?" He leaned against the counter and grinned at her, his eyes sparkling wickedly.

Tate O'Sullivan was tall and lanky, with blue eyes and blond hair that he wore in a thick ponytail. Though well into his thirties, he still retained the kind of winsome, boyish air that made women feel protective.

Among other things, Madeline thought wryly. In fact, she suspected that a lot of the women who pursued Tate around Aspen were suffering from pangs that weren't entirely maternal.

"Jennifer tells me that Kelly spent the night again on the weekend," she said.

"I don't think she likes Kelly very much." He frowned in concern and stroked the tip of the brush with a rare expression of seriousness. "I'd give anything to make life stable and happy for that kid, Maddy. I wish my marriage had worked out differently."

"I know you do. But I think Jennifer is probably as happy as most children." Madeline gave him a stern glance. "Even if her father is a bit of a ladykiller."

"Come on, Maddy," he coaxed, his eyes sparkling again. "You must love me a little bit."

"But of course. I love you to distraction." She headed briskly for the alcove where they kept office supplies, coffee-making equipment and a small fridge. "Just as I love my son Beau, who's about your age."

"Well, you certainly don't look old enough to be my mother." He followed her to the rear of the shop, loping along in his paint-stained jeans.

"Tate, did we get the new shipment of agates?" she asked.

"The invoice is in there somewhere. I think they're still in the storeroom. Look, are you sure this is a good idea?"

She riffled through a pile of invoices without looking up. "What do you mean?"

"Going back to your old hometown."

"Here it is." Madeline found the invoice, then turned to him. "Don't you think it's a good idea for me to visit my children?" she asked.

"I don't know." He poured a couple of mugs of coffee, handed one to her and spooned sugar into his own, then indicated the pair of rattan armchairs near the desk. "Sit down. Let's talk about it."

"There's nothing to talk about. I've already booked a flight and a hotel room in Bayou Beltane. I'll be arriving on Saturday." But she sank obediently into the chair and sipped her coffee, waiting for him to continue.

"How did you ever wind up in that backwater bayou town anyhow, a classy lady like you?" he asked. "What's there, besides your kids?"

She shrugged and lifted her hands with Gallic expressiveness. "Not much. It's lovely and peaceful, quite rural, utterly different from New Orleans. After growing up in Paris, I really found it quite charming."

"But why did your parents live out on the bayou, all the way across the lake?"

"The Twin Span had been constructed by the time we moved to Bayou Beltane, so it was an easy trip across Lake Pontchartrain to the city. When my mother took the lecturing post at the university, I think they were convinced—" she gave a wry smile "—that I'd be safer in a rural setting. After all, I was the only child, their darling, the apple of their eye."

"And how did you reward their parental concern?" He leaned back and rested his feet on a carved wooden box containing giant chess pieces. "You fell madly in love with one of the local yokels."

"Justin Delacroix was scarcely a yokel, Tate. Still," she

added reflectively, "everybody was utterly horrified when Justin and I announced that we wanted to get married. My parents most of all, because they'd wanted so much more for me."

"Why? Isn't a lawyer a pretty good catch?" Tate said idly.

Madeline's cheeks turned pink. "You must realize that my parents considered themselves...well, several cuts above the Delacroix. They had planned such a brilliant future for me. I'd been taught four languages, and my art training was coming along nicely. I have no doubt they expected me in due time to make an impressive match, both socially and financially, and go on to distinguish myself in an art career as well."

"And instead there you were, hanging out with a small-town lawyer's kid."

"It was dreadful. His parents were as upset as mine. They wanted Justin to finish law school and get started on his career before he considered marriage."

"Just like Romeo and Juliet," Tate said with a theatrical sigh. "So romantic, isn't it?"

Madeline gave him a wry smile and sipped her coffee. "Perhaps, but not nearly as tragic. Justin and I didn't die for love. We just drifted apart. Still, we were..."

She looked out the window, where autumn colors blazed in the park across the street.

"Yes?" he urged, leaning forward. "What were you going to say, Maddy?"

She gave her young partner a faraway, thoughtful look. "I was going to say that we were happy at first, in spite of the coldness of our families. There was a time when Justin and I were the whole world to each other. But, of course, that was thirty years ago."

Tate gave her a keen glance. "When you go back now, will you be visiting with him at all?"

Madeline nodded reluctantly. "I'll probably have to see him at least once. I need to find out what he knows about Shelby's problems. But if I had my choice, I'd rather just avoid all of them, except for Aunt Mary and my children. The Delacroix can be rather...overwhelming."

She shivered and took another sip of coffee.

"So why go back," Tate asked, "if all this ancient history and family crap bothers you so much?"

"Because I'm worried about Shelby. I've told you what's been happening. I believe my daughter may have gotten herself into something dangerous, and I want to know what's going on."

"Come on, Madeline," he said cheerfully. "A couple of accidents don't necessarily add up to a conspiracy, you know."

"I know that." She brooded at the front window again, where Bare Bones Gallery was lettered in gold, then turned to the man beside her. "But I also know these people, Tate. Politics is a blood sport in Louisiana. Some of them can be utterly ruthless if they feel their interests are being threatened in any way."

"So what if they notice you snooping around and you become another target of this big conspiracy? Good business partners aren't all that easy to find, you know." He tried to make it sound like a joke, but his eyes betrayed his concern.

"I don't intend to snoop around," Madeline told him. "I know exactly who I'll need to talk to about this. Besides, I intend to give the impression, if anybody asks, that we're planning to open another gallery somewhere in St. Tammany Parish and I'm in town to research possible locations."

Tate raised his eyebrows and whistled. "Hey, that's not a bad idea," he said thoughtfully. "Another gallery in the heart of a busy tourist area. Do you think we should have a look at it?"

"I think, *chéri*," she said with forced cheerfulness, "that I would rather be torn apart by alligators than return to Bayou Beltane for anything more than a three-day visit."

Tate threw back his head and laughed. "Another of your wishy-washy responses. Why can't you ever be definite about anything?"

Madeline smiled at his teasing, then got up and set aside her empty coffee mug. "Time to open the doors and let the people in to spend their holiday money."

"Okay. But it's my turn to work in the back today, right?"

"Yes, my boy, you can paint to your heart's content. And since you're going to be looking after the shop on your own for the week I'll be away, you get a whole extra week in the studio after I'm back."

"Fair enough. Say, Madeline?" He paused on his way back to the workroom.

"Yes?"

"Where will you be staying? Is there a decent hotel in this little town?"

"There's quite a nice place, actually. A bit rustic, as I recall, but very clean and comfortable. It's called the Bayou Inn. I've booked a room there and I'll probably take most of my meals in the hotel dining room, except for a few visits with Aunt Mary and my children. Jax will be having our...my first grandchild soon, you know."

"That's right. I'd forgotten. Okay, I guess it all sounds harmless enough." Tate smiled and tipped his paintbrush at her in a lazy salute, then ambled through the gallery and disappeared into the workroom.

JUSTIN GOT UP EARLY the next day and made his way to the attic, where he spent a frustrating half hour poking through assorted bits of family memorabilia and discarded sporting equipment.

Again he thought of Madeline. During her stay in this house, the attic had been clean and well organized, with neatly labeled boxes and clothes hung away on racks, covered in careful shrouds of plastic. Now it was all a hopeless jumble.

But at last he found a pair of old steamer trunks filled with the varied castoffs of four young women. Most of the clothes in the trunks were outgrown or outdated but too good to throw away. If Madeline had been here she would have sorted through them regularly, arranged for the mending and laundering of better-quality garments, then given them away to local charities. Instead, the trunks were messily jammed with more than ten years' accumulation of odds and ends.

Justin knelt on the dusty floor and struggled with his unfamiliar task, trying to pick things that looked at least a little stylish but also small enough to fit Claudia. He'd selected a fairly nice array of shorts, slacks, sweaters and blouses, along with some loafers and other casual shoes, when he hit paydirt.

One of his girls, probably Shelby, had taken a charm-and-modeling course in her early teens, and the textbooks were still piled at the bottom of the trunk. Justin leafed through them and found detailed instructions on makeup, deportment, conversational skills and grooming.

He bundled the volumes into a plastic sack along with assorted clothes and shoes, then took a few moments to select some novels and a couple of high school grammar textbooks from a bookshelf on one wall.

Finally he hauled his whole bundle of treasures downstairs, stashed them in his car and dressed for the office.

On the way past Remy's place of business he approached the cluster of buildings and stopped in front of the bait shack. Looking as ragged and unkempt as ever, Claudia crouched on the dock, tipping buckets of rotten mealworms into the green waters of the swamp, where fish circled, waiting to snap them up.

"Hi," Justin said, getting out of his car.

She glanced up at him and flushed painfully with embarrassment. "Hi," she muttered.

Justin opened the trunk and hauled out the sack of clothes and books. "These are some things my daughters have discarded over the years," he said, feeling almost as awkward and shy as the girl on the dock. "I thought you might be able to use some of them."

She approached him uncertainly, her dirty bare feet padding on the wooden causeway, and peered into the sack.

"But them are..." Claudia leaned forward to touch a pair of folded khaki slacks and a soft cotton shirt. "Them are real nice things, Mr. Delacroix. Too good to give away."

"The clothes were in trunks up in my attic. Nobody's worn them for years. It's all pretty casual stuff, though. We'll have to buy something more formal if we're going out to dinner at the Bayou Inn."

She shifted nervously. "I ain't...I'm not real sure I can do this, Mr. Delacroix. I'm scared to death of goin' there."

"People never get anywhere by giving in to their fears, Claudia. Now, there are also some books in here that might help you. And I'll meet you at Rick's this afternoon at two o'clock so we can go shopping. All right?"

"Look, Mr. Delacroix...why're you doing all this for me?"

He shifted on his feet, considering her question thoughtfully. In fact, it was the same thing he'd been asking himself ever since their conversation the night before.

At last, he said, "I want to do something for somebody else, Claudia. I've spent my whole life concentrating on myself and my career, and it's brought me nothing but loneliness. There are some important things about life that I need to learn. I'm hoping maybe you can help."

She picked up one of the books and leafed through it, then smiled wanly. "Seems like you ain't the one who needs to learn things."

"I think we're both going to have a real adventure, Claudia. And we might as well get started. Is two o'clock all right, or do you have to work?"

"We're mostly shut down for this week while Remy's away. I'm just cleaning up and getting ready for the fall tours."

"So you'll be able to meet me in town this afternoon?"

She gulped and swallowed hard, then set her jaw with touching gallantry. "I'll be there. God help me," she muttered under her breath, heading back to her buckets of mealworms.

"SOMETHING QUITE SHORT," Justin told Mae-Belle Schwartz, who stood at her hairdressing station, hands on ample hips, regarding him in openmouthed astonishment. "Claudia has a pretty busy life. I'm sure she doesn't want to fuss with her hair."

Claudia gripped the arms of the padded leather chair, peering at them fearfully through her long tangle of black hair like a frightened little animal hiding in a thicket. She was a bit more presentable this afternoon, having selected a pair of slacks and one of the cotton blouses from Justin's sack of discarded clothes instead of her usual shirt and overalls. She also had a clean, freshly scrubbed look that he found touching.

"Short," Mae-Belle repeated, still dazed. "Like, how short?"

"Like Charlotte had her hair cut last spring," Justin said after a moment's thought. "I always liked that hairstyle."

"I can do that." Mae-Belle turned her attention to Claudia. "Land's sake, child, this is some god-awful mess of hair you got here."

"I know," Claudia whispered.

"It'll take me a while," Mae-Belle said to Justin, all business now that a course of action had been determined. "You gon' wait, or what?"

"I'll slip down to the office," he said, "and come back in half an hour."

The last he saw was Claudia's panicky expression as he left her in the beauty shop, trapped in the big chair as Mae-Belle approached with a pair of scissors.

WHEN HE WENT BACK to pick her up, Claudia was a different girl.

She stood by the front desk and examined herself in the mirror with a look of wonder. Her glossy black hair, which had been shampooed, cut short and layered, seemed to glisten with natural highlights. The stylish haircut revealed a long graceful neck and a delicate line to her cheek and jaw that had been hidden until now.

Justin paid Mae-Belle, including a generous tip, and escorted Claudia from the shop.

"You look beautiful," he said with genuine admiration.

She touched her cropped head, overcome with shyness. "Ain't never... I've never had a store-bought haircut," she whispered. "Thanks, Mr. Delacroix."

"Don't thank me, Claudia. I told you, this is an adventure for me. How old are you?" he asked curiously as they paused outside one of the dress shops that his daughters liked to patronize.

"I'm almost twenty-four."

Justin glanced down at her in surprise, a little taken aback. Because of her ragged clothes and tomboy manner, he'd assumed the girl was still in her teens.

But when he thought about it, he realized Claudia had been working at Remy's place at least three years now, maybe four. And she'd been working at other jobs even before that, so she'd probably never had the chance to finish high school. As long as he'd known her, the girl had been living in a shabby houseboat moored in the swamp. She rode to town on a bicycle, after her old clunker of a car had finally quit forever, looked after herself and asked for help from nobody.

"I never got much high school," she said, as if reading his thoughts. "But I do like to read. I get books from the library all the time. I even took a couple of courses at the college. It's just real hard to—to try and change yourself. Specially," she added bitterly, "when I got a family of brothers who always wreck things for me, no matter how hard I try."

"You could move away from them," Justin suggested.

"Not really. I got a good job working for Remy, and I don't know nothing else."

"Anything," he said automatically.

She gave him a shaky smile and followed him into the store, looking around nervously while Justin talked with the owner.

"Something in a plain dark color, Emily," he said. "Kind of simple and elegant, don't you think?"

Emily Colbert was very elegant herself, a slim black woman with an attractive face and a wonderful sense of style. If she thought it odd that Justin Delacroix was buying clothes for the young operator of his brother's bait shack, she gave no indication.

But Mae-Belle wasn't likely to be so discreet. Justin knew well enough that this story would be all over town by dinnertime.

Speculation was going to be frenzied.

Let them talk, he thought with another surge of the

strange recklessness that had overcome him lately. *Let them say whatever they want to. I intend to help this poor child, and there's no reason on earth why I shouldn't.*

He waited on an upholstered gilt chair while Claudia went into the mirrored cubicle with an armful of dresses. She ventured back out after a few minutes, looking so marvelous that he could hardly believe his eyes.

The girl wore a black, high-waisted dress set off by a white lace collar. With her graceful, cropped head and flushed cheeks, she looked like a beautiful gamine.

"Do you like it?" Justin asked as she studied herself in the mirror, holding the skirt out with both hands and twirling awkwardly.

"It's..." She looked at herself, then back at him. Tears glittered in her eyes. "God, I ain't—I mean, I don't... Oh, Mr. Delacroix, I can't never pay for all this stuff. I got enough cash to pay you for the haircut, but this here dress, it costs—"

"Never mind. We'll work something out."

"Like what?"

"Well," he said after some thought, "Odelle and Woodrow could use some help around the house. Maybe in your free time you can do something like that."

"But how? I ain't—"

"We'll get something organized later," he interrupted. "For now, let's just buy the clothes. It's bringing me pleasure, Claudia," he said earnestly. "My girls are all grown and don't need me anymore. My wife's been gone for years. The fact is, I'm not much good to anybody these days. It's really fun to be able to help someone."

"Okay," she said at last. "I reckon I can mow your lawn or something, can't I?"

"We'll take this one," Justin told Emily, who was listening with a thoughtful smile. "And I guess we'll need some shoes and things. Write it all down and I'll stop back later to settle up, okay?"

Emily gave him a shrewd glance. "You're a nice man, Justin Delacroix," she murmured, standing next to him as Claudia moved hesitantly toward a rack of shoes. "A real nice man."

"I'm having fun, Emily," he said simply. "More fun than I can remember having in long time. She's got a crush on somebody," he whispered, bending down conspiratorially. "And we've decided she's going to become the kind of girl who can get his attention."

Emily chuckled. "Seems to me this girl could get anybody's attention."

It was true. The haircut and the new dress were magically effective. Already the gangly tomboy was transformed into a lovely ingenue.

"So what's next?" Emily asked him, her eyes bright with amusement.

"Some practice in building confidence and social skills. First of all, we're going out to dinner on Saturday night at the Bayou Inn."

Emily shook her head, still smiling. "Better be careful, Justin. She's going to be a beautiful girl when you get done with her. This whole town's going to be talking."

"You know, Emily," he said calmly, "I've tried all my life to be the kind of man who never got talked about, and it did me no good at all. So let them talk."

DURING THE WINTER, after Charly was released from the hospital, Madeline had made a trip to Louisiana to see her daughter. But she'd been frantic with worry the whole time, and her visit had been so rushed that she could hardly remember anything except arriving at the airport in New Orleans, being whisked off to a hotel in Beau's car and spending some anxious hours at Charly's bedside.

This time it was Shelby she was worried about, and that feeling of suffocating, helpless dread was just the same.

But other things about this trip were different. For one thing, nobody except Aunt Mary knew she was coming, so there wasn't a welcoming reception at the airport. Instead, Madeline collected her own luggage, rented a car and headed out of the city and onto the Twin Span early on Saturday afternoon.

The road across the lake was crowded with weekend traffic. Madeline gripped the wheel, overcome with memories.

This swampy landscape seemed different in some ways after ten years of absence, but poignantly familiar in others. She'd probably driven the same highway a thousand times, taking children to doctors' appointments and dance lessons in the city, to concerts and sporting events and holiday excursions.

Almost invariably it had been Madeline in the car with one or more of her offspring, doing duty as chauffeur and chaperon.

Justin was always working....

Her hands tightened on the wheel. She rolled the window down to let the damp breeze into the car, breathing deeply. She'd forgotten that warm, caressing feeling the air always had in Louisiana. There was something almost tangible about it, a sense that you could sink down and be supported on billowing clouds of fragrance.

In Colorado, the sun-dazzled atmosphere was so thin and crisp that it seemed to burn your lungs if you breathed too deeply....

She pulled off the bridge and drove along the bayou toward the small town where she'd spent so much of her adult life. The place seemed smaller than she remembered, drowsy in the mellow warmth of October. A few of the street names were different and some houses looked more modern, but the atmosphere hadn't altered in the least.

Probably, Madeline thought, it hadn't changed much in a hundred years. There was a timeless feeling to Bayou Beltane, as if the little weathered houses on stilts and the gracious mansions behind their screens of mossy trees had been here for centuries and would endure forever.

She had a sudden urge to take the long way around, down Magnolia Street, where their cottage had been. In the past, while she'd been living in the Delacroix mansion out on the bayou, she'd often driven that way to brood over the little place with all its sweet memories.

But as time slipped by, the memories got to be more painful than sweet and eventually she stopped driving down Magnolia. It must have been twenty years at least since she'd seen the little vine-covered house with its pale green shutters.

Her face clouded and she kept to the main thoroughfare, avoiding the lure of side streets as she headed toward the Bayou Inn.

The girl at the reception desk was a stranger to Madeline, as were the rest of the hotel staff. All of them, to her relief, seemed far too young to remember a quiet, dark-haired woman who'd lived out at Riverwood more than ten years ago.

"My name is Madeline Belanger," she said, using her maiden name. "I have a reservation."

"Let's see. Belanger." The clerk checked her computer. "We have you in the old part of the building, ma'am, facing the courtyard. Is that all right?"

Madeline smiled politely. "Yes, that will be lovely. Thank you."

She climbed the stairs to her room, following a young man who carried her luggage. As they moved down the corridor, she gazed around her with a dazed sense of unreality.

So much the same, and yet everything seemed so different.

The room was charming, with a deep window seat, chintz draperies and slipcovers, and heavy rosewood furniture. After years of living in Colorado, with all the vibrant earth tones and uncluttered western style of decorating, she found this faded opulence vaguely comforting.

She unpacked and ironed a few of her clothes, then tried to decide where to begin her telephone calls. But she was both tired and restless, reluctant to get down immediately to the business that had brought her to Bayou Beltane.

It was Saturday afternoon, not a good time to make calls, she decided at last. Nobody would be around now. She might as well wait until after dinner and see if she could get hold of some of the children.

Finally she dressed in slacks and a cardigan, went outside and wandered up and down the quiet green streets hung with flowering baskets. As she walked, Madeline had a feeling of breathless suspense, knowing that at any moment she might stumble on somebody she recognized.

One of her children could be walking down these very streets. She could suddenly encounter an old neighbor or friend.

Or even Justin himself...

But though she passed many townspeople who smiled at her with casual friendliness, there was no sign of recognition.

I've been forgotten, she told herself, and felt relieved by the knowledge. *I'm no more than a stranger in this place.*

The atmosphere was heavy and languorous, and the heat began to grow oppressive. She took off her sweater and hung it over her shoulders as she walked, feeling drowsy, almost light-headed.

Finally she went back to the hotel and climbed the stairs to her room, letting herself into its air-conditioned stillness with a sigh of weariness. She curled up on the four-poster bed, pulled a comforter over her body and gave herself up to a sleep so deep and dreamless that it was like falling off a cliff.

After a couple of hours she woke, confused and disoriented. She lay for moment in the twilight shadows and struggled to remember where she was.

Bayou Beltane, she thought. *I'm in this town again. Justin is just a few miles away from me. And it's possible that somebody here is trying to hurt Shelby.*

Both thoughts made her feel edgy and troubled. She got up hastily, showered and dried her hair, then dressed in a simple gray linen sheath the same color as her eyes, set off with a strand of dark pearls.

She walked downstairs to the dining room, conscious of a few admiring glances as she passed through the lobby. But still, nobody seemed to recognize her.

Have I really changed so much? she thought. *Have I grown old in these ten years since I've been away?*

The hostess approached Madeline in the entry to the dining room and cast an inquiring glance behind her.

"I will be dining alone," Madeline said.

"Certainly, ma'am. Could you come this way, please?"

Madeline followed the woman to a pleasant table in an alcove near a mullioned window, with a view of the red-cobbled courtyard planted with magnolias, flowering bougainvillea and lush shrubbery. The hostess lit a candle in a blue glass jar and handed Madeline the leather-covered menu.

She murmured her thanks, shook out her napkin and placed it over her skirt, then froze in horror. A couple sat a few tables away from her, conversing earnestly in low tones.

One of them was a ravishing young dark-haired woman in a black dress with a simple white lace collar. And the man with her was Justin Delacroix.

CHAPTER FOUR

"MY BROTHERS, they ruin everything nice that ever comes my way," Claudia was saying, her head lowered so the flame from the hurricane lamp glistened softly on her dark hair. "They always done that, long as I can recall. And Joey, he's the worse. He's really awful, Mr. Delacroix."

"What sort of things do your brothers do?" Justin frowned. "Why would they want to keep terrorizing their sister? Especially a younger sister. You'd think they'd feel protective toward you."

"They say I'm uppity." Claudia gave him a bleak smile. "I reckon that sounds pretty funny to you, seeing the way I dress and all, but my brothers think I'm getting above myself."

"How?"

She shrugged. "I'm the first one in the family to hold down a steady job, move away from home and try to go to school and such. It makes them real mad. And when I won't loan them money, they get even madder."

The girl took a breadstick from a napkin-covered basket and began to toy with it aimlessly, breaking it into little pieces.

"They're all out on the shrimp boats right now, but when they get back home they'll hear about this," she murmured. "About me having this haircut and wearing new clothes and going out to fancy restaurants with somebody like you. Joey, he won't like it much, I can tell you that right now."

Not for the first time, Justin began to wonder about the

wisdom of what he'd gotten himself into, and whether his meddling was ultimately going to cause this poor girl more misery than happiness.

He recalled his grandmother once long ago telling him, "When you have a mind to interfere in somebody's life, my boy, you'd best be very sure of what you're doing. Because the consequences are going to be your responsibility...."

"So what will your brothers do if they're upset with you?" he asked.

She shrugged again. "I dunno. Most likely they'll just beat me up," she said, with an impassive calm that stunned him.

"Beat you up?"

"One time Joey came around wanting to borrow money and I wouldn't give him none. He was real drunk, and he beat on me so bad I had to go and stay at the hospital for a couple of nights."

"My God."

"But Jake charged him with assault and he spent a month in jail," she added reflectively, "so he might not try that again. Most likely he'll just come over some day with Nate, and Paul and Jim-Bob and they'll trash my place while I'm at work."

"Claudia, we can't allow something like that to happen."

She smiled and touched his hand briefly. "Don't look so upset, Mr. Delacroix. There ain't a whole lot in my place for my brothers to trash. They done it lots of times, and it only takes me a little while to fix everything up again." She lifted her chin bravely. "I ain't afraid of my brothers no more. Not a bit."

This time it was Justin's turn to give her hand a comforting pat. Along with the caution, he felt another emotion growing within him, a protectiveness as deep as if this girl were one of his own daughters, and a warm resolve to keep her from being harmed.

"If they come around to bother you, Claudia, just let me know and we'll have another talk with Jake. Your brothers need to learn that it's not a good idea to bully a girl."

She smiled, her eyes sparkling suddenly. "I ain't afraid of them," she repeated.

"Not," Justin said, smiling back at her. "Let's try hard to drop the 'ain't,' shall we?"

"I'm...not afraid of them," Claudia repeated, cutting a huge piece of her steak and spearing it with a fork. "I am not afraid of them boys. Oops!" She grinned at him and shook her head. "I mean, those boys."

"That's very good," he said. "Oh, and another thing, Claudia..."

"Hmm?" She paused, still gripping her steak knife, with the forkful of meat halfway to her mouth.

"Not such a big piece, all right?" Justin said gently. "You should try to cut pieces of meat about a quarter that size, and eat each one as it's sliced. While you're using the fork, you lay your knife across the upper corner of your plate like this."

He demonstrated while Claudia watched, fascinated, then tried to imitate him.

"It seems so finicky," she complained. "How do folks ever get the whole steak done with before it's time to go home?"

Justin chuckled. "It may take a little longer, but not much. This is what we call 'gracious dining.'"

"Gracious dining," Claudia repeated, clearly tickled by the phrase.

She concentrated on slicing a small piece of steak, then put the knife down carefully and transported the meat to her mouth.

"Mr. Delacroix..." she murmured after chewing and swallowing.

"Yes, Claudia?"

"There's a lady a few tables away from us who seems like she knows you. She's barely took her eyes off us since she sat down."

"Where?"

"Behind you. Starboard side. Looks like she's all alone."

It must be Virginia Carmichael, or somebody else from the office, Justin decided, feeling suddenly nervous. He leaned forward, lowering his voice. "What does this woman look like?"

Claudia slid her eyes to one side under the pretext of reaching for more bread, then bit off a hefty length of breadstick and talked through it. Justin was about to correct her, but held his tongue.

"Real pretty," she said in a muffled voice. "Not all that young, more like you."

Justin smiled privately at this but said nothing. "Classy-looking," Claudia added, "dressed in something that looks like it's nothing fancy, but prob'ly cost a thousand dollars."

Then it was Virginia.

Justin braced himself for a stilted exchange of greetings and the curious examination the older woman would no doubt give Claudia, who was looking prettier by the moment as her delicate face flushed with excitement and a few sips of wine.

"A string of gray pearls, pale complexion," Claudia continued, obviously taking her reporting job seriously, though she pretended to address the bread basket. "Slim and sitting up real straight like a queen, dark hair all nice and smooth."

Dark hair and...

That certainly didn't sound like Virginia. In fact, it sounded more like...

Justin's heart began to pound noisily. He sat erect in his chair, turned and found himself looking straight at Madeline.

For a moment the room swam around him dizzily. His chest constricted so tightly that he wondered if he might be about to have a heart attack. He was vaguely conscious of the blur of candle flames, of talk and laughter and the clatter of dishes and cutlery all around him, of drifting scents of flowers and perfume.

And in the center of it all was Madeline's face, her wonderful eyes regarding him gravely.

At last the mists began to clear, Justin's heartbeat slowed a little and he was able to push the chair back and get to his feet.

"If you'll just excuse me for a moment, Claudia," he murmured huskily to his young companion, "I'll be right back."

Like a man in a dream he walked among the linen-draped tables to pause in front of Madeline. For a long, tense moment they looked at each other. In Justin's mind, the seconds dragged on until they felt like years, and he couldn't think of a single thing to say.

It was Madeline who finally broke the charged silence with her customary grace.

"Hello, Justin," she said, smiling. "What a coincidence, meeting you here. Could you sit down with me for a moment, do you think?"

He couldn't believe how composed and casual she sounded, as if their last conversation had taken place only the previous day instead of all those long, bitter years ago.

Numbly, he pulled out one of the chairs and sat opposite her, staring hungrily, drinking in the details of her face.

"You look exactly the same," he murmured. "You haven't changed a bit."

Her cheeks turned faintly pink. "Nonsense," she said with a brief laugh. "We're not children anymore, you know. I'm a woman of fifty, Justin, and I've earned every one of these character lines. Don't deny them to me."

"But the—the essence of you." He floundered awkwardly, surprised by his own words. "You're the same person you were more than thirty years ago when we were kids. Except that your hair's a little shorter," he added. "I like it, Madeline."

"Well, I doubt that any of us ever changes much, when all is said and done." There was a sudden edge to her voice. "We just get older, but not necessarily different at all."

"Do you really think so? You believe people can never change?"

Justin knew he was behaving irrationally. He should be making small talk, inquiring about her reasons for being in town, acting suave and gentlemanly. But he was so shaken, so deeply moved by her unexpected appearance. So unnerved to see her again like this in the quiet elegance of the Bayou Inn.

He also realized that he was passionately interested in her opinion. He'd always been intrigued by Madeline's thought processes, fascinated by her quietly offbeat view of the world.

In fact, looking back, Justin found it hard to understand why he'd stopped talking with her and asking her questions. What aspect of his life could possibly have been important enough to take him away from this woman, ignore her for so many years that she'd finally given up on him?

The old pain, so long buried, began to throb through his body, leaving him feeling desolate and bereft all over again as he waited for her answer.

But she only shook her head and looked down at the table, concentrating on her place setting. She moved the knife and the spoon into precise alignment, then traced their heavy silver engraving with her fingertips.

"Do you remember how we used to laugh, Madeline?" he asked wistfully. "Remember in the little house on Magnolia Street, when one of the twins would do something funny and we'd sit on the floor and laugh together until our sides ached?"

Something happened to her face. It was as if a shutter had dropped over her clear gray eyes, enclosing her mind and emotions and blocking him out. Suddenly she was like a woman sculpted of marble, gracious and lovely but impossible to reach.

Justin looked at her, chilled, and realized she wanted no part of him. There would be no shared memories, no laughter or teasing, no warmth. She was finished with him, and she had been for years.

The finality of her expression was like another blow to his heart. It was all he could do not to give way to tears, though Justin Delacroix was a man who'd seldom cried in his life.

The young waiter arrived, bringing her a seafood salad. She smiled up at him. "Thank you."

"Now, is there anything else you'll be needing, ma'am?"

"Oh, no, I don't think so. This looks perfectly lovely. There's nothing quite like fresh Louisiana crabmeat, is there?"

Still the boy hovered, looking solicitous. Justin realized the waiter wanted to see Madeline smile again, and hear more of her gentle words of praise. She'd always had that effect on people. Even strangers went out of their way to please her.

At last the waiter left and Madeline poured a dribble of oil and vinegar over her salad.

"Justin, I need to speak with you about something," she said. "Would it be possible for me to come to the office on Monday?"

"Well, I'm not in the office much anymore," he said. "I drop in a couple of times a week for meetings and consultations, but that's about it." He grinned ruefully. "I'm a judge now, Madeline."

"So I've heard." She smiled back at him with automatic politeness, but her eyes were worried.

"What did you want to see me about?" Justin asked, feeling a quick tug of alarm. "Is there some kind of problem?"

"That's what I want to find out. I'm concerned about Shelby."

"So am I," Justin said. "But you know what she's like. I can't talk to her about anything these days. It's so frustrating."

"Well, maybe you and I can discuss it, just to set my mind at rest. If you're not in the office any longer, would it perhaps be possible to meet for breakfast tomorrow?"

He felt a boyish surge of excitement but repressed it sternly, keeping his face as grave as hers. "That would be fine. Are you staying here at the Inn?"

"Yes. I have a very nice room overlooking the courtyard."

"Then we could meet here in the dining room. Would that be all right?"

She inclined her head.

"Nine o'clock?" he said.

"Thank you. That would be fine." Again she smiled, but he heard a tone of polite dismissal in her voice.

Justin knew it was time to get up and leave. The problem was, he couldn't seem to tear himself away. He wanted to sit there all night, looking into her eyes and hearing her voice.

"You must have come without telling anybody," he said. "None of the girls mentioned this to me, and neither did Beau."

"I haven't spoken to the children since I made my plans. In fact, I didn't tell anybody but Aunt Mary that I was coming."

"But will you be seeing the children before you leave?"

Her face softened. "I certainly hope so. And their partners, if they're around. I've yet to meet Marshall, Lucas and Holly, though I must say, I've heard a great deal about all of them. I was even hoping that Jax might...have the baby a little early," she said. "I'd love to see the baby."

"Would you like me to arrange something? Maybe we could all meet at the house, and the kids could bring along their—"

"No!" she said in obvious panic, then smiled quickly to soften her response. "Thank you, but I think I'll make my own arrangements with the children, Justin. I'm not anxious to visit Riverwood. Although," she added wistfully, "I'd love to see Charles again. How is he?"

"He's just fine. He drops in a few days a week at the office, but mostly he spends his days reading and puttering in the garden. Though I do think," Justin said reflectively, "he tends to suffer a bit lately from problems with the housekeeping."

"What do you mean?"

"Riverwood has changed, Madeline. It's not the household you used to run."

"Why?" she asked.

"Well, right now there's no food in the fridge, hardly any clean sheets to be found, and there's a nasty smell lingering somewhere in the dining room that makes me think one of the dogs might have had a little accident."

"Oh, dear," she murmured. "Where are Odelle and Woodrow?"

"Visiting relatives in Florida. And the housemaid's gone, too. Marie has filled the kitchen with candles and dried herbs, hanging from the beams. It's like a jungle. I can barely find my way around the table to cook and eat my Kraft dinner."

Her eyes widened. "Justin, for heaven's sake. You must be joking."

"Oh, no. I'm afraid none of this is very funny."

Nevertheless, he found himself chuckling ruefully as he told her about the state of the kitchen, the absence of any kind of household help, and the doleful need to eat hamburgers in town when he was hungry.

She joined in with the exquisite bubble of laughter that he remembered so well. Her face lit up with amusement, and all at once she was the sweet companion he remembered from so many years ago, the same graceful girl who'd bewitched him when he was a boy of eighteen.

"Madeline," he whispered, reaching out to touch her arm. "If you only knew how much I—"

Again her face stilled and that remote look came into her eyes. Almost imperceptibly, she moved her arm away.

"I don't want to keep you any longer, Justin," she said. "Your companion has been alone for some time already."

"My..." Justin followed her gaze and felt a little jolt of chagrin when he saw Claudia sitting at the other table. The truth was, he'd completely forgotten about the girl.

She caught his eye, smiling radiantly, and looked so pretty that he was startled all over again.

"She's very beautiful, isn't she?" Madeline said quietly.

"Claudia? Why, she's just..." Justin paused abruptly, thinking about the cautious, distant look on his ex-wife's face when he'd spoken of their shared past.

And hadn't Shelby mentioned something recently about

a wealthy businessman from Denver who was Madeline's current escort? "Incredibly rich and sexy" was her description of the man.

"Yes," he said after a moment. "Claudia is very beautiful. And a delightful person, too. She's so…unspoiled and natural."

"She looks very sweet." Madeline returned to her salad, picking bits of crabmeat from among the mound of greens.

Reluctantly, Justin got up and started to move away from the table. "Nine o'clock, then?" he said, pausing to glance down at her.

She nodded. "I'll see you then. Justin…"

"Yes?"

Madeline looked up at him directly, her gray eyes full of worry. "Do you think Shelby's in some kind of danger?"

He hesitated, wondering what to tell her. "I think," he said at last, choosing his words carefully, "that some strange mischief is afoot, something Shelby's been stirring up without really knowing what she's doing."

"But do you believe anybody would actually set out to harm her?"

"If I truly believed that," Justin said, "I'd be moving heaven and earth to make sure it didn't happen."

Madeline nodded, still looking troubled. "We'll talk more about it tomorrow, shall we?"

"All right. Until tomorrow, then?"

"Until tomorrow," she murmured.

The last Justin saw of her was that sleek dark head bent over the table, and a glow of candlelight on her elegant cheekbone.

MADELINE FINISHED her salad and declined an entrée, but chose to sip another glass of wine and have a light dessert.

Though the food and drink seemed dry and tasteless as dust, she didn't want to give the appearance of rushing away.

Instead she sat calmly at her table, watching as, just a few feet away, Justin talked and laughed with his lovely young companion.

Natural and unspoiled, he'd called her. Well, she certainly appeared to be both. In fact, the girl kept gazing around at her surroundings with a kind of awe, as if she'd never seen the inside of a fine restaurant before. But her dress was tasteful and expensive, and her accessories looked perfect. Still, there was a shy, touching gaucheness about her manner that Madeline found both puzzling and appealing.

No wonder Justin was attracted to the girl. But really, this Claudia was just a child. She had to be younger than Shelby.

Not that this fact in itself was particularly upsetting. Back among the jet-setting Aspen crowd, Madeline saw situations like this all the time—wealthy middle-aged men squiring beautiful young girls barely into their twenties.

And during her childhood years in Europe, the sight of an older man with a young mistress had been very common, so she wasn't terribly shocked by Justin's choice.

Still, it wasn't really the sort of thing she would have expected of her former husband. He'd always been so buttoned-down and conventional, so conscious of his public image. But this May-September relationship must be causing all kinds of gossip among the staid citizens of Bayou Beltane.

Madeline was a little confused, as well, to realize just how much it hurt to imagine Justin in bed with this delicious child.

She herself certainly had no personal interest in Justin Delacroix. After all, the man had hurt her terribly, neglected

her for years, destroyed their marriage and their home with
his carelessness and ambition.

No doubt her reaction was simply a normal part of life.
What woman wanted to see her ex-husband with a woman
so much younger than herself? It was human nature, nothing more.

But when Justin and his companion got up to leave, it
was all Madeline could do to smile courteously and conceal
the sudden, wholly unexpected burst of pain she felt as he
took the girl's arm protectively and escorted her into the
lobby.

He was still so handsome, with that dark, slightly silvered hair and finely molded face. She'd rather hoped he
might be balding and paunchy after all these years, but
Delacroix men tended to age well.

Madeline thought about the way he'd looked as he sat
across the table from her and watched her with such a
warm, intent expression. And the feel of his hand when
he'd reached out to touch her arm…

She shivered, experiencing a distressing sensation of
melting and warmth at the core of her body, a flood of
purely sexual response she'd thought never to experience
again in her life.

"Oh, my God," she whispered. "Please, God, not
that.…"

She should never have come back to Bayou Beltane. It
was madness, talking to Justin again.

Hastily, Madeline made plans to protect herself. She'd
spend just enough time in town to learn what she could
about this vague threat to Shelby. Then she'd be gone, back
to her home in Aspen where she was safe from all these
haunting memories and turbulent emotions, and far away
from Justin Delacroix.

She finished her meal and exchanged a few casual pleas-
antries with the young waiter, then climbed the stairs

slowly to her room. But her fatigue was gone, replaced by a tumult of nervous excitement that didn't subside when she undressed and soaked in a long, luxurious bath, then pulled on a nightgown, robe and slippers.

Sitting at the little rosewood desk, Madeline called her children one by one, but found nobody at home on this Saturday night. She left a message on each machine saying she was in town and would be available for visits after breakfast on Sunday morning.

Finally she went to bed and lay thinking about the coming day.

Tomorrow morning, just a few hours from now, she'd see Justin again. They'd be eating together, talking about their family and people they'd known in common for dozens of years.

The situation was fraught with danger.

She had to be firmly on her guard, Madeline realized as she lay in bed and stared at the ceiling. She couldn't let any of those treacherous old feelings draw her into letting down her defenses.

The best thing was to keep thinking about that lovely young woman who'd been dining with Justin tonight, and the way he'd held her arm so protectively as they left the restaurant.

Who was the girl, and what did she mean to Justin?

Claudia, he'd called her. It was a quiet, dignified name, one that Madeline had always been fond of.

Was it more than simply a physical relationship? He'd talked about how sweet the girl was. When he'd spoken of her, his face had registered genuine affection.

Madeline had known the man for more than thirty years. She could tell when he liked somebody. For some reason that hurt more than anything—the fact that he truly liked this girl.

Madeline had grown up in a cosmopolitan setting, where

the ways of men were looked on with amused tolerance.
She wasn't shocked by the knowledge of Justin's sexual
relationship. But ten years after their divorce she was still
distressed at the idea of him laughing with another woman,
reading the newspaper with her in bed, sharing jokes and
memories—enjoying the kind of companionship that Madeline had always craved during her marriage.

"Ridiculous," she muttered, rolling over in bed and
clutching the pillow. "Simply ridiculous."

Again she felt an urgent longing to be gone from this
place, back to her own pleasant condo nestled among the
towering peaks around Aspen.

It was more than an hour before Madeline finally dozed
off. Her sleep was troubled, filled with scraps of dreams
about Justin and his new girlfriend, about Charles and William and Mary, about the children and their years together
in the old house on the river.

CHAPTER FIVE

CLAUDIA WOKE EARLY on Sunday morning and slipped out
of bed, stretching and yawning, then padded across the
braided rug next to her bunk bed and onto the deck of her
little old houseboat.

The sun was rising in the east in a pastel swirl of clouds,
and a southern wind blew lightly over the water. She stood
by the railing in her flannel pyjamas, breathing the sweet
salty air from the distant gulf and looking across the tranquil expanse of the river.

Palmettos and cypress trees massed along the edge of the
water, trailing their branches into the still, green depths.
Near the boat, a banded water snake swam lazily among
the lily pads, its head held high, forked tongue darting. Off
in the center of the river a snowy egret rose clumsily and
flapped its wings, turning and drifting into the mist above
the other shore.

Claudia sighed with pleasure, then frowned when she
remembered the previous evening. She picked at a faded
splinter of paint on the deck railing, wondering if she'd
made a complete fool of herself.

Mr. Delacroix was so nice, a true gentleman. He was
gracious and patient, and seemed genuinely interested in
helping her to learn things.

But she was such an idiot, so totally ignorant about all
the things a grown-up woman should know without being
told.

Her cheeks flamed when she remembered being gently

remonstrated over her table manners, instructed to cut her meat properly and not talk with her mouth full. A person was supposed to know those things from childhood, but she'd never been taught.

After her mother died, Claudia and her brothers had eaten like animals, grabbing whatever chunks of food they could find in their little shack on the bayou. They'd never gathered around a dinner table and concerned themselves with which fork to choose, where to put the knife when it wasn't in use or how to talk politely and use proper grammar.

She wandered back inside the single room of the shabby rented houseboat, where everything she owned was tucked away. Claudia loved keeping the place spotlessly clean, from the tiny galley at one end of the room to the neat little head at the other.

A small closet was jammed between the bunk and the galley. Claudia opened it and took out the black dress. Unwrapping its plastic covering, she held the gown against her body, examining her wavy image in the mirror on the closet door.

She'd forgotten about the new haircut, and she felt a little start of surprise when she looked at herself. It seemed like an entirely different person gazed back at her, somebody wide-eyed and graceful, the kind of girl who'd know automatically which fork she was supposed to use.

"Well, you really gone and done it, ain't you?" she told herself soberly. "And you sure can't back out now. Whatever happens, you gotta go on with this, Claudia Landry."

Still, she felt a little shiver of fear when she turned away from the mirror and looked around at her tidy floating home.

Despite her brave words to Justin Delacroix, Claudia really was afraid of her brothers, and she dreaded the prospect of them coming around to trash her boat. After the last time, it had taken so long to repair the mess, to get everything neat and shipshape again, the way she liked her home to be.

Besides, old Hiram Skettle, who rented the boat to her, had threatened to put her out of her home if it got damaged again.

"Nothing personal," he'd said, hitching up the strap of his overalls and scratching himself lazily. "You're a real good girl, Claudia, and you always pay your rent on time. But I cain't have them animals coming around here and wrecking my property. You know I cain't."

"Bastards," she muttered angrily, gripping the dress as she thought about Joey, Paul and Jim-Bob with their swaggering ways and crude speech, and their constant refusal to let her live her life in peace. "Dirty bastards."

She clenched her hands into fists, then breathed deeply and forced herself to relax. For a moment she stroked the delicate black fabric with a lingering hand before hanging the dress away carefully in its shroud of plastic.

After brief consideration, she chose one of the other new outfits to wear—a pair of pleated khaki slacks with a brown leather belt, and a cream-colored linen shirt with the sleeves rolled up and held by buttoned tabs.

Claudia put on the stylish clothes and looked at herself in the mirror again, smiling with pleasure.

What an amazing difference it made to dress like this. She was still tomboy Claudia Landry from up the bayou, but the truth was, she looked more like one of Mr. Delacroix's pretty daughters.

Claudia glanced out the porthole and watched as a leggy gray kitten approached the boat. He paused at the dock to lick a front paw and swipe it over his whiskered face a couple of times, then ran lightly down the walkway, leaped to the deck and came in through the open door to jump onto her bed.

Nestled in the middle of the rumpled blankets, the kitten returned to his morning grooming. He hoisted one hind leg in the air and twisted to lick his glossy flank with furious energy.

Claudia smiled and scratched behind his ears. "Hi, Socks. You been out there tearing around again, you bad kitty? I ain't seen you for three days. I was getting real worried."

The little cat rubbed against her hand, then looked up at her, his green eyes wide and inscrutable.

"Aw, c'mon now, what're you staring at?" Claudia asked dryly. "Socks, you never seen a girl with a haircut before?"

The kitten relaxed and settled back among the blankets, lifting his head to be petted.

"I must really be nervous," Claudia muttered, "if I'm worried my own cat don't recognize me."

Socks closed his eyes and began to purr noisily.

"Doesn't recognize me," she corrected herself. "I know what you're thinking," she added, turning away to get a loaf of bread from the tiny fridge. "You're wondering how I can wear fancy clothes like this when I'm heading off to work. Ain't—aren't you, Socks?"

The kitten yawned, then watched with sudden alertness as she reached for a can of cat food.

"Well, I won't be doing any dirty work today," she told him. "I'm just going over a bunch of paperwork for Remy. Fact is..." She scooped the cat food into a plastic bowl and lowered her voice as if eavesdroppers might be nearby, listening. "Lots of times I'm not doing dirty work, Socks. I just wear them old overalls because, well, I don't want to be bothered with nothing else." Claudia put the bowl on the floor. "Anything else," she corrected herself automatically.

And because the overalls feel safe, she told herself, but didn't say it aloud.

Inside that baggy denim, with her old plaid shirts and the tangle of hair covering her face, she felt more or less invisible. She could hide and be safe.

But Mr. Delacroix was right. It was time to stop hiding.

Claudia watched while Socks leaped down from the bed and began to eat daintily. She made herself a few slices of toast and gulped some instant coffee, then tidied her bed and locked the houseboat while Socks napped on the deck in a thin pool of sunlight.

She rode her bicycle along the bayou to Remy's cluster of shacks, enjoying the freshness of the morning and the whisper of wind as it rippled through the tall, coarse grasses lining the road.

At the swamp tour offices, she parked her bike and checked the outbuildings. Then she went inside Remy's office, made a pot of coffee, switched on the radio and settled at the desk to go through a pile of invoices and enter them in the ledger.

Sunlight streamed through the windows and the screen door, falling in slanted rectangles across the wooden planks. The radio was playing a country ballad, haunting and sweet. Claudia hummed along with the music and reached up absently to touch the short hair around her ears, surprised again by its sleek, clipped feeling.

Still humming, she took her empty mug and got up, carrying it across the room to the coffeepot. Suddenly a shadow fell across the floor and she whirled around, startled.

A tall, broad-shouldered man stood in the doorway. Claudia stared at him without recognition, her eyes dazzled by the sunlight pouring over his shoulders. When he moved into the room and closed the screen door behind him, she suddenly caught her breath and stood rigidly, searching for words.

The man was Bernard Leroux. Claudia took in every detail of his appearance while she gawked at him, still unable to speak.

He was wearing a white T-shirt and faded jeans. His brown hair was cut short, and in his handsome tanned face, the eyes were piercing blue. He'd obviously been out on his boat and hadn't shaved for a couple of days, but the shadow of dark stubble, so unattractive on other men, just made Bernard look more sexy and virile.

She clutched the mug nervously, drowning in embarrassment.

Her visitor was also silent, watching her in obvious surprise.

This is ridiculous, Claudia told herself. *Somebody has to say something, we can't just stand here and stare at each other all day.*

But she was so painfully self-conscious in her stylish clothes, her leather sandals and elegant haircut that she couldn't think what to say.

"My goodness," she murmured at last, turning away with an awkward laugh. "You scared me half to death. I ain't—I'm not used to folks dropping by the office when Remy's not here."

"Where's Remy?"

"Gone to New Orleans for a few days. We'll be open for business again on Tuesday. I'm finishing up some paperwork before he gets back."

"You're..." He looked at her in confusion. "Did Remy just hire you, or what?"

Claudia returned his gaze, speechless with surprise. "Bernard...I been working here for more than three years!" she said at last.

His eyes widened and he took a step forward, peering at

her in the shadows of the office. "You're Claudia?" he breathed. "Claudia Landry?"

A male voice on the radio crooned in the stillness, singing about love and passion, about sorrow and heartbreak and a woman he couldn't forget.

Claudia smiled dryly and poured coffee into her mug, turning away to hide her flaming cheeks. "Ain't—isn't it amazing," she said with forced lightness, "how much difference a haircut can make?"

Bernard leaned against a metal filing cabinet and watched while she hurried across the room with her coffee and settled behind the desk again.

"It's not just the haircut," he said at last. "You look completely different, Claudia. Like a whole new person."

She felt a little more composed now that she was sitting down and had the big wooden desk between herself and her visitor.

"Well," she said, "I reckon I'm pretty much the same person I always was, haircut or not." She adjusted the ledger in a businesslike manner and picked up a pen, hoping her hands wouldn't start shaking too badly. "Can I do something for you, Bernard?"

"I wanted to ask Remy about..." He shook his head. "It's okay. He'll be back tomorrow, you said?"

"That's right. Tuesday at the latest."

"Okay. I guess I can talk to him then." Bernard turned toward the door, then paused. "Will you be working here all day?"

Claudia shook her head. "Just till I get the rest of these entries made. I need to go home this afternoon and paint the railing on my boat before it starts raining."

He smiled, his teeth flashing against his brown face. "Need any help?"

Claudia's heart began to pound so loudly under the

cream-colored linen that she was afraid he might hear it. But she shook her head and looked down at the ledger.

"I don't need nobody's—anybody's help with my boat," she murmured. "I been looking after it myself for a whole lot of years."

Bernard reached for the doorknob. His hands were finely made, square and strong, and there was a light dusting of golden hairs on his tanned forearm, gilded now in the sunshine. Claudia shivered and felt her mouth turn dry.

"Well, if you ever need any help," he said, "you just let me know."

"Thank you." She summoned the tattered remnants of her dignity. "I'll remember that."

Bernard lingered for a moment, smiling at her. Then he was gone, and Claudia sat alone, staring at the empty doorway while she gripped the coffee mug so tightly that her knuckles turned white.

ON SUNDAY MORNING, Madeline slept late in the four-poster bed at the Bayou Inn. After her restless night, she almost drowsed through a wake-up call from the front desk.

Finally the persistent ringing dragged her from the morass of troubled dreams.

"Hello?" she said breathlessly, hauling the receiver toward her and resting it on the pillow.

"Ms. Belanger? This is your wake-up call. It's eight o'clock."

"I...yes," she murmured, twisting her head to look at the clock. "Thank you very much."

She hung up and lay for a moment with her eyes closed, longing to fall back into sleep and not have to face the upcoming breakfast.

But when she opened one eye to examine the clock again, panic set in and she climbed hastily out of bed, tossing the covers aside.

Eight o'clock!

Madeline was normally an early riser. Despite the time change and the wake-up call, she'd fully expected to be up for at least an hour already, showered and groomed, possibly having a pot of clear tea with lemon sent up to the room so she could compose herself at leisure before meeting Justin.

But instead, she found rushing around frantically to get ready. There was something treacherous in the bayou air that affected even the most disciplined—a languorous, do-it-tomorrow kind of feeling that crept into one's very bones.

"Dreadful place," she muttered as she pulled the door of the shower stall closed behind her and turned on the spray of steaming water at full force. "Lazy, corrupting place where everybody knows everybody else's business and there's nothing to do all day but sit in the sun and gossip...."

But it was also a lovely place, she had to admit when she emerged from the shower with her hair wrapped in a towel and crossed the room to look out the window. Forgetting her rush, Madeline curled up on the window seat as she rubbed the towel through her damp hair and gazed down at the courtyard.

The terrace had been freshly washed and the steaming bricks glistened bright red in the sunlight. An old gardener in overalls moved slowly among the trailing bougainvillea, trimming and watering, his dark skin and faded denim making a pleasant contrast to the bright green of the leaves, the brilliant flowers and shiny washed brick.

Madeline found herself longing for a sketch pad and some tempera paints, a feeling she'd had frequently since arriving in Louisiana. Everything here was a picture, a stimulus to her artist's imagination.

But strangely enough, when she'd actually lived on the bayou, she hadn't painted much at all.

Once again Madeline gazed thoughtfully at the courtyard with its rich palette of colors.

All those early years, she'd been so passionately in love with Justin, and then so busy with their growing brood of children, that she hadn't touched a paintbrush. And finally, when the children were in school and she would have had some free time, she was too lonely and sad to feel like painting.

Only when she escaped, moved away to Colorado and began a life of her own, had she been able to start recovering her gift.

She got up and rummaged through her carry-all, looking for the hair dryer.

Maybe it would be different now, since she'd developed some strength of character and a sense of her own identity. Perhaps now Madeline could actually live here in Bayou Beltane, near her family, and not be swallowed up by the pressure of everything that went on in this closely tied community.

"What nonsense is this?" she asked herself, staring gravely at her own face as she dried her hair. "Surely you can't be considering anything so ridiculous."

But all the children are here, she told herself silently. *And I miss them so much. Soon there'll be grandchildren…very soon, in fact.*

"That's no excuse for moving back to a place where you were miserable for so many years. The children are all grown and perfectly capable of visiting you in Aspen. In fact," she added dryly, "all of the children love visiting in Aspen."

Still, the woman in the mirror seemed unconvinced. Her eyes looked wide and tearful, and there was a stubborn set to her mouth.

"Utter nonsense," Madeline repeated firmly. "The sooner I can get finished and away from here, the happier I'll be."

She fluffed the hair around her face, then turned to rummage through the closet and give serious consideration to the problem of what to wear for this breakfast meeting with Justin.

Nothing too formal, since she didn't want to give him an impression their relationship mattered to her at all....

Perhaps a pair of khaki slacks and this silky brown T-shirt?

Madeline frowned, then shook her head.

Too casual. That wasn't the right message, either. It implied she was comfortable and relaxed with him, and perhaps they were about to set off on some kind of outdoor jaunt for the rest of the day.

Definitely not the mood she wanted to create.

Finally she settled on a long skirt of finely combed denim, a white cotton blouse with silver buttons, a pair of leather sandals and some engraved silver earrings from the Bare Bones Gallery.

The look was perfect, Madeline decided as she dressed. Not too formal, not too casual, and just different enough to make the point that she wasn't a Louisiana resident any longer. She lived in the West, where she had a life-style completely different from the one Justin had always known.

She took some time over her makeup, still smiling ruefully at herself and her concern over this meeting. Just before nine o'clock she tidied the room, closed her door and descended the curving staircase. Her heart began to pound and her palm felt clammy on the railing when she saw Justin waiting in the lobby below.

He, too, must have given some thought to the matter of dress for this Sunday brunch with his ex-wife. Instead of his usual jacket and tie, he wore a pair of tan linen slacks and a yellow cotton shirt printed with a small seahorse logo over the left pocket.

He seemed as young as she remembered him despite the silver at his temples. The man was tall, erect, tanned and amazingly handsome. Maddeningly, his nearness made her knees feel weak.

"You look beautiful," he said with warm sincerity as she reached the lobby and approached him. "Positively radiant."

Madeline smiled. "Thank you, but I'm afraid it's mostly these cowgirl clothes. They tend to be very flattering."

"So the elegant Parisienne is a cowgirl now?" he teased.

"That's right," she said. "I've even learned the two-step."

He gave her a warm glance that shook her composure even further. "Well, I'd love to see that. Madeline, you look about nineteen years old."

"Ah, but you forget, Justin." She gave him another wry smile as they entered the dining room. "Most of the time when I was nineteen, I was pregnant with twins and looked positively dreadful."

"That's not true." Justin nodded at the waiter, then pulled out a chair for Madeline and sat down opposite her. "Matter of fact, I was just thinking the other day…" He paused and cleared his throat, then continued huskily, "I was thinking how pretty you looked when you were pregnant with Beau and Jax."

She glanced up at him in surprise, wondering what to say, and was a little taken aback by the intensity of his expression.

"Now, whatever brought that ancient memory into your mind?" she asked lightly, smoothing the napkin in her lap.

"I happened to be passing along Magnolia Street and I went to look at our first house. Remember that little cottage, Madeline?"

"Vaguely." She frowned, concentrating on the menu. "Do they do the eggs Benedict nicely here?"

"It's not green and yellow anymore," Justin said. "Our old house, I mean. They've gone and painted it some god-awful trendy color. But otherwise it seems pretty much the same."

"I could have beignets, or the *pain perdu*," she murmured, gripping the leather cover of the menu. "But I don't know if I..."

He smiled at her. She'd forgotten the way his eyes crinkled at the corners, and that surprising dimple just above the edge of his jaw where the skin had always felt so silky when she kissed him....

"I didn't know you liked rich things for breakfast, Madeline," he said. "As I recall, you always used to eat half a grapefruit and nibble some dry toast while the rest of us were loading up on fat and sugar."

"I still eat that way," she said, then smiled when she remembered little Jennifer O'Sullivan sitting gravely across the dining table in her tartan outfit. "Unless..."

"Yes?" Justin opened the menu and glanced at it. "Unless what?"

Madeline shrugged. "Unless I have company for breakfast. Then I sometimes break my own rules, just for a treat."

This time it was his turn to tighten his fingers on the menu. He shot her a quick, guarded look. "And do you often have company for breakfast, Madeline?" he asked quietly.

"It's not..." Automatically she began to protest the implication, then remembered the lovely young woman he'd escorted the previous evening. "Yes," she said calmly. "On occasion I do."

He was silent a moment, giving the waitress a brief, courteous smile as she filled their coffee cups.

"Shelby tells me you're dating a businessman from Denver."

"Dating?" Madeline made a little grimace of distaste. "That's such an unattractive word for people our age, don't you think?"

"So how would you describe your relationship with this fellow?"

"I wouldn't describe it at all," Madeline said calmly. "I would leave it in the background where it belongs. After all, Justin, we're not here to bare our souls to each other. We only want to talk about Shelby, that's all."

The waitress came to take their orders. When they were alone again, Justin sipped from his coffee cup and looked at Madeline over the rim. "So what have you heard about Shelby?"

"Aunt Mary told me last week about the shotgun blast on the bayou road. That was the first I've heard about any direct threats to her."

"We're still not certain it was a threat," he said. "It could just as easily have been an accident."

"Do you believe that?"

He frowned, tracing the cup handle thoughtfully. "I'm not sure what to believe. There have definitely been some strange things happening."

"Like Charly's accident? And the fire in the horse barn?"

He glanced up quickly, his eyes widening. "That's not what I was thinking about. Why? Do you really believe the two things are connected somehow?"

"I have no idea what to believe. You're the one who lives here, Justin. I only want to know if there's some kind of threat to my children, and if so, what can be done about it."

He stared at her, clearly troubled. "If I believed for a

minute that what happened to Charly was somehow linked to the accidents Shelby's been having..."

"Why is it so hard to believe? You know well enough what people around here are like."

"Oh, there's always been plenty of mischief along the bayou, but I don't believe anybody would set out deliberately to harm one of our children. For God's sake, either of them might have been killed!"

"Charly almost was," Madeline said quietly, remembering all over again the pain of that dreadful time during the winter. "And Beau was seriously burned, I hear."

"You could be right," Justin muttered after a long silence. "Maybe I'm too close to everything to be sure about what's going on. Around here, the bizarre can get to seem normal after a while."

"That's certainly true."

He looked at her across the linen and silverware and a little vase of scarlet dahlias in the center of the table. "So what do you think is happening?"

Madeline stared down at the tablecloth. "Well, for one thing, I believe Shelby made a very dangerous enemy when she won that custody case against Lyle Masson. And there are people in her own family who are closer to the likes of Lyle Masson than they are to her."

"You mean Uncle Philip?"

She made a wry grimace, then watched as the waitress delivered their food.

"Madeline?" he asked when the young woman left. "Is that what you're thinking?"

She reached for the pepper and sprinkled it judiciously onto her poached eggs. "Well, let's be reasonable. If there's a threat, it's more likely to be coming from that side of the family."

"But I can't believe Philip would actually... Those girls could have been killed. No matter what he's like, the man wouldn't go that far. Or allow anybody else to, for that matter.''

''Maybe they just intended to frighten Shelby a little, to show her who's boss, but things got out of hand.''

''I've considered that,'' Justin admitted with some reluctance. ''But I still don't want to believe it. If I did,'' he added fiercely, ''I'd go over there right now and—''

''Do more harm than good, no doubt,'' Madeline said dryly. ''I think it's probably better if I have a little talk with Philip myself. He and I have always gotten along quite well, you know.''

''Philip's such a snob,'' Justin mused. ''He was thrilled when you married me because he thought it added some class to the Delacroix.''

''What utter nonsense,'' Madeline said with feeling. ''I'm glad that sort of thinking is finally being left behind, even here in the South.''

Justin watched her curiously. ''So you'll really go and talk to Philip about all this?''

''I certainly will.'' Madeline spread strawberry preserves on a slice of toast. ''In fact, I intend to go to his office tomorrow and ask him if his unsavory friends have been trying to harm any of my children. And,'' she added, ''to request that he pass on a message about what will happen if it goes any further. I think that should be quite effective, don't you?''

Justin smiled suddenly and gave her a look of warm admiration. ''I'd like to be a fly on the wall during that interview.''

''Don't worry,'' she told him serenely. ''It will all be very civilized and courteous.'' She nibbled her toast and took a sip of water, then dabbed her mouth with a napkin. ''It's the *other* interview I'm planning to conduct that could produce some fireworks.''

''The other interview? Who else do you intend to see?''

Madeline took a sip of coffee and set the cup down. "Flora," she said.

"You're going to talk to Flora Boudreaux?" he asked in astonishment.

"I certainly am. Some of these things Mary told me about have the look of Flora's kind of mischief. Especially that fire."

"I've thought the same thing," he admitted. "She's been acting even wilder than usual lately, very erratic. When Steven died, she was almost out of control with grief."

"Aunt Mary told me about that. And I have a lot of sympathy for her, but I also know what kind of cruelty Flora's capable of. I simply won't have that woman doing harm to my family."

"Would you like me to come along when you talk with her?"

"I don't think so, Justin. Flora and I will just have a little chat, woman-to-woman, and I'll see what she's up to. That's one of the reasons I'm here."

"But, Madeline...aren't you afraid of talking to Flora?" he asked. "You always used to find her so intimidating."

"I still find her distasteful. But I'm not at all intimidated by her or Philip. In fact..."

"Yes?" he prompted.

"I filed a document with my lawyer in Aspen before I left, Justin. It outlines a few things I know about Philip, and some additional things I've learned about him and Lyle Masson through some business colleagues who have connections down here. My letter also gives detailed instructions what to do with the information if I meet with some kind of...accident. I intend to tell Philip about that document, so I'm not at all afraid."

Justin's admiring look turned to one of awed surprise. "You're so different," he said. "You've become a real tiger."

"Just last night," she told him with a brief smile, "you were telling me I hadn't changed at all."

He studied her thoughtfully. "I'm not sure you have. Maybe this fearless woman was inside you all the time but I never saw her."

Madeline ate her meal quietly, thinking about his words. She knew exactly what he meant. In fact, she was thinking much the same thing about him. This boyish, relaxed Justin was a person she'd never really seen before.

All during his early manhood, responsibilities and ambition had rested heavily on his shoulders. He'd been serious to the point of pomposity. Now his smile flashed at unexpected times, lighting his face like sunshine, and he had a casual, almost reckless air that she found dangerously appealing.

"Let's not get into the analysis game," she said lightly. "It tends to destroy friendships." She looked up at him. "Justin, these old papers that Shelby keeps talking about..."

"Yes?"

"Do you know anything about them?"

"Only that they relate to a legal case more than sixty years old that my grandfather lost, one where the judge exhibited some very odd behavior. It's all a bit of a mystery."

Madeline sighed. "There are so many mysteries down here. You feel mysteries in the air when you walk along the streets."

For a moment she was tempted to ask him why nobody had told Uncle William the truth about his parentage. But it was none of her business, Madeline told herself firmly. She was already getting too involved in family affairs for her own comfort.

"That's the way of the South, Madeline," Justin was

saying. "Tell me, is there anything at all I can do to help you?"

She shook her head. "I only wanted you to know what I'm doing. Let's talk about the other children for a while, all right? I'd like to hear your opinion about all these new partners. And," she added with a wistful smile, "how you feel about becoming a granddaddy."

They talked quietly for the rest of their meal, avoiding any personal observations or other dangerous topics. The waitress brought the bill and Justin reached for it, refusing Madeline's offer to pay her share.

"Would you like to come out to the house for coffee?" he asked.

She considered, tempted by his offer. The chance to see Riverwood again, to visit with Charles and see how her children were living...

As well, Madeline couldn't deny that she was curious about Justin's life. He'd already mentioned Odelle's absence and the general disarray of the household. It was something she could hardly imagine, Justin Delacroix living in less-than-perfect surroundings.

Finally she gathered herself together, pushed her chair back and smiled at him. "I don't think so, Justin," she said quietly. "But thank you for the offer, and for breakfast, too. It was very pleasant."

With a gracious nod she turned and left the dining room, painfully conscious of him watching as she walked away.

CHAPTER SIX

IN THE LOBBY, Madeline paused at the desk to inquire about messages.

"I'm expecting quite a number of them," she told the clerk, who looked up in a distracted fashion from his computer screen. "At least five."

He rummaged in a cubicle and took out a single scrap of yellow paper with a handwritten message.

Madeline watched him in confusion, her heart sinking. "But...I was hoping there would be more."

The clerk shook his head. "I'm afraid that's all we have for you now, ma'am."

"All right." She smiled automatically and moved away, carrying the slip of paper. "Thank you. I'll be in my room for a while if anybody should call."

The clerk nodded and returned to his computer. Madeline climbed the stairs, examining the scrap of paper. "Shelby telephoned," it read. "Will be home all day Sunday. Call ASAP."

Madeline went into her bathroom and washed her hands. She studied her face in the mirror, trying to imagine how she would have appeared to Justin across the breakfast table. Despite his compliments and his look of warm admiration, she could hardly compare with that radiant young woman he'd been escorting the night before.

She wandered back into the other room, picked up the phone and dialed Shelby's number.

"Hi!" Shelby croaked, her voice husky. "What a wonderful surprise. I can't believe you're actually in town. When I got your phone message last night, I was amazed."

"You sound terrible, darling," Madeline said with quick concern. "Do you have a cold?"

"I'm coming down with something, that's for sure. Yesterday I just had a little sore throat, but today I'm croaking like a bullfrog."

"Any other symptoms?"

"Well, let's see. I seem to be running a bit of a fever and I feel sore all over."

"That sounds like flu. Is there anybody with you?"

"Not a soul," Shelby coughed hoarsely. "Even the housemaid's taken off, and Odelle's been gone for days. This big old place is like a mausoleum. I don't even know where Grandfather is. Probably over at Aunt Mary's, where he can find something to eat."

"But..." Madeline gripped the phone cord. "But darling, who's looking after you?"

Her daughter made an odd, strangled sound that Madeline recognized as laughter. "Heck, I don't need looking after. I'm almost thirty years old, for heaven's sake."

"Nonsense," Madeline said. "I happen to know what that house is like. It's a long way from your rooms to the kitchen, and you should be staying in bed when you're sick with the flu. Who'll fetch you hot tea and bring you something to eat when you're hungry?"

"And put a gooey old mustard plaster on my chest?" Shelby asked.

"Don't be impertinent, young lady." Madeline smiled into the phone. "Every one of my French nannies used to swear by mustard plasters. They're a very effective treatment."

"And I have the burn scars to prove it," Shelby said dryly. "It's nice to hear your voice," she added, sounding so wistful that Madeline began to worry again.

"Is nobody else there at all, dear?" she asked. "Where are your sisters?"

"Everybody's away. You should have let us know you were coming, because they're going to feel just terrible about missing you."

Madeline felt another stab of disappointment. "Where has everybody gone?"

"Well, let's see. Beau and Holly…" Shelby paused, overcome by a coughing fit, then continued. "Beau and Holly went with Remy and Kendall to do some business in the city and have a little holiday. Remy's looking for a new boat, Beau's shopping for horses and Holly and Kendall want to pick up some clothes."

"I see. So they'll be gone until…"

"Tuesday, likely. Will you be staying that long?"

"I'd planned to leave on Wednesday morning, but perhaps I can arrange to extend my visit a little. What about your sisters?"

"Marie's in Orlando taking a course in alternative medicine. She won't be back for two weeks…speaking of which, you should see this house. The place is a total disaster zone, not just because Marie left her herb harvest all over the kitchen."

"Yes, I know," Madeline said with a brief smile. "Actually, your father's told me quite a lot about the state of the household."

"You mean you've already talked to him?" Despite her hoarseness, Shelby sounded both startled and pleased.

"Your father and I had breakfast together this morning."

"But that's wonderful! Why, it must be the first time you two have spoken for years."

"Justin and I weren't 'not speaking,'" Madeline said. "It was just that the—the opportunity never came up before."

"So what did you talk about?" Shelby asked. "Don't you think he's looking great?"

"Yes, Justin looks very well. As a matter of fact, he was…"

"What?" Shelby asked when her mother paused.

"Nothing important," Madeline said, more curtly than she'd intended.

"Oh, come on," Shelby coaxed. "What were you going to say?"

"Just that he seems to be doing quite well for himself these days. Justin was escorting a most attractive young woman last night. She was positively radiant."

"Well, I don't know," Shelby said dubiously, "if you could really describe Virginia Carmichael as young. Although I must admit, she certainly knows how to dress."

"This woman's name wasn't Virginia," Madeleine said. "He introduced her as Claudia."

She heard her daughter's sharp intake of breath, followed by a lengthy silence.

"Shelby? What is it?"

"You know, I heard something about this," Shelby murmured. "But I never believed a word of it until now. You actually saw them together? He was with Claudia Landry?"

"They were sitting about ten feet away from me in the dining room at the Bayou Inn, and they seemed to be having a wonderful time."

"No kidding," Shelby said. "Was Claudia wearing her denim overalls?"

"Her…" Madeline frowned in confusion. "She was wearing a black dress that looked like a Donna Karan. Very simple and elegant. She was lovely."

"My God," Shelby breathed, then lapsed into a coughing fit and was unable to speak for a while. "I still can't believe it," she said at last. "This is all just too bizarre."

"Who is this girl, Shelby?"

"She works for Remy down at his tour business. Mostly she runs the bait shop and ticket sales. Claudia's really a sweet kid, but I've never seen her wearing anything except rubber boots, baggy overalls and plaid shirts about six sizes too big for her. And she's got a tangled mess of hair that hangs in her eyes all the time."

"Not anymore."

Madeline thought about the lovely gamine sitting opposite Justin. Once again she found herself marveling at how drastically the man had changed. This was more evidence of a transformed personality.

The old Justin would never have concerned himself with the kind of person Shelby had just described, no matter how young, pretty or sexy the girl was. Justin would have made a more cautious, socially acceptable choice in a romantic partner.

Madeline felt a sharp pang of jealousy and realized to her alarm that she was becoming dangerously attracted to this new, devil-may-care incarnation of Justin Delacroix. In fact, she could hardly manage to get his image out of her mind.

"So?" Shelby was asking with breathless interest, "do you think he and Claudia are really together? I mean, did it look as if they—"

"I don't think it's appropriate for me to be discussing your father's private life," Madeline said with considerably more calm that she felt. "You'll just have to direct your questions to him, I'm afraid. Now, where are Jax and Charlotte?"

"Jax and Matt have taken the kids to a horse show in North Carolina. It's something they've all been looking forward to for a long time."

"Oh, yes," Madeline said in growing dismay. "I remember Jax mentioning something about that. I just didn't realize it was happening quite so soon, or that Jax would make the trip so close to her due date."

"Well, you know Jax. Nothing slows her down...not even a baby. And Charly and Marshall are off in west Texas, sleuthing around on some mysterious case that she won't even talk about it."

"Is Charly feeling all right?" Madeline asked anxiously.

"She's so happy. She loves this private-investigation business. And," Shelby added, sounding bleak again, "she's pretty crazy about Marshall, too. They're real happy together."

"That's nice." Madeline's voice tightened, and she felt sick with disappointment. "But it looks like I might not get to see any of them."

"I still don't understand.... Why did you just drop in like this? You should have let everybody know you were coming."

"I didn't want my arrival published too much in advance. I wanted a chance to look around discreetly and make my own judgments about what's been happening in this town."

"Happening? What do you mean?"

"Oh, I think you know," Madeline said quietly. "Tell me, has you car windshield been fixed yet?"

"It's going to be ready in a... For heaven's sake, you didn't come all the way to Louisiana because of a stray load of buckshot!"

"It wasn't only your shotgun blast, although that news was disturbing enough, let me tell you. But it seems a lot of very strange things have been happening to you lately, my dear, and I've only recently become aware of them."

"There's nothing in the world to fret about," Shelby said, obviously trying to sound breezy and offhand despite her raspy voice. "It's just a lot of coincidence, that's all."

"So your father's been telling me. Is that what you truly believe?"

"Of course it is. I've lived in Bayou Beltane all my life. I can't believe anybody around here would want to cause me any harm."

Her words were casual enough, but Madeline, who knew her daughter better than anybody, sensed an unfamiliar note of tension, even fear, in that raspy young voice.

"I think perhaps we should talk about it some more," she suggested. "But not over the phone, Shelby, because this is too tiring for you. I want you to go to bed now, dear."

"Maybe you could come out here," Shelby said tentatively. "Just for a visit, since I can't come to town."

Madeline looked at the telephone, feeling torn.

She knew how deeply Shelby had suffered over her mother's departure all those years ago, and how long it had taken for this stubborn daughter to forgive her. The invitation, offered with seeming casualness, was an important step for both of them.

"Shelby," she said after a moment, "you know how much I'd love to see you. But I really don't want to visit Riverwood."

"If you don't come here, I won't be able to see you. I feel so rotten, I couldn't drag myself out of bed and go somewhere else to talk with you. Anyhow, I'd have to borrow a car, and I don't know if—"

"All right," Madeline said reluctantly. "I'll come. Just rest and try to sleep for a while. I'll drive out there this afternoon."

"That'll be so nice." Shelby coughed again. "When will you get here?"

Madeline glanced at her watch. "Well, it's close to eleven now. I'll tend to a few things here in my room and let you have a little sleep, and get there around two. Is that all right?"

"Mmm," Shelby murmured sleepily.

Madeline pictured her daughter curled up in bed with the receiver nestled against her ear, and was shaken by a warm flood of tenderness.

"Mama?" Shelby asked.

"Yes, dear?"

"Will you rub my forehead and make me a pot of herb tea with honey?"

Madeline looked at the phone in astonishment and felt tears stinging her eyes. "Yes, darling," she murmured. "I'll be happy to."

"I love you," Shelby said drowsily.

"I love you, too, my dearest," Madeline said, trying to keep her voice steady. "Have a nice sleep, and I'll see you in a few hours."

JUSTIN WANDERED across town to the law office, where he'd left his car. He couldn't help thinking about Madeline, and was still shaken by the unexpectedness of her arrival, the turbulent emotions aroused by speaking with her again after all these years.

She was amazing, he thought, remembering her clear gray eyes, her lovely face and quiet bubble of laughter.

And she was so *interesting*. The woman had been his wife for all those years, but he'd taken very little time to really talk with her. Now, when it was far too late, he found himself fascinated by her outlook on life, her wry humor and gentle wit.

Madeline was every bit as competent and strong as Virginia Carmichael. But in a strange way, she was also as vulnerable and winsome as young Claudia.

She was beautiful, desirable and completely beyond his reach.

He stopped as a car passed, and kicked idly at an uneven patch of concrete sidewalk, overcome by sadness and a crushing sense of loss.

As often happened during emotional times in Justin's life, he recalled one of his grandmother Delacroix's homely aphorisms.

"A woman can start out by hating a man and find herself falling in love with him," she'd once told her grandson. "But if her love should turn to hate, she'll never, ever come back to loving again. Women aren't made that way."

Had Madeline's love for him really turned to hate over the years of their marriage?

Justin remembered his shock and outrage when his wife had quietly announced that she was leaving him. At first he hadn't believed it. Only when she'd started packing her things and making arrangements to move out, ignoring all of his arguments and their children's impassioned pleas, had he finally begun to realize she was serious.

Even now, years later, Justin could still recall his bafflement and frustration as he struggled to adjust to the new reality of his life, and get used to being a single man.

He'd never really had any experience with being single. Madeline had come into his life when he was eighteen years old. She'd been the first for him in every way—his first real love, his very first sexual experience. No other woman could ever move him in quite the same way.

But the emotions he was feeling now were also unfamiliar, and vastly disturbing. For the first time in his adult life, Justin Delacroix suspected he was falling in love. And the woman who filled his heart was the same one who'd rejected him all those years ago.

He headed down the sleepy main street, so lost in his brooding thoughts that he was scarcely aware of the traffic as it moved slowly past him, of townspeople walking home from church or out for Sunday morning brunch at Rick's Café.

"Justin!" a voice called from one of the stores as he passed.

He turned and saw Emily Colbert standing in the front door of her dress shop, watching him.

"Good morning, Emily," he said.

"You're certainly deep in thought," she commented. "I called twice before you heard me."

"I had breakfast with somebody I haven't seen for a long time. I guess I'm a little preoccupied."

Emily held the door of the shop open and made a gesture of invitation. He entered with automatic politeness, pausing by the front counter.

"And who was that?" she asked.

"It was Madeline."

Her eyes widened. "Really? I had no idea Madeline was in town."

"Neither did I." Justin looked up, trying to smile. "Until I practically ran into her last night at the Bayou Inn."

"How is she?" Emily asked, her voice softening. "You know, I've always loved Madeline. When I opened this shop, she was the first to come in and buy her dresses from me. Once she led the way, all the others followed."

"I didn't know that," he said, looking curiously at the woman's beautiful dark face.

"Well, it's true. And things were different back in those days, Justin. It took a lot of courage and generosity for Madeline to do what she did for me."

"I'm just beginning to realize how much courage she has," he said slowly. "Emily, I was a pure fool to lose a woman like that, wasn't I?"

"You certainly were." She smiled to soften her tart reply. "But we're all fools at some time in our lives, aren't we? It's allowed, as long as we manage to get smart before we're too old to do anything about it.''

"That sounds like something my grandmother Delacroix would have said."

Emily laughed. "The reason I called you in here is that I found some more outfits that would be perfect for your little protegé. I've got a few pieces set aside. Some skirts, slacks and blazers that would all coordinate with turtlenecks and blouses. She can have a complete wardrobe without a lot of fuss or expense."

"Thanks, Emily," he said. "I didn't expect you to go to all that trouble on your free time."

She waved a slender hand, glittering with rings. "It's really kind of fun," she said. "That girl is such a pleasure to dress. She really looks marvelous in good clothes."

"You should have seen her last night, having dinner with me at the Inn. She was a knockout."

"So I've heard," Emily said dryly.

Justin grimaced. "The story's all over town already, is it?"

"With a number of variations. The most interesting rumor claims the girl is actually your daughter by an illicit affair, and Madeline left you after she found out. But most of the folks in the coffee shops seem to believe she's just your mistress."

Justin sighed. "What a town. Tell me, Emily, should I put a notice in the paper denying everything?"

"That's the one thing you shouldn't do. It would only set them twittering all over again. The best thing is to ignore them, and they'll soon find something else to talk about."

"I suppose you're right. Would you like me to take the clothes now?"

Emily shook her head. "The slacks need to be fitted, and

I may have to take in the jacket seams a bit, too. And the sweaters and blouses should be tried, too."

"Tomorrow, then?"

"Well..." Emily hesitated. "I understand Remy's getting back tomorrow or Tuesday, so Claudia will probably have to work. It might be best to bring her today, if that's possible."

"But you're not open for business, are you?"

"I'm going to be here all day doing paperwork. I'll be happy to fit her if you've got the time."

"Oh, I've got the time, all right," he said, feeling another bleak flood of loneliness. "I've got nothing but time, Emily."

She smiled gently and patted his arm. "Then bring that young lady here to me, and we'll have some fun dressing her up."

"All right. Whatever she wants to keep," Justin said, "just put it on a tab for me and I'll settle with you later. All right?"

Emily shook her head, setting her earrings tinkling. "I'll do nothing of the kind. You paid for the dress and shoes. Anything else you buy for this girl is on the house."

He looked at her in astonishment. "But, Emily...how can you do something like that?"

"You know how I can do it, Justin."

"Oh, for goodness' sake," he said after a moment. "That old lawsuit...it was all over and forgotten about years ago."

"By everybody else, maybe. But I've never forgotten. Without the help you gave me back then, I wouldn't be in business today. And if you want to play Santa Claus to this poor child..." She smiled again. "Well, then, I'll just be one of Santa's little elves."

JUSTIN FOUND CLAUDIA at Remy's place, getting ready to drag her rusty old bicycle from its parking place and head for home.

"Don't you look nice," he said, smiling at her as he came up the wooden causeway.

She flushed at the compliment and turned around to display her outfit. "It's from them—those sacks of clothes you gave me. They fit like a dream."

"One of my daughters must be exactly the same size as you. I think it's probably Shelby."

She dropped the kickstand on her bicycle and leaned against the handlebars. "How was your breakfast, Mr. Delacroix?"

His smile faded. "It was kind of sad. My wife—my ex-wife—" he corrected himself, "doesn't really want anything to do with me, Claudia. She only wanted to talk about one of the children, that's all."

The girl looked up at him shrewdly. "But you still got feelings for her, don't you?"

He hesitated. "Yes, I do," he said at last. "I'm only now beginning to realize how much."

"So whyn't you tell her?" She began to wheel the bicycle along the dock again, and Justin fell into step beside her.

"It's too late for us," he said. "She has a man in her life. But even if she were alone, she wouldn't want me anymore. I had my chance years ago, and I ruined it."

The girl paused and looked at him with sympathy. "I'm real sorry, Mr. Delacroix."

"Why don't you call me Justin?"

She smiled ruefully and shook her head. "I can wear these nice clothes and maybe learn to use the right fork, and even sit in the dining room at the Bayou Inn," she said. "But I could never, ever call you nothing—anything but Mr. Delacroix. Never in this world."

"Well, we won't make an issue of it, then."

"Bernard came by," she told him shyly, looking off toward the water. "Just this morning while I was inside doing the books. He didn't recognize me."

"Really?"

"He asked if Remy just hired me. When I told him my name, you'd of thought he seen a ghost."

"Saw a ghost," Justin said automatically. "Did he say anything else?"

"He asked what I was doing today when I finished work, and I told him I was painting the deck rail on my boat. Then he wanted to know if I needed help."

"Claudia!" Justin said, forgetting his own troubles for a moment. "What did you say?"

"I don't even remember. I was too surprised to say much of anything." She sighed. "I felt real stupid about it afterward, but Bernard, he's just… He's so handsome, he purely takes my breath away."

Justin smiled. "Well, if you can wait an hour or so to start your painting, I have something for you to do. Emily Colbert spoke to me this morning. She's got some more outfits for you to try on."

"But, Mr. Delacroix," Claudia said in distress, "I can't take no—any more stuff from you. You done so much already."

Justin took the bicycle and moved it behind a shed, then led her toward his car.

"Nonsense," he told her, opening the door for her. "The fact is, I did some legal work for Mrs. Colbert a few years back, and she's always been grateful for it. These clothes you're getting are sort of a payment for that old favor, no cost to me."

"Really?" Claudia asked doubtfully.

"Absolutely. And you'll need some pretty things to wear," he added with a teasing smile, "if Bernard Leroux's started coming around to call."

CHAPTER SEVEN

AFTER HER CONVERSATION with Shelby, Madeline went down to the front desk and made inquiries about more phone messages in the vain hope that one of the children might have returned home unexpectedly. Then she went back upstairs and called Aunt Mary, promising to stop by for Sunday dinner following her visit to Riverwood.

Once all these arrangements were made, she still had at least two hours to fill. She called room service for a pot of tea and a newspaper and spent an hour reading and doing the crossword puzzle, then wandered outside for a walk.

The little town was sunny and slumberous on this Sunday noon. Few people seemed to be out on the streets. Even the dogs and cats were napping on front verandas and in the shade of trees.

Madeline drifted along the sidewalk, lost in memories. Despite all the years that had passed since she first came to Bayou Beltane, the place made her feel strangely young. She found herself reliving the breathless sensations of girlhood, when each day was a new adventure and romance waited around every corner.

If she half closed her eyes, she could almost see a young, carefree Justin strolling toward her, his dark hair shining in the light, and feel her heart pounding with excitement.

But those days were lost and gone in the mists of time. More than thirty years had passed since the first time she ever saw Justin Delacroix, and felt his arms around her....

She glanced at her watch, feeling restless.

Time passed so slowly here. Back in Aspen the days flew by in a multicolored blur of activity, but since she'd arrived in Louisiana, the world seemed to have stopped turning. The air was flower scented and languorous, the breeze off the lake gently caressing. The sleepy ambience was almost hypnotic, making her forget why she'd come here in the first place.

She passed Rick's Café and smelled the rich scents of espresso and cappuccino, of warm beignets and croissants. Madeline glanced into the darkened interior, tempted to enter those cool depths and sip a cup of espresso to pass the time.

But she resisted the urge because she couldn't see who was inside, and she was reluctant to meet old acquaintances without some advance warning.

At the corner of the main street, she glanced along the row of shops and recognized Emily Colbert's clothing store, still in the same location. The front door of the shop stood open, propped by a little gilt chair wedged under the doorknob.

Madeline smiled, wondering if the owner might be inside on this Sunday afternoon. It would be nice to have a chat with Emily again. They'd always been good friends. Maybe Madeline could even try on a couple of dresses and help to pass these seemingly endless hours before she headed out to Riverwood to visit Shelby.

She quickened her steps, heading for the dress shop, then paused in alarm and ducked into a doorway to peek around the corner.

Justin was coming out of the shop, accompanied by the pretty, dark-haired girl who'd been with him the night before at the Bayou Inn.

While Madeline watched, Emily Colbert followed the pair out onto the sidewalk and stood chatting with them, looking as slim and stylish as ever. But Madeline was hardly conscious of her old friend. She had eyes only for Justin, and for the girl at his side.

Claudia Landry was certainly a lovely young woman. She wore tailored khaki slacks and a cream-coloured linen blouse, simple clothes that showed off a slender, rounded body. Her sleek head glistened in the sunlight and her cheeks were pink with excitement as she talked and laughed with the others.

The girl's arms were full of packages, all bearing the distinctive gold logo of Emily's dress shop. Justin stood next to her, also holding a couple of large boxes. He looked extremely pleased with himself.

So he was actually buying clothes for his young girl-friend.

Madeline made a wry face at her reflection in the window of her hiding place, thinking about men. They obviously did a lot of strange things when they reached their middle years, and the man standing out there on the street was proof of that fact.

Madeline Delacroix would never have been able to drag her busy husband out to a dress store to watch while she tried on clothes. Even the thought of such a thing was ludicrous. Yet here he was, big as life, spending his Sunday afternoon shopping for clothes with a woman young enough to be his daughter.

Madeline felt sudden hot anger at him and all the rest of the world. It seemed so unfair, but the same thing happened over and over again. A woman sacrificed her youth and passion on one man, then found herself alone while he gave some young girl the kind of tenderness his wife would have received with such joy.

All thoughts of visiting with Emily vanished from her mind. Madeline wanted only to get away from this sun-washed street, back to the privacy and safety of her hotel room, and wait there until she could go to see her daughter.

She huddled in the shop entrance until Justin and the girl finally left and got into a big car sitting at the curb, laughing together as they settled their packages in the back seat. Emily waved while they drove away, then vanished inside her shop again, removing the chair and closing the door behind her.

As soon as all of them were out of sight, Madeline ducked out of the shop entry and headed up the street in the direction of the hotel without looking back.

ALTHOUGH THE MAIN street of Bayou Beltane was almost deserted, Madeline wasn't the only one who saw Justin and Claudia leaving the dress shop. Across the street in the open door of the billiard hall, Joey Landry leaned in the entryway and watched as his sister talked with the lawyer and a classy woman in front of the store.

Joey was thin and wiry, wearing a black T-shirt and a pair of jeans that rode low on his skinny hips. He had tattoos on both forearms, a gold hoop in one ear and a greasy dark ponytail. In his right hand he carried a pool cue, gripping it tightly as he stood looking across the street.

For a long time he stood without moving, coiled like a snake in the shadows, studying Claudia's glowing face and pretty new clothes.

So it was true, the rumor he'd been hearing. She really was hanging around with this rich middle-aged lawyer, shaming herself and her family.

Joey's lip curled with scorn and outrage.

Not for a moment did it occur to him to think about the things he'd done himself—the jail time and suspended sentences, the drunk-driving convictions and fines for fighting. After all, those things were just normal, youthful hell-raising. But a girl making a fool of herself over a rich older man who only wanted one thing was a shameful disgrace.

It also didn't occur to him to be angry with Justin Delacroix. You couldn't blame a man for reaching out and grabbing something juicy when he had a chance. Joey would have done the same thing himself.

No, it was Claudia he blamed for this situation. And Claudia was going to pay.

He had to admit he was a little surprised by the way his sister looked, even though she'd always been uppity and had notions that she was too good for the rest of the family.

Now she actually looked the part. If you didn't know who she was, you could have mistaken her for one of those rich girls who drove around town in their fancy cars and played tennis at the country club.

He grinned unpleasantly, showing a couple of broken front teeth.

"Well, you ain't one of them, little sister," he muttered aloud as Claudia got into the lawyer's big car. "You ain't a bit like them fancy girls. And I reckon maybe you need a little lesson to help you remember where you come from."

Time enough, Joey decided, watching as the car drove away. He knew where she lived.

Later in the day would be a good time to go and pay her a visit, after she'd kissed her sugar daddy goodbye and gone home to the little houseboat. When she was alone, maybe her big brother would drop around and pay her a visit.

And after that, maybe little Claudia wouldn't be quite so uppity anymore.

From the shadows he leered at the departing car, still holding the pool cue like a weapon, then turned and strolled back inside the smoky billiard hall.

JUSTIN DROVE CLAUDIA around by the houseboat to store her packages away, then dropped her back at Remy's so she could retrieve her bicycle. He waved off her thanks with a smile.

"It was a pleasure, Claudia. Go home and paint your deck railing. And you know," he added, "I wouldn't be surprised if Bernard Leroux came around to help. Even though you told him not to bother."

"You really think he might, Mr. Delacroix?" She stood on the wooden deck, gripping the handlebars of her old bicycle.

"Well, if I were his age and met a girl like you, I'd certainly be looking around for a paintbrush right now," Justin told her, and was rewarded by another of her shining smiles.

He pulled his car around on the dusty road and headed for Riverwood, watching Claudia in the rearview mirror as she vanished along the bayou. He felt a growing affection for the girl, and considerable gratitude for the diversion she'd provided after his unsettling conversation with Madeline that morning.

What a nice person she was. And what an amazing difference some new clothes and a dash of self-confidence could make!

He was still thoughtful when he pulled into the garage at home, climbed the stairs and entered the empty house, where the silence and untidiness seemed even more jarring than usual.

Justin paused in the foyer, looking around, then went through the halls to the other wing where Shelby lived. He listened for a moment outside her suite of rooms before knocking on the door.

Shelby answered his knock sooner than he'd expected, dressed in furry slippers and an old red jogging suit. She gazed up at her father blearily and sneezed, clutching a wad of tissues in her hand.

"Feeling any better?" Justin asked.

"A little. I've been sleeping like a log for the past couple of hours."

"That's good. Can I get you anything? A bowl of soup, maybe, or some hot tea?"

She shook her head. "I'll be all right. Guess what?" she added, brightening a little. "Mama's coming out here to see me."

He stiffened with alarm. "Your mother? She's coming here?"

Shelby nodded. "She called this morning. It must have been right after you two had breakfast together. When I told her how rotten I was feeling, she said I should have a nap and she'd drive out later this afternoon to visit me."

"Your mother's coming here?" Justin repeated, feeling dazed. "But Shelby...the place is a mess! We've got to get things cleaned up. How can I..." He looked around with rising helplessness.

"Relax," Shelby told him dryly. "I don't think she's coming out here to make any kind of formal housekeeping inspection. She only wants to talk with me for a while. Don't get all upset."

"Do you remember how your mother used to keep this place?"

"Vaguely. But I was only seventeen when she left. And back then, I was too wrapped up in my own business to take much notice of housekeeping."

"So was I," Justin told her with a sudden wave of sadness.

She smiled and patted his arm. "Well, don't worry. She'll probably come to the side door, anyhow, and straight into my rooms. I don't think she's all that anxious to visit here."

"But she's going to want to say hello to your grandfather. In fact, I should find him now and tell him she's..."

Justin turned and rushed off down the hall again, conscious of Shelby watching him from her doorway with a thoughtful expression.

He found Charles out on the porch swing, reading a paperback detective novel. Two liver-spotted spaniels drowsed at the old man's side, muzzles buried on their paws, long ears trailing onto the floorboards.

Justin lowered himself into one of the wicker chairs. "Madeline's coming out here this afternoon."

"Is she?" Charles lowered the book and glanced up at his son in surprise. "I knew she was in town this weekend. In fact, she's going to be having dinner with Mary and William tonight. But I had no idea she'd come out to Riverwood."

"You knew Madeline was here at Bayou Beltane?" Justin asked.

"Mary told me."

Justin shook his head ruefully. "Seems like everybody around here knows things except me."

"Is that so?" Charles's eyes sparkled with amusement. "Well, I guess these folks have never heard they're supposed to tell it to the judge."

Justin got to his feet and started toward the door again. "I'm going to see if I can clean things up a little before she gets here."

"You'd better keep Madeline out of the kitchen," Charles said. "That place is not in good shape."

Justin glanced back at his father's white head, silhouetted against the rich green of the live oaks in the front yard.

Charles put a finger between the pages of his book to mark his place, then turned to his son. "Have you seen her yet?" he asked.

"We had breakfast together this morning."

The old man's eyes widened. "Really, Justin? How is she?"

"She's as beautiful as ever," Justin said quietly. "And not the least bit interested in me."

Charles looked out across the lawn. "I've always loved that woman," he said. "She's a real, true lady, Madeline is."

"But you were so opposed to our marriage," Justin said in surprise. "Back in those days you didn't have a single good thing to say about her."

"You were both children," Charles said calmly. "You didn't know what you were doing. Our opposition had nothing to do with Madeline."

Justin hesitated for a moment, feeling a brief stab of anger. Finally he opened the door and went back inside, looking in dismay at a trail of muddy paw prints across the foyer.

Swearing under his breath, he went in search of a mop and bucket.

That entailed going into the kitchen, where he found Charles hadn't been exaggerating. The place really did smell musty, and nobody had yet tackled the dishes piled in the sink.

Justin stood in the doorway, wondering if he had time to roll up his sleeves and do them himself.

Although the housekeeping was admittedly slapdash these days, circumstances didn't normally reach such a dreadful state. Odelle still had a pretty stern hand when a whip was needed, and in her absence Shelby was usually willing to pitch in and clean things up, even though management of the household wasn't supposed to be her job.

But Shelby was feeling so rotten at the moment, she could hardly drag herself out of bed, let alone do any housecleaning.

He edged his way across the grimy tiles and opened a cupboard door, looking for cleaning supplies, then abandoned the search when he heard voices out on the veranda.

Justin slammed the cupboard, wiped his hands on his slacks and hurried out onto the porch, where Madeline was sitting in one of the wicker chairs next to Charles, laughing and talking.

Her presence brought the whole world to life. Even the two dogs were wide awake, sitting on each side of her chair as she leaned forward to pat them by turns. She looked up when he arrived.

"Hello, Justin. I came out to have a visit with Shelby because she's not feeling well."

"I know," he said, feeling nervous, almost shy. "She told me. Would you like a drink? Or I could make us a pot of coffee, if you prefer."

"You could?" she asked, her eyes widening. "Really? I had no idea you'd become so domestic."

"You don't know the half of it," Justin said ruefully, conscious of his father's eyes resting on him again with sardonic amusement.

"Well, thank you so much for the offer," Madeline said. "I don't need anything myself, but I'll be going to Shelby's room in a minute and I can see if she wants something to drink." She leaned forward again to pat one of the dogs. "Charles tells me these young fellows are Topsy's pups."

"That's right," Justin said. "I guess Topsy was just a pup herself when you…"

"When I left," Madeline said quietly as he paused. "Yes, she was a silly, happy-go-lucky baby with great big paws. Charles, do you remember the time she tangled with a skunk out in the woods, and Jax and Beau had to bathe her in tomato juice?"

The old man laughed. "You know, I'd forgotten that. As I recall, the tomato juice smell was harder to get rid of than the polecat's."

Madeline stroked one of the dogs, taking a silky ear in her fingers and touching it thoughtfully. "You're so much like your mother," she murmured to the dog. "Where is Topsy now?" she asked.

"We had to have her put down last year," Justin said. "There was no other choice. The veterinarian told us she had stomach cancer."

Madeline's face clouded briefly with pain. She picked up her handbag, then reached out to touch the old man's arm. "Well, I guess I'll be seeing you a little later, Charles. Aunt Mary tells me you're coming over for dinner tonight, too?"

Charles avoided his son's quick glance. "Yes, I was lucky enough to be invited. Mary's roasting a brace of Cornish hens and making pecan custard," he added, looking blissful.

"After I've finished my visit with Shelby, I'll come around and meet you here. We can walk over together. All right?"

"I'll look forward to your company, my dear." When she rose, Charles struggled out of the rocking chair and bowed with all of his old gallantry. "It's been a pure pleasure to see you again, Madeline. You're lovelier than ever."

"And you're just the same silver-tongued rascal you always were." She kissed his cheek affectionately, then headed for the veranda steps with a polite nod at her ex-husband.

At the steps, Madeline shaded her eyes with her hand and squinted at the burned-out hulk of the barn, its ruins still blackened. She shivered and glanced back at them.

"Where's Bear? What has he done with all the horses?"

"They're farmed out with the neighbors," Justin replied, "until we can start rebuilding."

Madeline nodded and began descending the steps.

"Madeline, wait a minute," Justin said.

"Yes?" She paused and turned to look at him.

He hesitated. It was so unbelievable to have her right

here, standing in the shadows of the veranda as she'd stood countless times in the past, and in his dreams and memories over the last ten years.

Justin was so moved that he hardly knew what to say. He was conscious only of a passionate desire to keep her near him, even for a little while.

"Don't go all the way around outside," he said. "It's easier to come through the house."

She looked at him uncertainly, then glanced over her shoulder at the leaf-strewn pathway around the side of the old mansion. "If you're sure..."

"Of course I'm sure. Come, I'll walk you through the house."

He held the door and she entered ahead of him, passing so close that he was sharply aware of her perfume, a delicate scent of gardenias that stirred a host of memories.

"That's the same perfume you used to wear," he said as she stood next to him in the entry hall and gazed down thoughtfully at the smears of dirt on the marble tiles. "Isn't it?"

Madeline looked surprised and wary. "Justin, I had no idea you ever noticed my perfume."

"There are a lot of things you didn't know," he said huskily. "And I guess that's my fault. I should have told you."

She opened her mouth to speak, then fell silent abruptly, wrinkling her nose in a way he recognized.

Justin grinned at the old fastidious expression, feeling a flood of love so intense it almost took his breath away. He had to struggle to find his voice.

"Speaking of fragrances," he said with forced casualness, "what you're smelling right now is coming from the kitchen, I'm afraid."

"The kitchen?" she looked up at him in astonishment. "But what's happening in there?"

"Nothing's happening," he said grimly. "That's the problem."

She crossed the foyer, heading for the kitchen door. Justin could tell by her step and the set of her slim shoulders that she wasn't about to be dissuaded. He hurried to keep up with her.

She opened the door and took a few steps into the kitchen, then stood looking around, openmouthed. "But this…" she said at last. "This is terrible. It's positively dreadful. Justin, what on earth is going on here?"

"It's not usually so bad," he answered lamely, watching as Madeline ran a fingertip across one of the counters and grimaced with distaste. "One of the housemaids just quit and the other went on holidays at the very same time Odelle and Woodrow left for Florida. And Shelby's been sick, so nobody's—"

"But what are you eating?" she interrupted. "Who prepares your meals?"

"Nobody. I told you, most nights I whip up a box of Kraft dinner."

"I thought you were joking." Her cheeks turned pink with annoyance. "All those girls of mine were taught the proper way to care for a household. They're just being careless. I wish they were here right now so I could give them a piece of my mind."

"Why would you do that?" Justin asked.

She looked up at him, her wonderful eyes stormy.

"Because you deserve better than this. How are you supposed to work when you're forced to live in conditions like this?"

She crossed the room to peer inside the fridge, then slammed the door with a murmur of outrage.

"If the kitchen is in this state, I can just imagine what your clothes are like, and how the linens are being looked after. It's a disgrace, that's what it is."

Justin watched her, enchanted.

Madeline hardly ever got angry, and when she did, she was always careful to conceal her emotions. This was a rare display of feeling, and it touched him deeply that she seemed to be angry on his behalf.

He moved across the room toward her, overcome with emotion, longing to reach for her and take her in his arms. But when she saw the intensity of his expression, Madeline's anger turned to a cautious, frightened look and she edged toward the door.

"I'll just...I think I'll run along and talk with Shelby now," she murmured, then escaped, leaving Justin all alone in his untidy kitchen, aching with sadness.

MADELINE INSISTED that Shelby stay in bed for their visit, and was a little concerned by how readily her daughter agreed. Normally, keeping Shelby in bed in the daytime had always been like trying to cage a tiger.

But today she snuggled gratefully among her pillows and gazed up at her mother with pathetic gratitude when Madeline brought her a glass of ice water and a damp cloth for her forehead.

"I'm being such a baby," Shelby said, then coughed noisily into her wad of tissues. "But my head aches, my bones ache, my throat hurts and I'm all stuffed up. I feel just lousy."

"Of course you do, sweetheart. Just settle down in bed and visit with me for a little while, and then I'll bring you a nice bowl of soup and you can go back to sleep."

Shelby snuggled under the covers while Madeline tucked them cosily beneath her chin.

"Tell me..." Shelby began.

"Yes, dear?"

"Did you really come all the way down here because of my car windshield?"

"Among other things. I want to know precisely what's going on with you before I talk to Philip."

Shelby's eyes widened. "You're going to talk to *Uncle Philip?*"

"Why ever not?" Madeline asked with a touch of impatience. "The man isn't living on the moon, after all. He's right here in Bayou Beltane, and if there's mischief afoot, he's likely to be at the center of it. Philip or Flora," she added darkly.

"Or both. Did you hear about the fire in the barn?"

"Yes, and I was outraged." Madeline hugged her arms, shivering. "When I think of Beau, and what might have happened…"

"But I can't figure out why Philip and Flora might be doing these things," Shelby said, frowning. "I tried to talk to Uncle Philip myself a while ago, you know."

"And?"

"And I got nowhere, as usual."

"Do you think it might have something to do with Lyle Masson?"

"It could," Shelby admitted. "And he and Uncle Philip are thick as thieves. Literally," she added with a grimace. "Yvette told me all about their creepy little Men's Club."

"Well, I intend to chat with Philip about all that, so let's not waste time on it now. Tell me what else you've been doing. Your father mentioned something about some old family papers?"

Shelby grinned. "He doesn't want me to snoop. That's the actual word he used. Like I was ten years old, playing Nancy Drew."

"So what has your snooping turned up?" Madeline got up to refresh the damp cloth.

"You really want to know all this?"

"I certainly do."

"Well, I guess I have to go right back to the beginning,

then." Shelby looked up at her, trying to smile. "Do you have time to hear a really long story?"

"I have nothing but time, my dear."

While Madeline listened and offered occasional sips of ice water, Shelby told all about the old legal papers and transcripts showing conclusively that Hamilton Delacroix should never have lost his final case, which resulted in the murder conviction of his client, Rafe Perdido.

"You're saying there was some kind of wrongdoing on your great-grandfather's part?" Madeline asked in confusion.

Shelby shook her head. "It looks more likely there was some odd behaviour on the part of the judge, but for the life of me I simply can't understand why. I know there are some missing journals out there, books kept by Judge Alvarez, and I even suspect I know who's got them. If I could only get my hands on those journals, I could solve the whole mystery."

Sick or not, Shelby had what Justin described as her "bulldog look." Madeline sighed.

"Is it so important, my darling?" she asked gently. "Couldn't you just let this go?"

Shelby ignored her. "And then after Travis came and told me about those letters," she continued, frowning, "it cast things in a whole different light. The letters prove Camille was pregnant when she died, that she'd been determined to marry a Delacroix and that our family was involved with her somehow. Travis said it wasn't Rafe Perdido's baby."

Madeline looked at the girl in surprise. "So whose baby was it?"

"I think it was Uncle Philip's. Or maybe even Grandfather's," Shelby said reluctantly.

"What about Hamilton Delacroix himself? Perhaps he was the father."

Shelby's eyes widened. "Mama," she breathed, "do you think he could have been? The thought never crossed my mind."

"Well, Hamilton certainly had an eye for a pretty young woman," Madeline said calmly. "It seems to be a common trait with those Delacroix men."

Shelby cast her mother a quick glance, then returned to her own line of thought. "But then..." She sat up, frowning. "Maybe he set out to close the case so Rafe would be sent away to prison, because then nobody would be left to point an accusing finger at him. But Great-grandfather was supposed to be so fine and upstanding."

"Lie down." Madeline pushed gently on her daughter's shoulders, forcing her back down under the covers.

Shelby complied, staring up at her. "Can you get me the briefcase from my desk? The brown one with all the—"

"No, I certainly can't. And you're to stop brooding about all this ancient family history, Shelby. Do you hear me?"

"Why?"

"Because you're sick and you need your rest, not more excitement."

Shelby waved a dismissive hand. "Oh, come on. I'm not *that* sick."

Her daughter's mouth set in the stubborn line that had always made Madeline despair. Ever since babyhood, when Shelby looked like that, nobody could dissuade her from a chosen course of action.

"Darling," Madeline said, laughing, "you're such a trial to me."

"I intend to get to the bottom of this mystery."

"Why?" Madeline asked. "Why is it so important to you?"

"Because *something happened.*" Shelby leaned forward passionately and gripped her mother's arm. "Something happened in the bayou that night. A woman died, a girl who was pregnant with a baby. A man was found guilty after a mock trial that should never have resulted in conviction, and my great-grandfather was his defense lawyer. I want to find out what really happened.''

After this long speech, she subsided into another fit of coughing, her head rolling wearily on the pillows.

Madeline went to rinse out the damp cloth and came back to sit by her daughter's bed, stroking Shelby's forehead gently, her eyes looking faraway and troubled as she gazed out the window.

CHAPTER EIGHT

INSIDE THE HOUSEBOAT, Claudia put away all the pretty new clothes. Then she stood happily and considered the resplendent contents of her little closet, feeling like a princess.

She had so many slacks and skirts to wear, as well as blouses, sweaters and jackets to put with them, that she could spend her whole day just trying clothes on and taking them off again.

Claudia grimaced at Socks, who sprawled in his favorite spot in the middle of the bunk bed.

"Well," she told the cat, "I don't have time to be trying on clothes all day. In fact, for this painting job I'm wearing my old overalls, Socks-Cat, and I don't care what you say."

The kitten blinked and rolled over, waving his paws in the air, then went back to sleep.

Claudia dressed in a frayed T-shirt and her old denim overalls, just as she'd done every single day before Justin Delacroix made his surprising entry into her life. But when she looked at herself in the mirror she had another shock.

Even in her old clothes, she looked dainty and attractive, with a graceful, winsome look in spite of the baggy denims.

It must be the haircut, she thought in confusion, studying her reflection.

But Claudia knew it was something more than a hairstyle. In the last few days she'd acquired an air of confidence, a look of humor and directness in her eyes, even a different way of holding her head. A whole lot of things

Play "Lucky Hearts" for this...

exciting *FREE* gift!
This surprise mystery gift could be yours free

when you play LUCKY HEARTS!

...then continue your lucky streak with a sweetheart of a deal!

1. Play Lucky Hearts as instructed on the opposite page.

2. Send back this card and you'll receive brand-new Harlequin Intrigue® novels. These books have a cover price of $3.99 each, but they are yours to keep absolutely free.

3. There's no catch. You're under no obligation to buy anything. We charge nothing — ZERO — for your first shipment. And you don't have to make any minimum number of purchases — not even one!

4. The fact is thousands of readers enjoy receiving books by mail from the Harlequin Reader Service™. They like the convenience of home delivery... they like getting the best new novels BEFORE they're available in stores... and they love our discount prices!

5. We hope that after receiving your free books you'll want to remain a subscriber. But the choice is yours — to continue or cancel, any time at all! So why not take us up on our invitation, with no risk of any kind. You'll be glad you did!

The Harlequin Reader Service® — Here's how it works:

Accepting free books places you under no obligation to buy anything. You may keep the books and gift and return the shipping statement marked "cancel." If you do not cancel, about a month later we'll send you 4 additional novels and bill you just $3.34 each plus 25¢ delivery per book and applicable sales tax, if any.* That's the complete price — and compared to cover prices of $3.99 each — quite a bargain! You may cancel at any time, but if you choose to continue, every month we'll send you 4 more books, which you may either purchase at the discount price... or return to us and cancel your subscription.

*Terms and prices subject to change without notice. Sales tax applicable in N.Y.

If offer card is missing write to: Harlequin Reader Service, 3010 Walden Ave., P.O. Box 1867, Buffalo, NY 14240-1867

HARLEQUIN READER SERVICE
3010 WALDEN AVE
PO BOX 1867
BUFFALO NY 14240-9952

BUSINESS REPLY MAIL
FIRST-CLASS MAIL   PERMIT NO. 717   BUFFALO, NY

POSTAGE WILL BE PAID BY ADDRESSEE

NO POSTAGE
NECESSARY
IF MAILED
IN THE
UNITED STATES

added to her new look, all of them related to the way she felt about herself.

Claudia sighed with contentment and went aft to a wooden locker, where she took out a can of green paint, a brush and a small jar of turpentine. Padding around to the bow, she settled down on the deck and began painting the railing.

It was pleasant work. Sunshine filtered through the trees along the shore, dappling the water with shifting golden coins of light. Crickets hummed and the air was drowsy with afternoon warmth. Farther down the lagoon a deer came out of the brush and stepped daintily toward the shore, bending its head to drink.

Claudia dipped her brush in the green paint and smeared it across the weathered deck railings, enjoying the way they came to life and began to shine.

She loved painting. Even when she was a little girl, she'd tried to convince her father to paint the old shack they lived in. Claudia always had the feeling her life would be completely different if she could only live in a white house with bright green trim. In that sparkling little place there'd be no cruelty or sadness, no aching hunger or pain from beatings.

But her daddy always scoffed at her, and so did her brothers.

"Uppity notions," they'd sneer. "Painting the house! Next thing you know she'll be wanting them fancy drapes and wall-to-wall carpet."

And then Joey would hit her a couple of times, just to let her know who was boss.

But Claudia didn't want to think about sad things today. That whole miserable life was far behind her. Now she had a job and a snug little home of her own, and a closet full of pretty clothes.

Why, she'd actually eaten a meal at the Bayou Inn, sitting at a candlelit table in the dining room as if she were a rich girl. And just this morning, Bernard Leroux, as big as life, had smiled and talked with her.

Unless she was imagining things, he'd even flirted a little.

Claudia sat back on her heels, rested the paintbrush against the edge of the can and allowed herself to think about him again. She summoned up his image—the sun-browned face and broad shoulders, the wry, lopsided grin and shadow of stubble on his jaw.

She was so deep in her fantasy that when Bernard himself appeared on the deck she felt a confusing sense of unreality. It was as if the force of her imagination had somehow brought him to life before her eyes.

But he was clean-shaven now, wearing a blue cotton shirt, denim shorts and canvas deck shoes. And he was looking at her with a kind of warm intensity that made her feel all shivery inside.

"Hi there. Aren't you even going to say hello?" he asked.

Claudia scrambled to her feet, blushing furiously. "I'm sorry. I thought you was—I thought you were somebody else."

He looked disappointed. "You're expecting somebody else?"

"No, I'm just busy painting."

She struggled to regain her composure, but it was impossible while he was watching her like that. She knelt and dipped her brush again, biting her lip as she worked down the underside of the rail.

Bernard moved closer, standing near her. She could see the toe of his canvas shoe, the dense golden hairs on his tanned leg.

"Hey, Claudia, do you have another paintbrush?" he asked.

"No, I don't. Anyhow, you don't want to do this," she muttered, still not looking at him. "You'd get them—those nice clothes all dirty."

"No, I wouldn't." He dropped to one knee beside her, grinning. "I'm a very careful painter."

"I'm not." Claudia displayed some of the green smears on her overalls. "I start out okay," she told him, "but then I get to daydreaming and start being careless, and before long I'm covered with paint."

He laughed and moved away to seat himself on a deck locker, watching her. "What kind of things do you daydream about?"

You, she told him silently. *Most of the time I daydream about you.*

"Oh, I don't know." She edged along the deck, putting a little more distance between them so he couldn't hear the pounding of her heart, and started on a fresh stretch of railing. "About the future, I guess. About the kind of house I'd like to buy someday."

"What kind of house?"

He seemed so interested that she lost some of her shyness. It was incredible to realize they were actually having a conversation like normal adults. He was asking questions and she was answering them, not even making a fool of herself.

It had to be the haircut.

"I'd like a little house on the edge of town," she said, plying her brush carefully. "Close enough that I could walk uptown or ride a bike to pick up my groceries, but far enough away that I wouldn't have to be crammed in real tight with a lot of other folks. I like some space around me."

"So do I." Bernard settled back on the locker, feet extended comfortably. "I feel lazy," he said after a moment, "sitting here and watching you work."

"I like painting," Claudia said simply. "And," she added, amazed by her own daring, "I don't mind having the company, neither."

She glanced up and met his eyes. He smiled at her, looking so handsome and gentle that her heart began to thunder again.

"Come on," he said when she went back to her painting, "tell me more about this dream house of yours. What color is it?"

"It's white," she said promptly. "With green shutters and trim, the same color as this." She gestured toward the paint can. "It has a little front porch with a rocking chair, a red brick walk and a terrace out back, a magnolia tree and a whole lot of flower beds."

She gazed out across the water, sighing with bliss at the treasured vision, then gripped the brush in surprise when she realized she'd never in all her life confided this dream to another living soul.

And now she was telling Bernard Leroux, of all people.

"That sounds nice," he said. "I'd like a house just like that, too. But I'd want a shop out back where I could do some woodwork."

Claudia glanced at his callused brown fingers, thinking about those hands shaping pieces of wooden furniture for the house, maybe some kids' toys, a baby cradle....

Her cheeks turned warm and she dipped the brush hastily, then squeezed off the excess paint against the rim of the can.

"This is a nice place," Bernard was saying, looking around at the trim little boat. "It's real peaceful out here, Claudia."

"I like it."

"And you keep your boat nice, too."

"It's not mine. I rent from Hiram Skettle, but he lets me paint or do whatever I like."

Socks appeared on the deck and moved toward them, stiff-legged and cautious, his tail high in the air. He stopped abruptly and regarded the newcomer with a cold stare.

"Well, who's this fellow?" Bernard asked, reaching toward the cat. "Hi, kitty."

"His name's Socks," Claudia said. "He sort of owns me."

Bernard chuckled. "I know what you mean. I have a cat on my boat, too."

"Socks lives here, but sometimes he goes away for days at a time and worries me half to death. Then he comes marching back, smug as you please, just like he was never gone."

"Do you have a secret life, Socks?" Bernard asked. "Got a cute little girlfriend stashed away in town somewhere?"

Claudia looked up in amazement as Socks edged nearer and sniffed at Bernard's outstretched hand, then began to rub against the man's leg, purring noisily.

"He likes you!" she said. "He don't—doesn't tend to like people right off."

"But I'm a really nice guy," Bernard said, his eyes crinkling with humor as he smiled at her and lifted Socks onto his knees.

She returned to her painting so he couldn't see her face. But she was thinking how true it was, what he'd just told her.

Bernard really was a nice man. He was gentle and kind; you could tell that from the way he handled the cat. And when she'd begun telling him all about her dream house, he seemed genuinely interested, as if her feelings really mattered.

Claudia couldn't believe how easy he was to talk with. He might have been Remy or Mr. Delacroix, lounging there in the sunlight and chatting away with her as if they were old friends.

For years she'd dreamed and fantasized over this man, followed his every move with a feeling of obsessive, helpless longing. But she'd never suspected he could be so downright nice.

By now Socks was stretched full length on the man's knees, purring in lazy contentment while Bernard patted him with long, gentle strokes.

Lucky cat, Claudia thought, and shivered all over again when she imagined how those hands would feel, touching her....

She resumed her painting as they talked. Bernard told her about his boat, which was almost paid for, and the growing success of his tour business. As soon as the boat mortgage was paid off he intended to get a bigger one and expand his trade, moving down the lake so he wouldn't be in direct competition with Remy.

From business they moved on to talk about themselves, the things they liked and disliked, their favorite colors and food, their childhood fantasies.

While they chatted and laughed, the sun dropped lower behind the trees and cast long shadows across the water. Claudia felt the coolness and realized to her sorrow that their afternoon would soon be over.

She'd never felt so close to anybody, so warm and accepted and happy in a person's company. Bernard Leroux, amazingly, seemed like a man who could be not only her dream lover but her best friend.

"Well, that's it." She got to her feet and looked at him shyly. "I'm out of paint. I'll have to pick up some more at the hardware store and finish this last stretch of railing another day."

She poured turpentine into her can and began to clean the brush while he watched.

"Claudia," he said, clearing his throat.

"Yes?"

"Would you like to…maybe go out and grab something to eat? We could have some burgers down at Rick's, or whatever you wanted."

She glanced up at him, too startled to reply. Bernard Leroux was actually inviting her out on a date? It was like a miracle.

Best of all, I have lots of nice things to wear, she thought in astonished delight.

She could dress in the slacks she'd been wearing that morning, or the long cotton skirt with the embroidered white blouse, or maybe the…

"If you don't want to," he was saying awkwardly, "that's all right. I just thought we could—"

"I'd love to," she said, scrambling to her feet. "Matter of fact, I'm real hungry, Bernard. A hamburger sounds great. Could you just give me a few minutes to finish cleaning up this stuff? And then I'll have to change my clothes."

"No rush. Take all the time you need. Say, do you think I could have a drink of water and use the head, Claudia?"

"Of course. The galley's just in through that door, there's glasses over the sink and the head's next to the bunk."

He got up, gently displacing Socks, who yawned in annoyance, then turned and followed Bernard inside, whiskers twitching sleepily.

Claudia sat back on her heels, watching them go, still dazed with happiness. Finally she went back to the job of cleaning the brush and putting a lid on the can of green-stained turpentine, preparing to stash it away in the bin on shore where they disposed of engine oil and fuel cans.

But as she was moving along the deck a shadow fell across the wooden boards in front of her, giving her a start.

She looked up and felt her heart stop, then begin to beat fast in alarm.

Her brother Joey leaned against a portion of railing she hadn't finished painting, watching her with a cold, surly look that she knew and dreaded.

He eyed her up and down with lazy insolence, his lip curling. She clutched the paint can and glanced over her shoulder, thinking about Bernard inside the houseboat. But there was no sign of him or the cat.

"So," Joey drawled, "you figure you're pretty hot stuff, don't you?"

Claudia lifted her chin. "Get off my boat," she said curtly.

"Even tryin' to boss your big brother around, are you? Well, you better not try none of that stuff, kid. Because your fancy friends ain't here to protect you now."

"I don't need nobody to protect me. You're not touching me, Joey Landry. Never again. Now, get out of here."

He moved forward with lightning speed, like a water moccasin uncoiling to strike, and slapped her face so hard that Claudia felt dazed. She tasted a salty trickle of blood inside her mouth.

"That's for talking back," he said. "And this—" he clenched his fist and moved forward again "—is for shaming your family, you little slut."

Rage suddenly washed over her, hot and red. She forgot about Bernard inside the houseboat, about her pleasant afternoon and the excitement of the past few days. All she could feel was a burning anger at these brothers who ruined everything nice that ever happened to her.

And along with the rage was a cold determination that it wasn't going to happen again.

Never again.

Claudia was tired of pain, finished forever with that terrible, violent childhood.

"Hit me all you like," she said, staring up at him defiantly. "God knows I can't beat you in a fight. But as soon as you're done, I'll go downtown to Jake's office and lay charges, and you'll go to jail."

"Like hell. You know what'll happen if you take any of this family business outside." He slapped her again, even harder this time, and gave her a taunting grin. "Them are just love taps, sister. If I wanted to hurt you, reckon I'd use this, wouldn't I?" Again he clenched his fist and waved it at her.

"Of course you would," she said bitterly. "You've done it often enough, you little weasel. Does it make you feel like a big man to beat up on a girl, Joey? Make you feel all tough and strong? Because you're just a worm. You're a pure coward."

Joey's face contorted with anger and his eyes glittered dangerously as he moved toward her. "I warned you, quit your sass."

"And I warned you, keep your hands off me or you're going to be real sorry. You're a skinny, pathetic little excuse for a man."

She could actually see the moment when he snapped. It terrified her, but Claudia stood her ground while he mouthed obscenities and grabbed her, the muscles bulging in his wiry arms.

"You got some kind of death wish, little girl?"

He clutched the front of her overalls and shook her furiously until her teeth rattled, then wrapped his callused hands around her neck and pressed his thumbs into the base of her throat.

Claudia stared at him through a haze of pain and fear, seeing the madness in his eyes, the chilling cruelty of his face as his hands tightened around her neck like bands of steel.

"Reckon maybe you're sorry now for what you said,"

he whispered. "Reckon you wanna apologize. But we gotta learn you some lessons, girl. You gotta learn that uppity girls ain't nice."

She struggled feebly, trying to free herself from his grasp, but her head felt like it was about to explode and all the strength seemed to have drained from her body. She flopped in his arms like a rag doll, feeling desperate and terrified.

Suddenly, miraculously, his hands were gone and she was free. Claudia stumbled along the deck, clutching her burning throat as she took in huge gulps of the blessed fresh air.

Still dazed, she turned and saw Joey crawling on his hands and knees. Blood was flowing from his nose and mouth.

Bernard stood over him, tense with fury. "You damned punk!" he was shouting. "Come sneaking around here to beat up on a girl. That's real easy, isn't it, Joey?"

"We was just talkin'," Joey whined, edging away, still on his knees.

"Shut up, you little creep." Bernard reached down and hoisted the smaller man roughly to his feet, glaring at him.

Claudia sank onto a wooden locker and watched, wide-eyed and trembling. She'd never seen anybody as angry as Bernard looked at this moment. If Joey made one false move, Bernard would probably kill him.

Despite her hatred for her brother, she prayed he'd have enough sense to keep his mouth shut.

But Joey had never learned any wisdom in his life, and he didn't show any now. He wriggled sullenly in Bernard's grasp and wiped at the blood on his face. "What goes on in our family ain't none of your business. Besides, she was askin' for it, the little bitch," he muttered.

Bernard grasped the smaller man's throat and began to throttle him. Joey's eyes bulged in panic. He flailed and struggled so wildly that Claudia was terrified for both of them.

"You like that?" Bernard shouted, his face twisted with rage. "Does it feel good, Joey? Because you were asking for it, you know."

Finally Claudia gathered enough strength to run across the deck and tug on his arms. "Bernard!" she shouted. "Don't kill him. He ain't worth it."

She continued to pull and yell at him. At last Bernard released the other man with a final shake for emphasis, then pushed him away.

Claudia patted the bigger man's arm. "He's not worth it," she repeated.

Joey fell to his knees against the deck rail, moaning and spitting. His greasy ponytail hung low as blood dripped once more onto the wooden boards.

Bernard moved closer and nudged him contemptuously with one foot. "Get up."

Claudia's brother kept his head lowered and muttered something unintelligible.

"I said, get up."

Joey struggled to his feet, grasping the railing for support.

"You get off this boat," Bernard said, "and don't you ever come near Claudia again or you'll answer to me. Do you hear?"

The other man glared at him sullenly, wiping his chin with a dirty forearm.

"Did you hear me, Joey?"

"Yeah, I heard you." Joey turned to go, then paused and looked back at them, his eyes hard with anger. "But I sure don't know why you're so interested in this tramp," he said to Bernard. "She's taken, you know."

"Get off the boat."

Joey leaped onto the dock and moved a few steps away.

"Ask her," he called over his shoulder. "Ask her about the rich ol' boyfriend she's sleeping with. She's just a cheap little slut."

Bernard clenched his hands into fists and strode along the deck, making Claudia's brother edge hastily toward safety.

But Joey couldn't resist a parting shot.

"Ask her where she got her haircut and her fancy clothes, Bernard. See if she'll tell you the truth, or if she's gonna start lying again."

Then he was gone, running up the slope to his truck. He climbed inside, gunned the motor and headed off down the bayou road in a cloud of dust.

Bernard and Claudia stood together watching him go. The sound of his motor died and the stillness settled around them, broken only by the chirp of crickets and the lazy cry of gulls circling overhead.

Claudia fingered her neck and cheek, wondering if she was going to have a lot of bruises. She moved away from Bernard and stood looking down at the green-stained toe of her sneaker.

"Claudia?" he said. "Are you all right?"

"I'm fine," she whispered, not looking at him. Suddenly she felt a flood of sadness, a despair so deep that it was all she could do not to burst into tears.

"What did he mean by that stuff he said? Do you have somebody else?"

She shook her head. "Joey's crazy. He's always been like that."

"But your new clothes and the haircut and all...where did they come from? I've been hearing some gossip this morning," Bernard added, watching her closely, "but I thought it was all just talk."

The misery pressed closer, billowing around her like a dark cloud.

"Claudia?"

"It's not the way it looks," she said.

But there was no way out of the situation. People were going to be talking, and she couldn't stop them. If Joey knew about her relationship with Justin Delacroix, everybody in town must know by now. And they'd all have an opinion that would be voiced in every beauty shop and coffee house in Bayou Beltane.

"Tell me what's going on, Claudia."

Suddenly she was weary of having people bully her and push her around. She didn't want her behavior to be questioned by any man, not even Bernard Leroux.

Claudia looked up at him, meeting his eyes steadily. "Mr. Delacroix is my friend. He paid for this haircut and gave me all my new clothes, and took me out for dinner on Saturday night at the Bayou Inn. But he's just a friend, Bernard. And that's all I'm ever going to say about him, whether you like it or not."

Bernard's face turned white beneath the tan. For a long time he stood gazing at her as if he was searching for something to say. At last he turned on his heel and walked off the boat, up the dock and behind the cluster of old buildings on shore.

Claudia watched him go, her heart aching with sorrow. For a while after he'd left she stood looking at the green tangle of leaves glistening in the pale wash of twilight.

Finally she sank onto one of the lockers, buried her face in her hands and began to cry, her shoulders heaving. She was so deep in misery that she didn't even notice Socks when he came out and rubbed against her legs, purring anxiously.

WHILE CLAUDIA was crying on her empty houseboat, Madeline was enjoying a pleasant meal in Aunt Mary's home. Always a gracious hostess, Mary sat at the head of the table, pouring wine and introducing varied topics of conversation.

Her brothers, William and Charles, sat on each side of her, two silver-haired old gentlemen enjoying their Cornish game hen with its spicy Cajun stuffing. While they ate they discussed the sugar beet harvest, the sorry state of Louisiana politics, Madeline's life in Colorado, the new arts program at the university and the exciting prospect of Joanna's baby coming in a few months, and Jax's at any moment.

Madeline exchanged a few glances with Mary and realized that Uncle William and Charles hadn't been told about Shelby's "accidents" or the other strange occurrences in the Delacroix clan. Mary was always protective of both her brothers, especially William.

"It's lovely to be here," Madeline said, putting her wineglass down with a sigh of contentment. "You know, I've missed this place in my very bones."

Charles smiled. "And we all thought you shook our dust from your shoes and headed off to the glamour of Aspen without a backward glance."

Madeline touched his arm in gentle reproach. "How could you believe that? I think about all of you, every day of my life."

William smiled at her with a benign look that concealed his shrewd perception. "You should come back to visit more often, Madeline."

She shook her head. "I don't think I could. It's too upsetting. But I'm still delighted to see all of you."

She glanced at William covertly while he sipped his tea. Now that she knew the truth, she could see Desiree's fine bone structure in the old man's gentle face, and marveled that she'd never noticed it before. Again she felt a flood of weary anger.

How dreadful they were, this whole family, with all their

dark secrets and lies. And how unkind not to tell Uncle William the truth about his heritage....

The little housemaid brought in an antique silver coffee-pot and a tray of custards topped with roasted pecans and whipped cream.

Madeline helped herself to the rich dessert, thinking about Justin's kitchen and his stories of dining on Kraft dinners and take-out hamburgers.

"Madeline?" Charles asked. "You look distressed."

"I was just thinking about your kitchen over at River-wood."

He grimaced and took a hasty sip of coffee. "Not a very pleasant thought, I'm afraid."

"Odelle will whip things into shape when she gets back," Mary said comfortably. "And perhaps Marie will come back and help out a bit from time to time."

William poked thoughtfully at his custard. "Mary's always had a soft spot for Marie. You spoil that girl," he told his sister.

"I know," Mary admitted. "But she's always needed a bit of spoiling. The others were all so beautiful, good in sports, popular... Poor Marie didn't have any of that, just her own kind of specialness. And she still does."

"I realize how special she is," Madeline said. "And I love her dearly. I love all of them. But I do wish they'd take it on themselves to give their father some help. The girls have all benefited over the years from being able to live there, and in return, Justin is entitled to have his house-hold properly supervised."

Charles spooned up his custard. "I never thought I'd hear you spring to Justin's defense. Especially now," he added.

"What do you mean, especially now?" Madeline asked.

Mary and Charles exchanged nervous glances but said nothing.

"You mean, because of this new young girlfriend?" Madeline asked.

Two red spots appeared in Mary's thin cheeks. She shook her head in distress. "I've heard some stories but I can't possibly believe... Claudia Landry, of all people! Justin must be out of his mind."

"Why? She's a very attractive young woman," Madeline said.

William looked around in confusion. "That little ragamuffin who works in Remy's bait shop? What does she have to do with Justin?"

"Nothing at all, dear." Mary told him. "Eat your custard."

"Nobody ever tells me anything," William complained. He grinned suddenly, his eyes sparkling. "Back when I was still hearing confessions, at least I used to know what was going on."

The others chuckled dutifully, though Madeline and Charles exchanged a quick, embarrassed glance that spoke volumes.

They returned to their desserts and coffee with no further discussion of the gossip swirling around Justin Delacroix. Afterward, Charles and William settled to a game of chess by the fireplace, while Mary and Madeline went out to sit on the veranda. They watched the sunset across the river, their shoulders covered by knitted afghans to ward off the freshening breeze.

"It's really heaven, isn't it?" Madeline sighed in bliss, gazing at the shimmering pastel colors of sky and water and the shifting world of green that bordered the river. "If only there were no people here, this would be paradise."

"Some of the people living here are your own children," Mary said quietly.

Madeline glanced at her. "I know. And I miss them more than I can say, Aunt Mary. But it's not possible for me to live in the same community with Justin. Seeing him again has made me…''

"What?" Mary asked when she fell silent.

Madeline shook her head and bent to pet a big ginger tomcat that paused by her chair and sat gazing up at her with a slitted green stare.

"It can't possibly be… Is this Marmalade?" she asked.

"Big as life."

"But that's amazing!" Madeline exclaimed. "He must be fifteen years old, at least."

"Closer to twenty, I'd guess."

Madeline stroked the old cat's ears, feeling ridiculously moved. With everything changing around her at such a dizzying pace, it was a huge comfort to find something still the same.

"Do you remember me, Marmalade?" she asked wistfully. "I always loved you. Such a gentlemanly, polite cat, as I recall."

Marmalade ducked his head and moved closer, rubbing an ear against her leg, then curled in a contented orange ball at her feet.

"Seems like he does recall who you are," Mary said with a smile. She rummaged in a canvas sack and took out the white shawl she was knitting for Jax's baby, plying the needles busily. "So tell me," she said, lowering her voice, "have you learned anything about this nasty business?"

Madeline shook her head. "Not much. Justin seems convinced it's mostly coincidence, and I suppose he could be right. If it were anything more sinister he'd be terribly concerned, but he isn't."

She leaned forward to pat Marmalade's big soft head, frowning.

"You know, Aunt Mary, I was so worried back in Colorado when you and I first talked about this, I was almost frantic. But now that I'm actually here, the worries seem to have drifted away. From this perspective, they even look a bit silly.''

Mary studied her knitting, peering down through the lower part of her bifocals. ''Maybe that's the problem,'' she said, picking up a dropped stitch. ''Maybe Justin's too close to it, too. This bayou town lulls people into a false sense of security, Madeline. But bad things can happen here.''

''Like what?''

Mary shrugged. ''Bad things have been happening ever since I was born. Look at Steven and Nikki. That was a real tragedy, right on our doorstep.''

Madeline looked at the old woman's aquiline profile against the misty line of trees beyond the veranda. ''So you think Shelby's really in some kind of danger?''

''I don't know what to think.'' Mary finished her row and turned the work over, tugging at her ball of yarn. ''But I wouldn't be too quick to dismiss all these things as accidents.''

''Well, I don't intend to dismiss them,'' Madeline said. ''I'm having a talk with Philip tomorrow. And,'' she added, petting the cat again, ''I'm going to visit Flora, too.''

She saw Mary nodding thoughtfully in satisfaction. ''That's precisely the right thing to do,'' the old woman murmured. ''A very wise course of action.''

''Do you really think so?''

But Mary wouldn't say any more. She held out the length of knitting and asked Madeline's opinion about the pattern, making it clear she wanted no further discussion about Shelby's problems, especially the possible involvement of her brother Philip.

Madeline understood what the older woman was trying to tell her. Mary, after all, had to live in this community, and her health was no longer good. All her life she'd waded bravely into family conflicts whenever she felt it necessary.

But in this instance Mary wanted somebody else to do the probing and questioning.

At last Madeline got up regretfully, gathered her handbag and slipped inside to say goodbye to the two old men, who appeared to be involved in an amiable wrangle over an illegally placed bishop and barely noticed her departure.

Smiling, Madeline went onto the veranda again to give Mary a hug and kiss.

"You'll come back again before you leave?" Mary asked, looking up at her from the rocker.

"I'll try. If I can't make it here for a visit, I'll definitely call and tell you how I manage with Philip and Flora."

"Thank you, dear. And Madeline?" the old woman called as Madeline descended the steps.

"Yes?"

"Be careful."

Madeline looked up at Mary's gentle, bony face in the glow of the porch light. She hesitated briefly, then nodded, heading off down the path toward the footbridge.

The bayou twilight wrapped around her like a warm scarf of gray-and-mauve silk. Moths fluttered above the path and glimmered in the dense shrubbery. Madeline wandered along the footbridge, hands in her skirt pockets, hoping she could slip into the yard at Riverwood and retrieve her car without being seen from the house.

But those hopes were dashed when she reached the other side of the bridge and rounded a bend in the path.

Justin sat on a large rock just a few feet away, with both spaniels next to him.

CHAPTER NINE

JUSTIN WORE JEANS and an old leather jacket. He lounged with his hands in his pockets, gazing into the shadows with a brooding air.

Breathless and alarmed, Madeline turned, hoping to retreat the way she'd come, but the dogs had already seen her and mounted a chorus of noisy greetings. Justin got up to peer along the path, smiling when he realized who was approaching.

"Madeline," he said, moving toward her. "What a nice surprise."

"Really?" she said dryly, and hesitated under a spreading live oak.

This had to be more than a coincidence, she realized. There was only one path leading from Mary's house to Riverwood. Justin had obviously known she and Charles would be passing this way when they returned to the big house.

The dogs tumbled around her feet, excited by the arrival of a newcomer but too well trained to jump. She bent to caress their silky ears, trying to regain her composure.

"Charles and Uncle William are finishing up a game of chess," she said. "Charles will be coming along in a little while. Or," she added with forced casualness, "if you wanted to go over there now, I'm sure Aunt Mary would be happy to see you."

"No thanks." He leaned against a tree, watching her so

intently that she was unnerved. "I'm quite happy to stay right here."

Madeline stood erect and shifted on her feet, feeling ridiculously uncomfortable. All at once she was a teenager again, shy and awkward, not even knowing what to do with her hands. Finally she stuffed them in the pockets of her skirt and tried to look nonchalant.

"How's Shelby?" she asked.

"Feeling a little better. We had split pea soup for dinner, and now she's soaking in a hot bath. I think a good night's sleep will help a lot."

"I'll call in the morning and check on her before I go to Philip's office."

"Are you still sure you want to do that alone?" Justin asked.

"Quite sure." Madeline began to edge along the path, moving away from him. "And now I suppose I should be going, because I—"

He gestured toward the flat rock he'd been sitting on. "Madeline, stay here for a minute and talk with me. It's such a beautiful evening."

She hesitated. It seemed graceless to refuse, but she was afraid of being alone with him, particularly in this setting where the twilight felt so caressing, and the shadows were deepening all around them.

"At this time of the evening I feel young again," Justin said, gazing at the dense shrubbery bordering the path. "I feel like all those years haven't passed by yet, and anything could happen. All sorts of wonderful things, just waiting out there in the shadows. Do you know what I mean?"

Madeline understood exactly what he meant. But at the same time she was so surprised to hear him express such an emotion that she forgot her awkwardness and stood gazing at him in astonishment.

At last she moved forward and sat on the rock, smoothing her denim skirt around her knees. Justin lowered himself next to her and both dogs wandered over to lie at their feet.

For a while they lingered in a charged silence while the crickets chirped beyond the path. She was painfully conscious of his nearness, the soft leather of his jacket and his clean, masculine scent.

"Aunt Mary and Uncle William seem quite well," she ventured at last. "But she's looking a little frail, isn't she?"

He nodded. "It worries me a lot. They have a housemaid living over there with them, but I keep thinking about what might happen if there were some kind of medical emergency in the middle of the night and I'd have no way of knowing about it."

She nodded. "Those things are always a concern, especially when her health hasn't been good. Still, I'm sure that Aunt Mary and Uncle William don't want to give up their independence."

"They certainly don't." He glanced down at her. "How have you been, Madeline?" he asked. "Don't just tell me you're fine, tell me what it's really been like. Was life hard for you at first, after you left?"

She considered, then nodded. "Yes," she said quietly. "In fact, it was terribly hard. We were married so young that I didn't know how to be anything but a wife and mother, and I had to spend quite a long time getting to know myself, trying to develop some confidence in my own abilities."

"But you've managed?"

"Yes, Justin. I've managed very well."

He stared thoughtfully into the shadows. "When you left, I was so angry," he said at last, surprising her again. "I went around nursing my hurt pride for years, feeling sorry for myself. Then I started to think about how much courage it must have taken for you to do what you did, and I was ashamed.''

"Really?" She looked up at his profile, the clean line of forehead and nose, mouth and chin.

Madeline had always loved his profile. Even in the years since their divorce, she'd sometimes been horrified to find herself drawing that face on her sketch pad without being aware of what she was doing.

"Why did you leave, Madeline?" he asked, still not looking at her. "Did you just stop loving me, or was life here so awful for you that you couldn't bear it any longer?"

She gripped her hands tightly in her lap, wondering how to answer. Though she'd often imagined the two of them having such a conversation, she still wasn't fully prepared for this.

"I was smothering," she said at last. "Toward the end, there were days when I literally felt like I couldn't breathe at Riverwood. All the children were practically grown, and sometimes I felt so—so lonely that I couldn't bear it."

"Oh, Madeline," he said, his voice rough with emotion. "God, I'm sorry."

"Don't be sorry," she said briskly, moving her arm away from his. "It's all turned out for the best. I have a very pleasant life now, and I've learned to take care of myself. I'm a much better person because I lived through all that trauma. And I suspect," she added after a moment, "that you are, too."

"Do you think so?" he asked. "You really think I'm a better person?"

Madeline considered. "You're certainly a different person," she said at last. "I'm really quite surprised by you, Justin."

He turned quickly to glance at her, his gaze so probing and intent that she was compelled to return it. His eyes were dark blue with little specks of green and gold. Seeing them again made her feel suddenly weak and dry-mouthed with emotion.

"How am I different?" he asked.

She looked down at her hands. One of the dogs stirred and sat up, and Madeline reached out nervously to stroke its silky ears.

"You seem more thoughtful than the Justin I remember," she said. "And yet...I don't know. Boyish, I guess."

"Boyish?" he echoed, clearly astonished.

Madeline allowed herself a brief smile. "When you were a younger man, you were really quite pompous," she said gently. "I suppose it was the responsibility of having a family when you were twenty, but you always seemed...very sober and self-absorbed."

"And now I don't?"

She shook her head. "You're different now. There are times when you seem even younger than Beau. Almost reckless."

He gave her one of those rare, shining smiles that transformed his face. Madeline felt a deep stab of pain and looked away quickly.

"I suppose it's partly because of—" she began, then fell abruptly silent.

Because of having such a beautiful young lover, she was going to say. After all, it had to be an exhilarating feeling for a man in his fifties....

"Madeline?" he asked. "What were you going to say just now?"

She shook her head and got to her feet. "Nothing. Look, Justin, I really should be going. It's getting late, and I have to—"

He gripped her arm and pulled her gently back down next to him. "Don't go yet. Not when we've just started talking to each other again. When did we stop talking, Madeline?"

"I don't think we have all that much to discuss," she murmured, looking into the shrubbery again. It was almost dark by now, and the moths glimmered along the path like tiny stars.

"Of course we do," he said. "We have five children in common, plus more than twenty years of shared history. And we've had ten years of separation when both of us have been living our lives and learning new things. We've got a lot to talk about."

"Oh, Justin." She felt a deep wave of sadness and anger, and turned away from him with a brief, impatient gesture.

"What?" he asked, leaning closer. "Tell me what you're thinking. Are you angry with me?"

Madeline was distressed to find herself fighting back tears. "You wouldn't understand," she murmured.

"Try me."

She shook her head again, afraid to trust her voice.

"Madeline?" he asked, putting a hand on her shoulder. "What is it?"

She drew away hastily. "It's just so...sad," she muttered at last. "Sad and terrible that you should want to talk with me now."

"Why?"

All at once Madeline felt a hot, bracing flood of anger that helped to steady her voice. She looked up at him coldly. "Because there was a time when I would have given anything to have you talk with me and show an interest in my feelings, Justin. That kind of interest would have meant the world to me. Now it's all too..."

"What?" he asked.

"It's too late to matter anymore."

"Is it?" He put his arms around her and pulled her close, his voice rough with emotion. "Is it really too late?"

She stiffened, conscious of his warmth and the hard

strength of his body. "Of course it is. Justin, what on earth are you doing?"

He touched her hands, stroking each of her fingers with lingering slowness, circling the smooth bare knuckle on her left hand.

"Do you still have your wedding ring?" he asked.

She tensed, wanting to ignore the question but afraid not to answer. "Oh, it's back home somewhere," she said with forced casualness.

Justin glanced up and lifted her hand to his mouth. "You didn't throw it away?"

"I thought one of the girls might want it someday. After all, it's a family heirloom."

He brushed his lips across her fingers, then turned her hand over and kissed the palm. She shivered, suddenly aching with desire.

"For goodness' sake," she said, trying to snatch her hand away. "Justin, this is so—"

But his mouth was on hers and she couldn't speak anymore. For a mad, breathless moment, Madeline gave herself up to the bliss of his embrace, realizing just how much she'd yearned for her husband during these lonely years. Hundreds of sleepless nights when she'd dreamed of having Justin's arms around her, his mouth on hers, his body pressing against her own....

He'd been her first lover, just as she had been his. In the years since their separation, other men had held Madeline, but none had ever thrilled her the way Justin did. He was unique, and utterly desirable.

She loved the feel of his skin, the strength of his hands, the softness of his mouth. Even the spicy, pleasantly familiar scent of his aftershave was enough to take her breath away and send her into a dizzying spiral of yearning. She felt a wave of sexual desire, so intense that it rose from the very core of her and engulfed her being.

Now he was holding her tightly in his arms, murmuring incoherently as he covered her face and neck with kisses and explored her body with his hands, and she knew she wanted this man more than she'd ever wanted anything in all her life.

A small part of her being, some tiny, cautious corner of her brain, shouted an urgent warning. With a last flicker of sanity, she tried to pull away. "No," she whispered. "Justin, please stop this."

"Maddy," he whispered against her throat. "Darling, don't push me away. You don't know how much I want you. I've always wanted you. All these years, even when they've been trying to force other women on me, I could only think of you."

He kissed her again, and she was undone. She felt herself drowning in longing, taking leave of any caution that remained to her.

Without her conscious awareness, they seemed to be walking together along the path, their arms entwined, stopping to kiss and murmur incoherently. They entered the silent house and stumbled upstairs to his bedroom, as furtive as teenagers.

To Madeline, the situation felt more and more unreal. She found herself in the same room they'd shared for so many years, standing next to the bed where all of her children except Beau and Jax had been born. And yet it was a man's room now, with an austere look and a dangerous, unfamiliar ambience.

It felt as exciting as being in a hotel room with a virile stranger.

But this was no stranger. This was a man whose body she knew intimately, hungered for, dreamed of....

He undressed her, pulled her blouse and her bra aside to stroke her breasts, then bent to run his lips over her shoulders and throat. Madeline moaned in pleasure and unbut-

toned his shirt, burying her fingers in the curly graying hair
on his chest and tugging gently.

She'd always loved that thick mat of hair.

"Justin," she whispered. "Darling..."

At the sound of her voice he groaned aloud and swept
her into his arms, carrying her to the bed. He laid her down
and unbuttoned her skirt, pulling it aside to expose her legs,
then stepped out of his jeans and tossed them onto a chair.

With a part of her mind, she was still able to laugh at
their panting urgency to rid themselves of their clothes. She
and Justin were behaving more like randy adolescents than
a dignified, long-married couple in their fifties, about to
become grandparents.

But soon even that humorous bit of objectivity was swallowed up in passion, and then there was nothing anywhere
but his mouth and hands and body, filling all the aching,
empty places that had needed him for ten lonely years.

Afterward they lay together, utterly sated, their faces almost touching as they shared a pillow and smiled at each
other.

"You still do it," he murmured huskily, brushing the tip
of her nose with a gentle finger.

"Of course I still do it. What do you think I am, ancient?" she grabbed the finger and bit it daintily, making
him chuckle.

"No, I mean you still make that little noise when
you're...you know."

"What little noise?" She smiled and touched the tousled
silver hair at his temples.

"Like a sleepy cat." When he imitated the sound, they
both laughed in recognition.

"And you're still my knight in shining armor with his
magic lance," she whispered, kissing his cheek tenderly,
then reaching to trace the fine line of his aquiline nose.

"Do you remember those silly games we used to play, darling? We were so young."

"Oh, Maddy," he whispered huskily, gathering her into his arms and squeezing her so tightly that she almost cried. "I've never forgotten anything. God, how I've missed you."

"I've missed you, too," she admitted cautiously, not daring to tell him how desperately she'd yearned for him or how passionately her body responded to him even now. She drew away. "But Justin, we need to—"

"Uh-oh," he murmured, looking pleased and guilty, exactly like Beau at about six years old when he'd been caught in some childhood prank.

"What?" she asked suspiciously.

"Something's happening," Justin said.

"What do you mean?"

He took her hand and guided it lower, pressing her fingers against his groin.

Madeline leaned up on one elbow and gazed at him in openmouthed astonishment. "*Again?* For heaven's sake, man, can't you act your age?"

Once more he looked both sheepish and delighted. He drew her close and whispered against her hair. "It's been a long time, darling. And nobody's ever turned me on the way you do."

"Such nonsense," she whispered, trying to sound severe. "I need my sleep."

But her heart was pounding and her body was arching hungrily toward him again, and it was a long time before Madeline got to sleep that night.

NEXT MORNING, SHE WOKE in the misty half light of dawn and stared drowsily at his sleeping face on the pillow. She smiled and stirred under the blankets, her body still glowing with sexual contentment and a rare sense of homecoming. Then reality flooded in and she sat erect in horror.

Justin woke and smiled up at her. "Hello, sweetheart," he whispered.

Madeline scrambled from the bed without answering, gathered her clothes and hurried toward the bathroom. When she came out he was wearing his jeans and shirt, pulling on a pair of moccasins.

"Are you all right, darling?" he asked.

She avoided his eyes, rigid with embarrassment. "I have to get back to the hotel right away," she murmured. "I was lucky enough to get an appointment yesterday afternoon to see Philip today, and then I have to—"

"Madeline," Justin said gently, "please sit down and talk to me."

"I don't want to talk. I have nothing at all to say to you."

He lifted his head, clearly stung. "What happened here last night? I thought we—"

"Whatever you thought, you were wrong," she said. "Nothing happened last night but an attack of lust. For what it's worth, I regret my behavior terribly and I'm very sorry."

Justin recoiled as if she'd struck him. "But I don't..." He stumbled for words. "The way we loved each other was so..."

She found one of her shoes and began to look around anxiously for the other, finally retrieving it from under a dresser.

"Look, Madeline," he said, beginning to sound angry, "what's this all about? Tell me why you're acting like this."

She stood erect, staring at him. "I don't believe it," she said. "You can actually ask me why?"

"That's right, I can. Why are you treating me this way?

Last night we were as close as two people could be. Now you act like I'm a stranger you've had some kind of embarrassing one-night stand with."

"You *are* a stranger," she said bitterly. "You and your family have always been strangers to me, Justin. I have no way of understanding you."

"What do you mean?"

"Well, for instance..." She noticed a button she'd missed on her skirt front and fastened it with trembling fingers, searching for a way to make him understand. "For instance, Uncle William," she said.

Justin looked at her blankly. "Uncle William? What about him?"

"He's Desiree's son. She gave birth to him and then she obediently handed her baby over to the family."

"Yes," Justin said, "apparently that's true."

"But William and Mary don't know a thing about any of this."

Justin's jaw tightened. "We thought it was best not to tell them."

"You thought it best!" she shouted, so furious she was afraid she might cry. "But nobody ever considered his right to this knowledge about himself, or how he might feel. Did they, Justin?"

"We thought—"

"Can't you see how incredibly arrogant that is? Don't you realize how this family has twisted everybody's life for generations by keeping its awful secrets? I can't *bear* it, Justin. I simply can't bear it."

To her distress she began to sob and rushed from the room, hurrying down the stairs and out across the veranda before he could stop her.

Her car sat beyond the fence in the pale wash of daylight. Madeline clambered behind the wheel, gunned the motor and was halfway into town before her hands stopped shaking.

There was some truth in what she'd said to Justin about William and about family secrets. But with uncompromising honesty, Madeline admitted to herself that the Delacroix family wasn't the whole reason for her wild flight this morning. They were merely an excuse.

Justin himself was what she feared. One more night in his arms and she'd lose everything. Her hard-won independence, her composure and detachment—all would be swallowed up in that passion she'd never been able to control. Justin would consume her again as he had in the past.

As a young woman she'd allowed herself to drown in that man's power, to suffer his rigid, unwavering arrogance, and twenty years of her life had vanished into the mist.

It was too great a price to pay, Madeline told herself, gripping the wheel and staring at the lightening sky.

Never again would she lose herself in the embrace of a man as arrogant as Justin Delacroix.

JUSTIN HAD FOLLOWED HER onto the veranda, his arms aching with the pain of holding her so briefly, only to have her vanish again. He wanted to get into his own car and drive after the woman, force her to confront him and explain why she was being so harsh.

But he knew her well enough to recognize the futility of such an action. After all these years, just looking at the rigid set of her mouth told him how passionately upset she was.

With Madeline it was always best to let a little time pass after a quarrel before trying to approach her. She was so intrinsically gentle and reasonable that if she went off to think about things in solitude, she could usually talk herself out of a mood.

This fight had seemed different, though, and utterly inexplicable.

He'd felt her passionate response when she was in his arms. After all those years of making love to one woman, a man could recognize when she was aroused. Madeline's body rhythms were exquisitely familiar to him, and despite their troubles and conflicts, he'd always been able to bring her to a rich, satisfying climax.

Hunger for her hit Justin again like a physical blow, making him reel. He'd never yearned for anyone as much in his life as he did for that slim woman who'd just fled down the road into the rising sun. And yet after responding to him with passionate warmth, she'd turned away and rejected him utterly.

He couldn't understand it.

Justin sank onto the steps and buried his face in his hands. He was accompanied by the dogs, who sensed his misery and stood nearby, whimpering anxiously.

The worst thing of all was that his feelings weren't just sexual. Making love to her had felt like a rich balm, as satisfying and comfortable to his lonely, wounded spirit as coming back to a beloved home after a long, long absence. Now he wanted to spend peaceful hours looking at her, talking with her, listening to her thoughts and dreams.

Justin Delacroix wanted his wife back.

The dogs stirred restlessly and barked a welcome as a footfall sounded behind him—his father's familiar tread.

He raised a bleak face, struggling to control himself.

"Good morning, son." Charles paused by the veranda railing, gave him a keen glance and bent to pat one of the spaniels. "Is there anything wrong?"

"Madeline just left."

"Ah. I see."

Charles seated himself in the rocking chair and smiled

absently as both dogs came to rest their muzzles on his knees. He cast another brief, sidelong glance at his son.

"Well, that's real nice," he said, "to have the two of you...talking again. All the children will be happy."

Justin paused, looking down at his hands. He thought about his wife's delicate face and huge gray eyes, that slim body, her tragic expression as she'd run away from him. The memory hurt so much that he shuddered with remembered pain.

"She hates me."

"Now, I don't believe that." Charles extended his legs comfortably. "She seemed quite cordial when she arrived yesterday. And I gather," he added delicately, "that she spent the night?"

Justin nodded wearily.

"Hmm." Charles stroked one of the spaniels, then raised its velvety lip to examine the rows of strong young teeth. "Strange that she'd get so angry all of a sudden, isn't it? But I guess you can't blame her."

Justin stared at him. "What do you mean?"

"I suppose," Charles said with a sudden edge to his voice, "nobody in this world likes a two-timer, do they?"

"A two-timer?" Justin echoed, startled by the old-fashioned phrase. "What on earth are you talking about?"

Charles gazed into the shrubbery. "I may be old, son, but I'm not dead. I've heard what's going on. Even Mary knows about it."

Justin leaned over to grasp his father's arm. "Look, you'd better tell me what you're talking about," he said tightly. "Because I have no idea."

"Oh, Justin." Charles shook his head. "The whole county knows about you and that girl."

"What girl?" Justin asked blankly.

"Little Claudia Landry. The girl who works for Remy in the bait shack."

A light dawned, and Justin's eyes widened in shock. "You mean Madeline thinks I'm...oh, for God's sake! Did she tell you that?"

"She didn't have to. The story's all over town. We even talked about it last night at dinner."

Justin felt a rising alarm, accompanied by growing outrage. "This damned town," he muttered. "Sometimes it makes me so..."

"You can't blame the folks in town," Charles said mildly when his son paused, clenching his hands into fists. "After all, what are they going to say when they see a man in his fifties squiring a girl who's younger than his daughters?"

"That girl is just a friend!"

Charles sighed.

"I mean it," Justin said. "I've been helping her to—to gain some confidence and learn to be comfortable around people. That's all."

"So it's just a nice, charitable act on your part," Charles said with a skeptical glance. "Is that what you're telling me, son?"

"Yes," Justin said, "that's exactly what I'm telling you. The truth is, Claudia's in love with one of the boat operators, and she's too shy and insecure to let him know her feelings. I happened to find out the whole situation has been making her very unhappy. So I sort of...took her under my wing."

Charles leaned forward to look closely at his son. "My Lord," he breathed at last. "You're telling the truth, aren't you?"

"Of course I am," Justin said impatiently. "Why would I lie to you?"

"But, son, this is Louisiana. You must have known what folks would say when they saw you with that pretty young thing."

"I didn't care." Justin kicked at a fallen pine cone. "That was before Madeline came back. If I'd known for a minute that she was going to hear about it, and think I was... God, she must despise me!"

Charles watched while Justin got his feet and began to stride away.

"Where are you going, son?"

"Over to the Bayou Inn. I have to talk to her, tell her I'd never do something like that."

Charles got up and gestured to the younger man. "You know, I haven't learned an awful lot about women," he said gently. "Even in eighty years of living and two marriages. But I know enough to tell you that right now's probably not a good time to talk to Madeline."

Justin hesitated, thinking about her blazing eyes and the anger in her stride as she'd hurried away. Finally he turned aside, sighing in disappointment.

"I guess you're right," he said. "She needs a little time to cool down before I try to talk with her. Otherwise we'll both say a lot of things and the situation will get worse than it was before."

"That sounds like the truth to me," Charles agreed. "I'd let her think on it and talk to her later today."

Justin nodded, then clapped a hand to his forehead. "But I can't talk to her today. I need to be in New Orleans all day for a special sitting of the judicial committee." He frowned. "Unless I could get her to see me in the evening. I was planning to spend the night with Toni and Brody, and come home on Tuesday, but they'd understand if I canceled."

"Of course they would," Charles said comfortably. "Madeline has things to do in town, too, and she's not going back to Aspen until Wednesday morning. Let her think this over and cool down. You can come back from the city and give her a call tonight. That's my advice."

"I just hate having her think I'm the kind of man who'd do something like that," Justin muttered.

"I reckon you do. But a day in your life isn't going to make all that much difference, is it?"

"I suppose not."

Justin headed toward the path while Charles watched in surprise. "Where are you going, son?"

"Over to the other house," Justin said quietly. He nodded to his father, then set off into the sunrise with the dogs galloping ahead of him. "I'm going to have a talk with Uncle William."

BACK IN HER HOTEL ROOM Madeline paced up and down, her hands pressed to her flaming cheeks.

How could she have been such a fool? She'd actually allowed the man to hold her, caress her, whisper sweet things in her ears. She not only hadn't resisted, she'd responded to him with wild, shameless passion....

Madeline turned restlessly and headed for the closet, hauling her suitcases out and dumping them on the bed.

"I need to get away from here," she said aloud. "I don't want to stay here another minute." She began to jam things into the larger suitcase, then paused.

This was craziness. She'd come all this way for a specific purpose. She still needed to talk with Philip, pass a message to Lyle Masson and his unsavory henchman, and pay a visit to Flora Boudreaux. After those tasks were accomplished, she could leave the shores of Lake Pontchartrain and never return.

But she didn't need two days to arrange a couple of meetings, Madeline realized.

None of her children were going to be available this week except for Shelby. And in light of recent happenings, Madeline certainly had no desire to hang around waiting for them to get back from their various activities.

Her mind began to whirl with plans.

She already had an afternoon appointment with Philip. Maybe she could change their meeting to the morning hours, and charter a boat and go out to the swamp to see Flora after that. Then she could have her flight moved up a full day or more, and get away from this maddening, seductive place.

Back to Aspen, with its sun-dazzled mountain peaks and cold, crisp autumn air, its riot of colored leaves. Back to the gallery, her artwork and her calm, uncluttered life.

Far, far away from Justin Delacroix...

Madeline crossed the room with sudden decision and sat at the desk. She flipped through the telephone book, then dialed the airline and asked about the possibility of an earlier flight.

"This evening, if possible," she told the young woman at the other end of the line.

"The earliest we could find a vacant seat would be Tuesday morning at ten forty-five."

Madeline calculated rapidly. She could finish up all her business here in Bayou Beltane today, check out of the hotel and spend the night in New Orleans, then catch the Tuesday morning flight. She wouldn't even have to spend another twenty-four hours in this place.

"Tuesday morning will be fine," she said. "Thank you very much."

She hung up and leaned back in the chair, running a hand through her hair, then picked up her little address book, consulted it and dialed another number.

"Could I speak with Mr. Philip Delacroix, please?" she said when the phone was answered by a soft, musical voice.

"May I say who's callin'?"

"It's Madeline."

"Yes, ma'am. Jes' one moment, please." There was a long silence while Madeline waited tensely.

"Madeline," Philip said at last, with warm hospitality. "How nice to hear your voice. My secretary told me you'd left a message yesterday but I was in New Orleans."

Madeline took a deep breath. "Hello, Philip. Sorry to call so early in the morning."

"Shoot, I'm always up with the birds. What brings you back to our little town?" he asked.

His tone was still courtly, but Madeline could also sense a note of keen interest. The old man was an avid observer of the other side of the family, always hoping for a breath of scandal or some juicy trauma.

"I was anxious to see the children," Madeline said evenly. "And as a matter of fact, I wanted to talk with you about something, Philip."

"Well, now, I'm real flattered to hear that," he said. "How have you been, Madeline?"

"I've been quite well." Madeline hesitated, then plunged ahead. "Philip, I have an appointment to see you this afternoon, but I wondered if we could meet this morning, instead. I've been forced to alter my schedule a little."

"My entire day is at your disposal," the old man said with his usual suave gallantry. "Name the time, Madeline."

"Ten o'clock?" she said.

"I'll be looking forward to it. I surely will."

"Thank you, Philip. Oh, and one more thing…"

"Yes, my dear?"

"I wonder if I might ask a favor of you."

"Why, anything, Madeline. Anything at all."

She grimaced at his effusiveness. "I wonder if you have somebody with a boat who could spare me an hour or two in the afternoon. I want to go up the swamp."

"Up the swamp?" he echoed.

Madeline gripped the telephone cord, wrapping it tightly

around her fingers. "I want to have a talk with Flora Boud-reaux."

"You do?" he said, his voice suddenly cautious. "Now, that's real odd. What on earth would you and Flora have to talk about?"

"Just some private family business. Do you think you could find me a boat, Philip? I'll want to leave right after lunch. I'd ask Remy but it seems he's away, too, and I don't have time to locate anybody else."

"I still can't imagine a reason on earth why you'd want to go up that old swamp."

"Can't you?" she said quietly.

There was a brief, charged silence.

Finally Philip laughed, sounding more relaxed again. "Well," he said, "I reckon what you talk to Flora about is your own business, Madeline. I'd be happy to supply you with a boat. Just remind me when you're at the office. I'll make sure all the arrangements are made."

"That's very kind of you."

"I surely do look forward to seeing you again," he said. "You were always such a lovely woman, Madeline."

"Thank you," she said, her voice curt and dismissive. "I'll see you in a few hours, then."

She hung up and stared at her reflection in the mirror for a moment, then moaned and hid her face in her hands, trying not to think about Justin's arms around her, and the feeling of his mouth on hers.

CHAPTER TEN

THE EARLY SUN VANISHED, leaving the morning cloudy and still with wraiths of fog drifting out across the bayou and lying over the little town. Madeline felt like a ghost, wrapped in cool shrouds of gray as she walked through the streets to Philip's office.

The melancholy day suited her mood. She was still badly unsettled by the visit to Riverwood, with all its old memories and unresolved emotions.

And the shattering, unbearable sweetness of a whole night spent in Justin's arms...

She pushed open the front door and climbed the broad oak stairs to Philip's suite, pausing to give her name to the receptionist.

After knowing him for more than half a lifetime, Madeline almost expected the wily old devil to keep her cooling her heels in the waiting room, just to show his power. But when the secretary buzzed, Philip hurried at once to the reception area, beaming.

"Madeline," he said, bowing over her hand in courtly fashion, then giving her a brief, awkward hug. "How wonderful to see you. Come on in."

She walked with him toward his office, her feet sinking into the rich blue plush as she glanced at him covertly.

All of them were showing their age, she realized. Mary was over eighty by now, and Charles and Philip would be eighty very shortly. The three old people had a fragile look, and just a lingering trace of the hearty vigor she remembered.

Philip, in particular, looked quite unwell. His normal high color had faded to a waxen pallor, and his hands trembled slightly.

Time was passing so quickly, she thought with a deep wave of sadness. Everybody was getting older, even her own children.

I should be here. I should be living close to all of them, because life is so precious and it goes by in an instant....

The random thought alarmed and unsettled her. She sank into one of the leather chairs and accepted a cup of coffee from the secretary, who arrived behind them with a loaded tray.

"So, Madeline," Philip said after the woman padded out of the office as silently as she'd come. "How are the children?"

Madeline considered for a moment, then decided there was no point in trying to mislead him. "I did rather a foolish thing, actually," she said, taking a sip of coffee. "I flew out here on impulse this weekend without telling anybody, and as a result none of the children are home except for Shelby."

He leaned back and smiled at her across the gleaming expanse of his desk. "Well, now, that's a shame. A real shame. How's Shelby?"

Madeline met his gaze levelly.

The old rogue, she thought. If he and his friends had been doing anything wrong, there was no way to tell from his behavior or appearance.

As always, Philip was impeccably, even elegantly dressed, in a well-cut gray suit and snowy white shirt, a crisp green bow tie and gleaming shoes. His manner was affable and warm, but she was conscious of those eyes watching her with a cool, guarded look.

At least his eyes haven't changed, she thought.

She shivered, half afraid that Justin's passionate kisses might be visible on her mouth, her throat and face and hair....

Aloud, she said, "Shelby's not feeling well, I'm afraid."

His eyes flickered, but their expression remained cautious. "Now, I'm real sorry to hear that. What's the problem, do you know?"

"Just a touch of the flu. She was quite ill yesterday, but when I called this morning she sounded considerably improved."

Philip propped his fingertips together and looked at them thoughtfully. "I reckon she's been working too hard lately," he said. "Driving herself into the ground. That poor little girl should slow down a bit. Otherwise she'll come to grief, don't you think?"

Madeline glanced at him sharply, wondering if there was a veiled threat in his words. But his voice was bland and his face showed nothing but concern.

"What makes you think so, Philip? I didn't realize you were so familiar with Shelby's schedule."

"I have a whole lot of concern for my nieces and nephew," he said mildly. "I like to keep track of them. And Shelby seems like a real..." He hesitated, still examining his manicured hands. "A real busy little girl. Got a finger in every pie. It can't be healthy for her, doing so much all the time."

Madeline felt a rising tide of anger. She leaned forward tensely. "Look, Philip, I wanted you to know that I—"

He pulled a legal pad toward him, picked up a gold pen and began to doodle aimlessly. "Did they tell you Joanna's pregnant?" he interrupted, as if she hadn't spoken.

"Yes, I know." Madeline settled back in the chair, a little unnerved by this abrupt change of subject. "I haven't seen her, but I understand she's blissfully happy about the baby."

"I don't see her much, either." Philip stared at the notepad, looking so bereft that Madeline felt an unexpected twinge of sympathy. But her compassion evaporated with his next words.

"Speaking of family news," he said, giving her a bright, malicious glance from under his eyebrows, "I hear Justin's been causing quite a stir, too. Now, that's real surprising news, seems to me. I never thought the boy had it in him."

"What do you mean?" Madeline asked, gripping the cup tensely.

Philip gave her a wolfish grin. "You just arrived on the bayou, so I reckon you haven't heard any gossip. It seems Justin's fallen for some little bit of a girl barely out of the cradle. Did you know that? Why, it's all over town."

"I've never paid much attention to gossip," Madeline said coldly, her heart pounding.

"The girl's so young, some folks think she must be Justin's own child and you found out about her so you left him." Philip gave her another bright glance. "But I reckon more likely she's just a bit of fluff."

Madeline looked past him to the huge picture window. "I don't want to talk about this, Philip."

"Well, like I said, it seems real funny to me," the old man said with a sudden edge to his voice. "After all the years Justin's gone around passing judgment on other people, being so upright and sanctimonious, it's purely amusing to find that he's just another dirty old man, after all."

"Look, that's such a..." Madeline began hotly, then subsided when Philip looked up at her with amusement.

"What were you going to say, Madeline?" he asked softly.

"Nothing." She made an impatient gesture with her hand. "I have no particular interest in Justin's social activities, and I'm certainly not anxious to discuss him. I'm only concerned about my children.''

"They're all doing real well, I hear. The family's prospering. You must be proud of them.''

"I am.'' Madeline looked at him directly. "But I'm also a little worried, and that's why I've come to see you.''

"Why, if you're worried about something,'' he said expansively, laying both hands flat on the desk top, "I'd move heaven and earth to help you, Madeline. Heaven and earth.''

She ignored the heavy gallantry. "Some strange things have been happening to Shelby lately,'' she said. "Threatening phone calls and so on. Just last week she had a load of buckshot fired at her car. It really concerns me, Philip.''

"I reckon it would, if you thought that gunshot wasn't an accident.''

Madeline met his gaze silently.

"Is that what you think?'' he said.

"I don't know what to think. Nobody around here seems overly bothered. Even Justin seems half inclined to think it's just part of life on the bayou. But looking at this situation from a distance as I do, I tend to find it rather more upsetting.''

Philip wheeled his chair around to gaze out the window at the black marble fountain in the courtyard below, then turned back to his guest. "Maybe Shelby's been doing a little too much lately,'' he said at last. "Could be she's gotten herself on somebody's wrong side.''

Madeline tensed. "What are you saying, Philip? That somebody's deliberately shooting at her because she's made an enemy?''

"Now, I didn't say anything like that,'' he protested mildly. "I just said it's not always healthy to be too…busy. Folks can get miffed.''

"Philip, I don't think you understand. Somebody shot a

gun at my daughter. That goes a long way beyond being miffed, don't you think?''

"Tempers can run high out here," he said blandly. "Especially in the summertime. You know how hot it gets down on the bayou, Madeline.''

She watched him in silence.

"And," he added thoughtfully, examining one of his gold cuff links, "there are a lot of secrets in this old place. I reckon some folks would prefer to keep it that way."

"Including you," Madeline said bluntly. "Is that what you're telling me?"

His eyes widened in exaggerated shock and hurt. "Madeline, surely you're not accusing me of trying to hurt Shelby? Why, I've always been real fond of that girl. You know I have."

"I think you…" Madeline took a deep breath and forced herself to play along with him. "I think somebody might be trying to give her a bit of a scare, Philip, to keep her from getting on the wrong side of your corrupt friends. Someone like Lyle Masson, for instance."

She glanced at him quickly. His eyes didn't flicker, but she thought perhaps his gnarled hands relaxed a little on the desktop at the mention of the Louisiana politician.

"And I know how much influence you have in this county, so I've come here to plead for your help," she continued. "I could never get close to Lyle Masson, but I know you have his ear."

This was clearly the right approach. Philip always liked to be flattered and appealed to. He leaned back in his chair again, smiling. "Just say the word. I'll do anything I can, Madeline. Anything at all."

"Good. I'd like you to tell Mr. Masson that I'm watching, Philip, even though I'm not living here. If anybody hurts one of my children, deliberately or…or *accidentally*," she said with emphasis, "then that person is going to be

very, very sorry. And if anything happens to me, there's ℯ
letter on file with my lawyer that could certainly embarras:
a few people. Could you let your friends know that?"

He met her eyes, and she was conscious of an unspoken
challenge hanging between them. But his voice was milc
when he spoke.

"Now, that sounds like kind of a grim threat coming
from a lovely woman like yourself. I've never known you
to go around threatening people, Madeline."

"I suppose you haven't. But I've become a lot toughei
over the years," she said coldly. "And where my childrer
are concerned, I'm a force to be reckoned with. I jus
want...people to realize that."

The state senator watched her with an unblinking, basi-
lisk stare, then nodded and looked down at his desk, reaching for the pen again.

"I lined up one of the boys to take you up the swamp,"
he muttered. "Unless," he added hopefully, "you've
changed your mind about going to see Flora."

"No," she said. "I haven't changed my mind. Thank
you for arranging the boat, Philip."

"I still don't know why you'd want to talk to that
woman."

"Actually, for much the same reasons I've just been discussing with you," Madeline told him calmly. "I'm concerned about Shelby's welfare, and I want Flora to be aware
of my feelings on the matter. Flora Boudreaux's been
known to have some rather dangerous friends. Maybe one
of them knows something about that fire out at Riverwood."

Philip gave her a long, measuring glance. To her surprise, Madeline detected a hint of grudging admiration in
his eyes.

"Well, you certainly have changed," he said at last.

"Not the same woman I remember at all. You used to be so gentle."

"I was a perfect Southern wife," Madeline agreed. "My European upbringing prepared me very well for the role. But I've been looking after myself for the past ten years and it's been quite a learning experience."

Philip sighed. "The perfect Southern wife seems to be a vanishing species," he muttered soulfully. "I feel real sad about it."

"I'll bet you do," Madeline said dryly. She got to her feet and gathered up her handbag. "Thanks for giving me so much of your time, Philip. I hope you'll think about what I've said and help me if you can."

"I surely will." He heaved himself from his chair and hurried around the desk. "I surely will. When did you want the boat?"

"The sooner, the better." Madeline glanced at her watch. "Right now, if it's possible."

"Is Flora expecting you?"

She shook her head. "No, but I'm hoping she'll be home. It's still early."

Madeline followed her host down the broad oak staircase, wondering if she really deserved the admiration he'd expressed.

No doubt it took some courage to confront both him and Flora on the same day, as well as a kind of initiative she'd never possessed during her marriage to Justin. But in her heart, Madeline knew she wasn't nearly as brave as she appeared.

In fact, the memory of Flora's bold face, her sullen dark eyes and contemptuous laugh, were almost enough to make Madeline repent of her decision as she followed Philip through the office building and out the back.

But that kind of shrinking timidity had never accomplished anything in the past, she told herself firmly. Flora needed to be confronted, and Madeline was the one who had to do it.

"This is Tommy," Philip said, indicating a strapping youngster with a bad complexion and a greasy tangle of hair. "He'll take you down to the dock and use one of my boats to run you over to Flora's place."

Madeline smiled at the boy, who returned her greeting awkwardly and hurried around to the driver's side of the truck while Philip opened the passenger door for her. She climbed into the vehicle, onto zebra-striped seatcovers that looked reasonably clean.

"Now take care, Madeline, you hear?" Philip reached through the window to pat her shoulder. "Tommy's gonna stay with you the whole time, but you should still watch yourself out there."

"Why?" Madeline said bluntly. "What should I be careful of?"

Philip shrugged. "Flora's been real strange since Steven…since all that trouble happened. Went right off her rocker for a little while, and hardly comes to town anymore. When she does, she's mean and surly. Folks don't know what to expect from her."

Madeline thought about the depths of the swamp and the weathered shotgun shack filled with herbs, voodoo paraphernalia and rotting bits of animals, the place where Flora had lived all her life with old Desiree.

She shuddered, then pulled her arm away hastily. "I'll be fine, Philip. Thank you for all your help."

The boy shifted the truck into gear and headed off toward the marina. His pimply jaw was tight, and his face looked pale as he gripped the wheel. Even this hulking youth, she realized, was afraid to go out into that swamp and confront Flora Boudreaux.

Madeline gripped her hands tightly in her lap, suppressed a sigh of nervousness and turned to stare out through the

windows at the fog-shrouded streets of the little bayou
town.

CLAUDIA WOKE in the dense fog that surrounded her houseboat like cotton wool. It shut out both light and sound,
leaving her suspended in a magic place that was dark and
peaceful.

Socks cuddled in the bed next to her, a rare treat. She
gathered him close and smiled drowsily, enjoying the gentle
rocking of the boat.

But gradually reality invaded her mind, the memories all
came flooding back, and she began to feel tense with misery.

It was awful. Everything was awful. Yesterday Bernard
had fought with Joey, right here on her boat. And then Joey
had told him those dirty lies about Mr. Delacroix, and Bernard had been so upset....

Claudia moaned, rolled over and buried her face in the
pillow, causing Socks to squeal and wriggle in consterna-
tion. He struggled out of her embrace, gave her a bitter
glance and jumped lightly down onto the floorboards,
where he sat combing his ruffled fur with a widespread
paw.

She should have lied to Bernard, told him she didn't even
know Mr. Delacroix, that Joey was making everything up.
But that wouldn't have helped. It was all over town, so
Bernard would have heard the gossip before long and felt
the same way about her.

Claudia began to cry. Slow, hot tears trickled down her
cheeks, as corrosive as acid.

Her life had been better in the days when Bernard hadn't
noticed her at all. Now he thought she was a tramp, a con-
temptible person who'd sell her body to get new clothes
and eat dinners in fancy restaurants. He probably despised
her, instead of not knowing she was alive....

Eventually, another reality intruded on Claudia's misery. It was Monday morning, and she had to get up and go to work.

Sniffling, she climbed out of bed, vanished into the little head for a moment and came out toweling her face and hands, then wandered onto the deck to peer at the heavy curtain of fog. The world was utterly silent and she could barely see her hand in front of her face, as if she were lost on a ghost ship.

Finally she went back inside, opened the door of her closet and stood in brooding silence, looking at the pretty new clothes that had brought her such intense pleasure.

Already, it seemed like a million years ago.

"No fancy clothes for me anymore. Tonight I'll pack these things up and give 'em back to Mr. Delacroix," she muttered to Socks, who lay on the bed watching her. "Joey's right about one thing, I guess. We're not the type for fancy stuff."

She dressed in her most ragged plaid shirt and the paint-stained denim overalls, then tied a pair of dirty sneakers onto her feet, one sole flapping against the hardwood floor.

Finally she selected an old baseball cap and tugged it low over her eyes, concealing both her new haircut and most of the bruises from Joey's attack the day before.

"At least," she told Socks as she made toast, "I reckon that nasty boy won't be coming around here for a long time to come. So you might say something good came out of this, after all."

But try as she might, Claudia couldn't see any good in a situation where Bernard Leroux had walked away from her thinking she was a slut.

Now that she was up and busy, fully into the routine of her day, Claudia couldn't hold her misery at bay any longer. Once again, tears welled over her eyelids and flowed down her cheeks, silently at first. But soon she was overwhelmed, and she leaned against the counter, her shoulders heaving with the force of her sobs.

Suddenly a heavy tread sounded on the deck, making her jump and stiffen in fear.

Joey! He'd come back to catch her alone and finish the job. Bernard's whipping hadn't scared him badly enough, after all.

She looked around frantically for something to use as a weapon—a baseball bat, a length of pipe, anything she could hold and swing. Because sure as sunrise, Joey was going to kill her this time. She'd seen the way he'd looked yesterday when he left.

Gradually a voice penetrated her terrified state—not Joey's at all, but a deeper, gentler voice, with a masculine timbre that made her shiver pleasantly in spite of her terror.

She dashed an arm across her eyes and looked up in confusion, but she was crying too hard to be able to say anything.

Bernard gazed down at her soberly. "Quite a fog out there," he said. "It wasn't easy driving over here, and then I practically had to use braille to find the dock and figure out where your boat was. Like to fell in the water about a dozen times. You ever seen it so foggy this late in the season?"

He was talking more than usual, Claudia realized gratefully, to give her a chance to regain her composure. But Bernard, too, seemed ill at ease.

She grabbed a towel, wet it and rubbed it across her face, trying to stop sobbing.

When she had herself under control, he moved over and set a paper sack on one of the lockers.

"You want to tell me what you're crying about?" he asked with elaborate casualness.

"I just feel so…" She choked and hiccuped, then looked nervously at the paper sack.

"Claudia?" he said. "Why were you crying?"

"I feel so awful," she whispered, stabbing the toe of her old running shoe aimlessly against the wooden deck. "About...everything."

"Why? Because I laid that whipping on your big brother?"

"No!" Claudia was so shocked at his words that she stared at him, then lowered her eyes again, overcome by his nearness and the handsome, tanned planes of his face. "No," she repeated more quietly. "That don't—doesn't upset me at all. Joey deserved what you gave him for all the times he's bullied other people. Maybe he'll behave a little nicer from now on."

"Then why were you crying? If you're not hurt and you're not worried about Joey, what happened to upset you?"

She muttered something under her breath, staring at the wisps of fog snaking across the water.

"I can't hear you," Bernard said.

"I hated having you think...I was bad," she said at last, unable to find any other way of expressing it.

"Bad?" he asked.

She nodded miserably. "That I'd be...running around with Mr. Delacroix, or something like that. Because I'm not that kind, Bernard. In fact I've never...even been with anybody."

Her face turned scarlet with embarrassment and she kept her eyes fixed on his shirt buttons.

There was a long, awkward silence. "What're you saying, Claudia?"

"I'm saying that I'm not Mr. Delacroix's girlfriend. Nothing like that at all. He's just been helping me learn how to talk right and giving me clothes to wear so I'd look half-decent. Most of them are castoffs from his daughters, and the others are from Mrs. Colbert, who runs the dress shop.''

Bernard stood at the railing and scowled across the water. ''Why would Justin Delacroix and Emily Colbert go to all that trouble to help you learn how to dress and talk?''

''I don't know.'' Claudia stole another glance at the handsome young man who stood so close to her. ''I think Mr. Delacroix is still in love with his wife, and she don't...she doesn't want anything to do with him. But I think maybe he feels like if he can do some nice things for other people, he'll get rewarded somehow by having her come back to him.''

Bernard was silent a moment. He took a jackknife from his pocket and trimmed some slivers from the deck railing, then smoothed it with his thumb.

''And how,'' he asked, ''did Justin Delacroix find out you were unhappy and wanted help?''

''He come—he came along one night when I was crying in the bait shack, just like you came along this morning. When I told him my troubles, he said he could help. And that's how it started. It was like a dress-up game, nothing more. He's such a nice man. I wish my daddy could have been half that nice.''

Claudia forgot her shyness in her desire to convince him. She looked up earnestly, meeting his eyes. ''I swear that's the whole truth, Bernard. Nothing bad ever happened between me and Mr. Delacroix. He's just a friend.''

''And at night in the bait shack when you were crying...'' Bernard gave her a keen glance. ''What were you crying about, Claudia?''

Color warmed her cheeks again. She searched for an evasive reply, then changed her mind. There'd already been enough lies and misunderstanding to last a whole lifetime. She didn't want it to go on any longer. Besides, after the way her whole life had been dragged out and exposed to public view, there was no point in keeping secrets anymore.

"I was crying over you," she said, looking down at the scuffed toes of her running shoes.

"Me?" he asked in surprise. "Why were you crying over me?"

She took a deep breath. "Because I've...liked you a whole lot since the first time I ever laid eyes on you, that's why," she said without looking at him. "And you didn't even know I was alive, and it 'most killed me sometimes. That's why I was crying."

His face turned red beneath the tan and he made an awkward gesture, watching her in startled disbelief. "So you and Justin Delacroix," he muttered at last, "you decided to do a little fashion makeover?"

She felt like writhing in embarrassment. "Something like that, I guess."

Bernard walked away abruptly. Claudia waited in silent agony, certain that he was leaving. But at the end of the dock he turned and came back, pausing next to the wooden locker.

"I brought you some green paint," he said huskily, gesturing at the paper sack. "I hope it's the right color."

Claudia moved forward unsteadily to lift the package and look inside. "Thank you, Bernard. It's perfect. Now I can finish them—those deck railings later today, if the sun comes out."

Bernard watched her, his face unfathomable. Claudia pulled herself together and turned away. She didn't have the slightest idea what was happening, or what she should say next.

And, she thought with a flash of grim humor, *I bet none of them fancy etiquette books tell you what to do in a situation like this, neither.*

"Would you...like a cup of coffee?" she asked timidly.

"I'd love a cup of coffee." He bent and scooped Socks into his arms, carrying the purring kitten toward the locker. "We'll sit out here on the deck where there's more room, okay?"

"Okay." She smiled and ducked her head, loving the way Socks nestled in Bernard's strong, tanned arms.

Like a baby, she thought wistfully. Bernard would make such a good father....

"What are you doing today?" he asked, pausing in the doorway.

"Going to work." She rummaged in the cabinets, looking for a spare coffee mug that wasn't chipped.

"You must be planning to swab every boat in Remy's fleet, dressed like that."

She looked down at the ragged overalls and felt her cheeks turn scarlet again. "Actually, I'm finishing up some paperwork."

He leaned against the door frame, still holding the kitten in his arms. "Then why the overalls?"

Claudia turned away to reach for the kettle. "I don't know," she whispered. "I guess I didn't feel like... dressing up today."

His eyes rested on her quietly, and she could tell that he knew exactly how she felt. Bernard understood everything.

There was a brief, charged silence. At last she forced herself to look at him again. "Reckon I could probably change into something a little nicer," she murmured. "I got lots of nice clothes."

"So I hear." Bernard grinned. "I'd sure like to see you in some of those pretty things, Claudia."

She smiled back at him, overwhelmed suddenly by a happiness as intense as her earlier misery.

Everything was all right. In fact, everything was wonderful. Miraculously, by coming and talking to her this morning, Bernard had somehow given her back her pride, her peace of mind and all the rich new pleasures of her life.

"Thanks," she whispered.

He waved a hand in dismissal, still holding Socks in the crook of his arm. "I'll go out on deck and give you some privacy while you change your clothes," he said.

But he didn't leave, just kept leaning in the doorway, watching her.

"You're so pretty in your new clothes, Claudia. I want you to dress up so everybody can see how pretty you are."

She hesitated, suddenly nervous. "I'm not so sure I want folks noticing me anymore."

"Why? Are you still worried about Joey?"

"I guess, partly," she admitted. "Them—those brothers of mine, they wreck everything nice that ever happens to me."

"Joey isn't going to hurt you again, Claudia," he said grimly. "You can count on it."

See nodded, believing him. "Maybe it's because this feels so…precious. I want to keep it all to myself, just for a little while."

She moved past him, back onto the deck, and looked over the shrouded water. Bernard set the cat down and came nearer to stand beside her.

"Once, when I was ten years old," she said, looking into the drifting fog, "some church ladies came up the bayou at Christmastime and left presents for us, all wrapped and everything. I'd never had a present in my whole life. It was so pretty I couldn't stand to open it. I wanted to leave that present under my bed and look at it all the time, touch the ribbons and the wrapping paper and know that I could open it whenever I wanted. It was the nicest feeling, Bernard."

His hands tensed on the railing. "Did you finally open it?" he asked.

"After a long time. It was a doll with yellow hair and big blue eyes. I loved that dolly so much—" Her voice broke and she sighed, remembering.

"What happened to the doll?"

"My brothers wrecked her," Claudia said in a matter-of-fact tone, though the memory still brought a sharp wave of pain. "They broke her head open and threw her into the swamp. I cried for days. My daddy had to whip me twice to stop my fussing."

His hand dropped onto her shoulder, holding her so tightly that she gasped. After a moment he released her and moved away, heading for the deck, but not before she saw the glitter of tears in his eyes.

"I'll wait out here while you get dressed," he said again, his voice husky.

"Don't be sad for me, Bernard," she whispered. "Them days are all over with."

"I know," he told her, turning to look at her directly. "Those days are gone forever."

Then he smiled, just as the sun broke through the fog and made the water shimmer all around them like a carpet of diamonds.

CHAPTER ELEVEN

DEEP IN THE SWAMP, it took a long time for the fog to lift. Madeline huddled in the prow of the boat while Philip's young employee peered into the mist and handled the tiller, trying to make his way through the shrouded maze of bayous and backwaters.

The scene was strange, almost surreal. Twisted mangrove roots reared out of the green depths and palmetto branches trailed down onto the surface of the water, appearing and disappearing in broken patches of mist. The boat slipped forward, passing so close to shore at times that wet leaves brushed Madeline's face like the touch of clammy fingers.

When her guide cut the engine to navigate around twisted roots and stumps, the air was silent and dense, broken only by the muffled chirp of crickets and the distant rattle of a kingfisher.

Madeline's young companion cleared his throat. "You gonna be talking for a long time to Miz Boudreaux?" he asked.

"No, I don't think it'll take very long. Why do you ask?"

He shifted awkwardly on the wooden seat. "Reckon I'll let you off at the dock and wait for you down here in the boat if that's all right. Or," he added hopefully, "if you was gonna be a long time, I could slip back into town and come out later to pick you up."

Madeline could tell the youth didn't want to go anywhere

near that shack in the swamp. She knew how much stock the locals put in Flora's "powers."

And now that the Cajun woman was half-crazed with grief and thirsting for revenge, no doubt she was doubly terrifying.

"I don't mind if you wait on the boat," she said. "But I doubt if my visit will take very long."

"Okay." He glanced beyond her into the mist. "I reckon this is her place coming up now."

Madeline peered back over her shoulder, but could see only more trees and mist, pierced by dark patches of swamp. After a moment, though, a weathered shack came looming out of the fog, sitting precariously on half-rotted piers.

The boy pulled up to a sloping walkway and cut the engine, then stood up carefully in the boat and moved forward to help Madeline onto the slippery planks. She braced herself by clutching the rope strung alongside, then turned to smile at him.

"Thank you. I'll try to come back down as soon as I can."

He nodded and settled back in the boat, sprawling against the gunwales and hanging his feet over the other side as he took a couple of worn comic books from his jacket pocket.

Madeline climbed the planks to the little gray shack, her heart in her mouth. She'd been here only once, and that was many years ago.

When Marie was just a young teenager, she'd begged to be brought out to the Boudreaux's place to talk with Desiree about herbal remedies. The family had tried to discourage her, but Marie, always stubborn, had threatened to come on her own. So at last Madeline had traveled with her daughter to the weathered shack in the depths of the swamp. Desiree had been away, but Flora was there.

Now, almost twenty years later, Madeline could still remember the sense of dank mystery that hung around the place, and the look of Flora's capable, broad-tipped fingers as she laid out herbs and potions in front of Marie's fascinated eyes.

"Well, well." A harsh voice intruded on her memory. "What have we here?"

Madeline looked up to see Flora standing in the doorway of the shack. She wore a long cotton skirt, plaid shirt and swamp boots, and her shock of black and gray hair stood out all around her head.

There was no trace of makeup or other feminine adornment on Flora's person, but she still had an undeniable kind of sultry allure. It came, Madeline realized, from the sheer power of the woman's personality. Flora had never doubted her own abilities in the least, and her self-confidence made her a compelling presence in any company.

But now the woman's strong brown face was ravaged by grief, and there was a wild look in her eyes that Madeline didn't remember.

"Hello, Flora," she said quietly, pausing at the end of the walkway. "I was very sorry to hear about Steven. It must have been terrible for you."

Flora's eyes flickered briefly, then hardened. "I just bet you're sorry. What you care about any of us down here on the bayou, Lady Madeline? You gone on to better things now."

Madeline became aware of another figure in the shadows, an old lady sitting in a rocker on the front porch, wrapped in a knitted shawl.

"Bonjour, Desiree," she said in French, moving forward to drop a kiss on the woman's thin, papery cheek. "It's so nice to see you again."

Desiree grasped Madeline's hand and held it in both of her own, peering up at the visitor with eyes that were still surprisingly bright.

"Justin…" she whispered hoarsely.

Madeline looked down at the old lady. "Yes?" she asked after a moment. "What about him, Desiree?"

"Justin has lost his way," Desiree said in her rapid, accented French. "He needs a friend."

While Madeline groped for a reply, Flora laughed harshly behind her.

"Oh, Mama." She doubled over and slapped her knee, shaking with mirth. "Reckon Justin found himself a friend. Ain't that so, Lady Madeline?"

Madeline turned to give the other woman a cold look. "I didn't come here to talk about Justin."

"Oh, I know you didn't. It must be a terrible sad thing," Flora said.

Grief and rage seemed to have affected the woman in some dark and primitive way, even broadening her broad Cajun accent.

"Terrible sad," she repeated, leering, "for a great lady like yourself to find she can't give a man what he needs. All those years Justin wanted some nice hot sex, not a woman so cold he needed permission to climb into her bed. And now he's got what he wants. Lucky Justin. No wonder he looks so happy."

Madeline felt a chill of misery as she thought about Justin in bed with Claudia Landry. Irrationally, she wanted to defend herself to Flora, because the accusation of coldness wasn't true at all. She and Justin had always pleasured each other physically. In fact, they'd kept having wonderful sex even after most of the foundation of their marriage had been eroded by loneliness and neglect.

And last night, though both of them were far beyond first youth, their mutual passion had transcended anything she'd ever known. Just remembering his caresses brought a flood of warmth to her cheeks. As she thought about Justin's hands and mouth, Madeline felt a sweet, melting sensation at the core of her body, a spreading warmth and yearning.

She was conscious of Flora watching her with sardonic amusement, and had the uneasy sensation that those dark, cold eyes could look directly into her soul.

"I told you, Flora, I didn't come here to discuss my former marriage."

Since there was obviously going to be no invitation, Madeline edged across the mossy floorboards and seated herself in a cane-backed armchair, while Flora leaned against the deck railing, arms folded, watching her sullenly.

"So why'd you come here?" Flora asked at last. "You need some medicine? A love potion? A curse put on somebody?" Her eyes glittered in the shadows.

Madeline felt the hair prickle on the back of her neck. She shifted in the chair, determined not to show her discomfort. "No, I don't need your professional help, Flora. I'm here to talk about my family."

"Well, I don't want to talk about your family, Lady Madeline. They never done much for me."

Desiree muttered something disapproving from her rocking chair, and Flora cast her a sharp look. "You keep your thoughts to yourself, Mama," she said in the Cajun dialect that Madeline, with her fluent French, had always understood quite easily. "Nobody want to hear what you got to say."

Madeline opened her mouth to protest, then thought better of it. The relationship between Flora and her mother was their own affair, and there was no point in trying to interfere. Besides, judging from the scornful curl of Desiree's wrinkled mouth, the old lady could still look out for herself.

Instead, Madeline turned to Flora again. "I'm worried about Shelby."

Once more she noticed that flicker of surprise, quickly

concealed. Flora sat down at the top of the steps and extended her legs, as graceful and sinuous as a cat. "What about her?" She grinned unpleasantly. "She got herself in the family way? Need some help?"

"Of course not," Madeline said, more sharply than she'd intended.

She gave Flora a level, measuring glance, wondering if the woman really could be involved in any threats to Shelby. After all these years, Flora was still impossible to read.

She probably no longer had a physical relationship with Philip now that he was so elderly. But the two of them had been tied together throughout the years in all kinds of dark and sinister ways. And any cohort of Philip's was always a potential enemy to the other side of the family.

Madeline sighed, feeling the old secrets and conflicts of the swamp closing in around her like a suffocating blanket.

What this whole place needed was a hot flood of cleansing sunshine. But it would take some kind of miracle to bring all the ugly, hidden things out into the open and wash them away so people could go about their lives in freedom and happiness.

"I asked you, what about Shelby?" Flora repeated, watching her closely.

Madeline shifted again on the chair and tried to put all the dark thoughts out of her mind. "I'm worried about her," she repeated. "Shelby's been threatened lately, and I'm afraid for her safety."

"Who's been threatening her?"

"That's what I'm here to ask you. Somebody made some nasty telephone calls to her a few months ago, and recently a load of buckshot was fired at her car. Did you know that?"

Flora's expression didn't change. "Oh, yes, I know about all that. Scary things for one of Justin's little princesses," she said. "Nothing bad ever happened to those girls before, right?"

Madeline tensed, but forced herself to stay calm. "You've never had any quarrel with my daughters, Flora. They've done nothing to hurt you."

"Yes? And what do you know about hurt, Lady Madeline?" Flora asked harshly. "You never been hurt in all your life."

"Oh, but you're wrong," Madeline said, hypnotized by the woman's dark, angry gaze. "I've been hurt, Flora. I've suffered through the things that happen to my children, just as you have. A mother feels more pain on her children's behalf than she ever does on her own."

Flora's face twisted and she turned aside, staring out across the misty swamp.

"The barn burned down at Riverwood," Madeline said quietly. "And I think I know how that fire started. I've left the information with my lawyer in case something happens to me or any of my children."

Flora glanced at her sharply. The dark, impassive mask slipped for a moment, enough to let Madeline see that her random shot had struck home.

"My son was badly hurt in that fire," Madeline continued. "He could have been killed. Flora, I know that you of all people can understand how I feel about that and how determined I am to prevent any other...accidents."

Flora was silent, still gazing into the water. Her shoulders quivered, and her callused brown hands were clenched into fists.

"That's why I came to talk with you today," Madeline added, more gently. "I want to appeal to you as one mother to another. If you know of anybody who wants to hurt my children, I wish you'd tell me. All I'm concerned about is their welfare."

"Shelby's been doing a lot of snooping around," Flora

muttered, keeping her face averted. "She may be upsetting a lot of people, I don't know."

"But what does it matter?" Madeline asked. "Lots of times rich and powerful people lose a legal case, but they don't go to such lengths to get even."

Behind her, Desiree muttered something from the depths of her rocking chair.

"Yes, Desiree?" Madeline asked, turning to the old woman. "What did you say?"

"You shut up, Mama!" Flora said fiercely, speaking in Cajun dialect again. "I told you not to start rambling on about nothing."

"I'll say whatever I want to Madeline," Desiree muttered defiantly. "And your filthy hard mouth won't stop me, child." Mother and daughter glared at each other in tense silence.

Flora was the first to back down, muttering a curse. Madeline looked from one to the other in growing worry and confusion.

"Flora?" she asked. "What's going on around here?"

"Nothing's going on," Flora muttered stubbornly. "You go away, Lady Madeline. Go back to that fancy place where you been living now. We don't want you here."

Madeline took a deep breath. "I don't care whether you want me or not. I'm only concerned about my daughter. And I want all the people around here to know..."

She paused, watching as the mists of fog began to curl away, leaving the swamp hot and glistening in the midday sunlight.

"I want everybody to know that I'm watching," she added. "I told the same thing to Philip Delacroix this morning, and asked for his help to protect Shelby."

"You asked Philip for his help?" Flora gave a loud snort of laughter. "I reckon *that* never happened before! Now I'm real surprised," she added, fixing her cold dark eyes on Madeline. "To think a proud lady like you would go begging to Philip."

"I'm not the least bit proud where my children are concerned," Madeline said quietly. "I'd do anything to keep them safe. And I believe you can understand that, Flora."

Flora made a brief, contemptuous gesture. "So what you want from me?" she muttered.

"Information, if you've got it. If not, then just your help in…" Madeline paused, choosing her words carefully. "In letting people know that if anything should happen to Shelby or any of the others, there'd be terrible consequences. Whoever hurt her would never get away with it."

"Nobody's gonna hurt that girl," Flora said.

Madeline cast her a quick glance, wondering if the words were a promise, a prediction or just a way to get rid of unwanted company.

But she could tell from the withdrawn look on the woman's face that she wasn't likely to get anything more from Flora this day. Madeline got out of the chair and went to give Desiree another hug.

"Take care of yourself, Desiree," she whispered in French, holding the old woman's frail little body, the bones as light and brittle as a bird's. "It was so nice to see you again."

"My sweet lady," Desiree murmured in Cajun, her withered face lighting with a smile.

"Is Shelby all right?" Madeline whispered.

Desiree nodded. "Only good things come to Shelby. Love and success."

Madeline felt warmed and moved by the promise. "Really?"

"But you, my lady, you're going to lose your love if you're not careful. Got to be careful." The ancient eyes fixed her with burning intensity.

Madeline hesitated, then patted Desiree's cheek with a loving hand and turned away.

Flora got to her feet and leaned against the railing again, watching silently as her guest started down the walkway toward the boat.

After a few steps, Madeline paused and turned. "I really was sorry to hear about Steven," she said. "I grieved for you, Flora. It must be so dreadful to lose a child."

Flora stood her ground briefly, but her face twisted and her eyes shone with tears. She muttered something and stamped inside the shack, letting the door slam noisily behind her.

Madeline clutched the rope handhold and looked at the closed door for a moment, gradually becoming conscious of Desiree watching her from the shadows.

The old woman muttered something, and Madeline took a few steps back toward her. "Yes, Desiree?" she asked softly. "What did you say?"

"Justin," the old woman whispered. "He needs a friend. Justin needs a woman and a friend."

The deep-set eyes were fixed on her with some kind of desperate appeal. Madeline stared back at Desiree, searching for words.

At last she turned and fled down the sloping planks to the boat, where her young escort was already starting the outboard motor.

FOR A LONG TIME after she returned to the hotel, Madeline was still haunted by the memory of the swamp with its shrouds of fog and clammy stillness, of Flora's enigmatic gaze and Desiree's strange words.

She drew a hot bath, added scented oil and bubbles and soaked for a long time, trying to wash away the feelings of fear and unhappiness.

Finally, after calling Shelby and being assured that her

daughter was feeling better, she began to pack, anxious to head back across the lake and far away from Bayou Beltane.

The closets and drawers were empty and she was putting the last few garments into a suitcase when the telephone rang, startling her.

Madeline straightened and looked across the room in alarm, tempted not to answer. She couldn't stand any more of this place, any invitations to visit or further changes in her plans.

But maybe one of the other children had returned early and wanted to speak with her. She wavered, torn by indecision. Finally she crossed the thick flowered carpet and picked up the phone.

"Hello?"

"Madeline? Is that you?"

It was Justin. She sank into the upholstered chair and gripped the receiver, struggling to remain calm. Just the sound of his voice was enough to call up a wealth of sexual images, and a raging hunger that she had no idea how to control.

"Hello, Justin."

"I'm glad I caught you," he said after an awkward silence. "I didn't know if you'd be in your room. I tried earlier in the day but you were out."

"In a few minutes I'd have been gone again," Madeline said. "I really don't have much time to talk."

"I'm calling from New Orleans," he said. "I've been tied up in a judicial hearing for most of the day. I just wondered if you'd managed to speak with Philip, or with Flora."

"Yes," she said. "In fact, I saw both of them earlier today."

"And?"

"And I still don't know what to think," Madeline said

after a moment's silence. "I can't tell if they're involved. But I really believe they bear watching, Justin. I warned both of them that nobody in this town could ever hurt Shelby and get away with it."

"Did you really?" She could hear the note of startled admiration in his voice. "I'll bet those were interesting interviews. Philip and Flora must have been surprised, both of them."

"I dare say they were," Madeline said dryly, smiling at the memory, then sobered. "I truly mean it, Justin. Don't let this place lull you into carelessness. Something's going on, and it could be dangerous."

"I know," he said. "I've been thinking about it ever since we spoke. In fact, I'm ashamed you had to come all the way from Colorado to open my eyes. I'm going to get to the bottom of all this."

"That's good," she said in relief. "I'm glad to hear it."

"How's Shelby?" he asked. "Have you talked with her today?"

"Yes, and she's feeling much better. Beginning to complain bitterly about being stuck at home and not getting any work done."

He laughed. "That sounds more like Shelby."

Madeline smiled automatically, twisting the phone cord around her fingers.

"Madeline," he said after another long, tense silence, "I need to talk with you. There are so many things I want to tell you. Could we meet tonight, do you think?"

Madeline glanced around the room. "I'm afraid that's impossible, Justin. I told you, I'm about to—"

She stopped abruptly. He'd mentioned being in New Orleans. If she told him she was on the way to the city, he would probably insist on meeting her there.

Of course, she could refuse and carry on with her plans, but she was haunted by an image of Justin going from one hotel to another until he found her. After all, even in a city as large as New Orleans there were only half a dozen hotels that Madeline would normally choose, and Justin knew every one of them.

"Madeline?" he asked. "Are you still there?"

"Yes," she said. "There seems to be…" She picked up a room service menu and tapped it against the receiver. "I think it's some kind of problem with the phone. There," she added, speaking directly into the mouthpiece. "What were you saying?"

"I was asking if we could get together for a talk tonight. When are you having dinner?"

"I'm not sure. The visit to Flora's shack has ruined my appetite, I'm afraid. It's not easy to think of food when your stomach is tied in knots."

"Poor Madeline. Were you scared?" he asked in quick sympathy.

"Flora is not a comfortable person." Madeline resisted a treacherous urge to tell him the whole story. He sounded so warm and interested.

"All the more courageous for you to go out there and confront her," Justin said. "I'm really impressed by you, Madeline."

"Please…" She stared at a gold-framed painting on the opposite wall, her heart racing. "Don't talk to me this way, Justin."

"You don't want me to tell my favorite lady that I find her behavior admirable?"

His tone was even warmer now, almost flirtatious, and it made Madeline feel panicky. She knew she was in terrible danger here.

Even before her ill-fated trip out to Riverwood, she'd begun to feel herself beguiled and tempted by this place. Madeline loved the warmth and peacefulness of the bayou, the colorful ethnic diversity, the beauty that thrilled her at every turn and made her long to reach for a paintbrush.

She could be happy here, a voice kept whispering. This time it would all be different.

And her family was here. More and more, Madeline realized that nothing really mattered except family. How could she endure a life away from her children, and the grandchildren that would soon be arriving?

A life in exile, she thought bitterly. *I've been exiled long enough.*

Now, after sleeping with Justin and having that whole tumult of emotions aroused again, she found her situation even more perilous.

"Madeline?" he said, sounding genuinely puzzled. "Can't we talk about this?"

Madeline took a deep breath. "You and I have nothing at all to discuss except for issues relating to our children," she said. "All these other topics you're attempting to introduce are completely...inappropriate," she concluded lamely, blushing.

"Inappropriate?" he echoed, beginning to sound exasperated. "For God's sake, Madeline! We were married for more than twenty years, and we've been divorced for ten. We went to bed together last night and had a wonderful time, as I recall. Why is it inappropriate for us to talk about anything under the sun, if we choose?"

She wanted to shout at him, to rage and scream and slam the phone down in his ear. But Madeline wasn't the kind of woman who would do any of those things. Instead, she took another deep, calming breath.

Because I love you too much, she thought, *and I know how arrogant you are. Because if I give in this time you'll smother me again, and I can't bear to make myself that vulnerable....*

But of course she couldn't say any of that. So she cast

around for something to attack him with, and seized grate-fully on the memory of Claudia Landry.

"Justin," she said, "you're already involved in a relationship. You've made serious commitments to another person. And while I—"

He began to protest, but she cut him off briskly. "While I understand your desire to patch things up with me to ease your own pride, I'm afraid I can't be any part of it. It's the same kind of manipulative behavior I hated so much during all the years I was living with you. You can be a very self-serving man, Justin."

There was a brief silence. She waited, staring at the wall again, her breath fast and uneven.

"And this other person to whom I'm committed...I assume it's Claudia Landry? Is that what you're talking about?"

"Of course it is," she said coldly.

She heard a swell of noise somewhere behind Justin, and urgent voices. He called an answer to them, then returned to the phone.

"I have to get back to the meeting soon. They're winding up and preparing for a vote. Look, Madeline, what if I told you there's nothing at all between me and that girl? What if I swore it was only friendship, nothing more?"

She cast a panicky glance at her open suitcase and began to twist the phone cord again.

"Madeline?" he asked.

"If you told me that," she said with forced calm, "I'd have to wonder why you were bothering to lie, Justin. Because everybody else seems to know the truth about you and your young girlfriend."

"Everybody? Who's that?"

"Every citizen of Bayou Beltane, apparently," Madeline said, trying to keep her voice light. "Everyone who's spo-ken with me the past couple of days, including Uncle William, Aunt Mary, your own father, Philip and Flora, Shelby, the hairdresser downtown, the waitresses in the restaurant... I'm afraid you haven't been very discreet, Justin. You must...'' Her voice caught briefly and she paused, unable to go on.

''Madeline?'' he asked. ''What were you going to say?''

''I was about to say that you must be very much in love to have behaved so rashly.''

''Oh, for heaven's sake,'' he muttered again, apparently looking away from the phone, because his voice faded. He came back on, sounding impatient. ''Look, Madeline, we really need to talk about this. Can I see you tonight? I'll get away as soon as I can and drive back to town.''

Madeline hesitated, her mind darting anxiously.

''I'll come over there to the Bayou Inn,'' he said, ''and meet you in the lobby around...''

He paused, and she could picture him lifting his cuff to glance at his slim gold watch. The simple image, remembered with sudden and startling clarity, was enough to make her feel weak with yearning.

''Around eight o'clock?'' he said. ''Is that all right?''

Madeline hated to deceive anybody. But in this case she thought it was forgivable. Still, she couldn't bring herself to tell an outright lie.

''I'm not sure I'll be here at eight o'clock, Justin,'' she said, crossing her fingers as she looked across the room at her open suitcases. ''I...still have a lot of things to do.''

''I'll take my chances. Please try to make some time for me, Madeline. There are really important things I need to tell you.''

Over the phone she could hear another series of impatient shouts. ''I must leave now,'' Madeline said. ''And it sounds as if you're required elsewhere, too. Goodbye, Justin. Don't forget to watch over Shelby very carefully.''

''I promise. But we'll meet tonight at eight?''

Madeline murmured something noncommittal, then hung up and sat huddled on the chair, her hands over her face. After a long time she got up and finished packing, rang for the redcap and settled her bill at the front desk. Then she got into her rented car and headed out over the Twin Span, anxious to get to New Orleans, if possible, before Justin started his journey in the opposite direction.

The last thing she wanted was to meet him in the middle of the bridge, then have him turn his car around and start chasing after her like a scene from some terrible movie.

Nervously, she adjusted her dark glasses and drove a little faster through the sparse Monday afternoon traffic. She felt as if the entire Delacroix clan, dead and alive, clamored in pursuit as she fled over the bridge from Bayou Beltane, back to a world where she could live in dignity and freedom.

"I can't bear this," she whispered aloud. "I simply can't bear it."

Tears burned behind her eyelids, and she lifted the sunglasses to rub at her eyes with her sleeve.

Misery settled over her like a dank and heavy blanket, wiping out sunlight, hope and optimism, leaving Madeline aware of only one thing in all the darkness. It was something she'd kept from herself for more than ten years. No matter how far she tried to flee, she couldn't escape this one truth.

She still loved Justin Delacroix. He was the only man she'd ever be able to love.

The full realization hit her just as she left the bridge and started toward the city. She took the first off-ramp and parked on a side road near a ragged stand of sugar cane.

Then she lowered her head to the steering wheel and began to cry.

CHAPTER TWELVE

JUSTIN FINISHED THE DAY in a blur of motions, votes and tedious legal discussions. None of the proceedings seemed comprehensible to him. He was so distracted by the turmoil of his own thoughts that one of the committee members even asked him if he was feeling unwell.

He murmured an apology, tried to pay attention and function normally for the remainder of the afternoon. But as soon as the meeting was over, he grabbed his briefcase and headed for the door, rushing out into the mellow autumn twilight.

At a snack bar he paused to grab a po'boy and call Toni, telling her that his plans had changed and he needed to leave the city immediately.

She and Brody were hosting a casual backyard party for about a dozen friends, to celebrate her newly announced pregnancy, and he didn't think they'd miss him if he didn't show up. But to his surprise, his half sister sounded genuinely disappointed.

"Justin," she wailed, "don't tell me you're not coming. What could possibly be more important than a plateful of Brody's barbecued ribs?"

He looked through the smeared window of the snack bar, watching a group of children drawing chalk pictures on the pavement. "I have a date with Madeline at the Bayou Inn," he said.

There was a brief silence. "You're right," Toni said quietly. "That's definitely more important. Justin, please give her my love, would you? Tell her I still miss her terribly."

"I'll tell her. Sorry to run out on you, Toni. I'm sure it's going to be a great party."

"I hope," Toni said with warm sincerity, "that your evening is very enjoyable, too."

He remembered Madeline's flight from Riverwood, her tentative manner on the telephone and her guarded references to his relationship with Claudia Landry.

"I'm not sure what it's going to be like," he said at last. "But I can tell you, Toni, I wouldn't miss it for the world."

"Go for it, sweetie. And let us know how she is, all right?"

Justin murmured a reply, then pocketed his change and headed outside to the parking lot. He pulled his car into the busy, late-day traffic and out onto the causeway.

The sunset was painting the lake with soft colors by the time he neared the other side. Clouds massed above the trees, a brilliant swirl of pink, green and violet, while sunlight rayed through rifts in the canopy, touching the calm water with long fingers of gold.

The beauty of the evening made him feel youthful, full of hope and plans. The years seemed to roll away and he was a young man again, finished with classes for the weekend, heading back across the causeway to his new wife who waited in the little house on Magnolia Street.

The fantasy was so real that Justin could almost see her face, hear her bubble of laughter and feel the warmth of her embrace as she greeted him.

"Darling," she called joyously, running down the path and throwing herself into his arms. "My sweetheart, I've missed you so much! I have a million things to tell you, but first I want you to kiss me and kiss me until I can't breathe...."

Justin gripped the wheel and stared at the blur of farms and houses along the road.

"I love you," he whispered aloud. "God, how I love you. Oh, Madeline…"

Somehow, miraculously, those far-off days had been restored to him. He was driving into the little town where he'd spent his whole life, and Madeline was waiting for him just as she used to. In a few moments he'd see her again.

Nothing else mattered.

He glanced at his watch in a fever of impatience. Almost eight o'clock. No time to stop by the house and change into something more casual…

His suit jacket lay on the front seat. He tugged off the tie, as well, then opened the top buttons of his shirt. Suddenly he was so happy that he wanted to sing, to shout his joy to the world as he started down the quiet street toward the hotel.

Madeline was waiting for him, prepared to give him another chance.

He'd tell her the whole truth and make her understand. For once in his life, he planned to hold nothing back. All those things he'd never told his wife, Justin intended to say tonight.

He'd tell her he'd always adored her, that no other woman could ever satisfy him and he was desolate without her. He'd tell her how beautiful she was, how easily she still could make him laugh, how the gentleness of her mind and spirit were like a balm to his tortured soul.

And then he'd take her in his arms, and she'd hold him and whisper that she loved him, too, and that all their loneliness was over.…

He parked in the hotel lot, sprinted for the front door and arrived in the lobby feeling as excited and full of anticipation as a teenager.

Inside the hotel, Justin looked around eagerly, but there was no sign of her. He felt a stab of disappointment and a brief uneasiness.

Of course, she wouldn't have chosen to sit alone in the lobby. No doubt she'd gone into the dining room and was waiting for him there.

He strode across the lobby, stood by the reception desk and looked into the other room.

Not there, either. But she'd probably have chosen one of the alcoves, knowing they were going to have a private discussion.

"Good evening, Mr. Delacroix." The hostess arrived, smiling. "Do you have a reservation?"

"I'm meeting somebody here. My wife is waiting for me, I believe."

"Your wife?" she asked in confusion, then looked embarrassed. "Excuse me," she said awkwardly. "But I'm not sure I—"

"My ex-wife," Justin corrected himself, peering over the woman's shoulder. "She's slim and very attractive, dark hair about this long...."

The hostess shook her head. "I'm sorry, Mr. Delacroix. There's nobody here who fits that description."

"But she's got to be here." Justin resisted an irrational urge to shake the woman. He took a deep breath. "Do you mind if I just stroll through the dining room and have a look?"

"Of course not. Feel free," the hostess said, a little stiffly.

Justin gave her an apologetic smile and walked among the linen-draped tables, accepting greetings from most of the other patrons.

Madeline wasn't among them.

"I'm sorry," he said, back in the doorway. "I was so

sure she'd be waiting for me here. I can't understand what's happened.''

''That's all right.'' The woman's brief annoyance had faded to a look of sympathy and concern. ''She's probably still up in her room. Would you like me to seat you somewhere so you can wait for her?''

He hesitated. ''No,'' he said at last. ''I think I'll wait in the lobby, thanks.''

Justin wandered out to the front desk, checked his watch again and spent a few minutes roaming around, studying the paintings on the walls, leafing through an array of magazines on a coffee table.

In one corner of the lobby an antique grandfather clock ticked loudly, dragging the minute hand down toward the half hour. He checked his watch, then looked at the clock with growing concern. It wasn't like Madeline to be late for an appointment. She'd never been one of those women who spent hours getting ready.

At last, when the clock tolled the half hour, he approached the desk. ''Could you tell me the room number for Madeline Delacroix?''

The desk clerk checked a computer screen and shook his head. ''This would be a lady traveling alone?''

''Yes,'' Justin said.

''There's nobody registered by that name. We had a Madeline Belanger staying here, though. Could it be the same person?''

''Yes, that's her.''

Justin felt a fresh wave of unhappiness. He hadn't known she was using her maiden name again, and the subtle rejection hurt more than he could have imagined.

''Ms. Belanger checked out this afternoon.''

Justin's mind reeled. He gripped the edge of the desk and leaned forward. ''This afternoon? But I spoke to her this afternoon. What time did she leave?''

"I think it was about five o'clock. She'd already paid for tonight, but wasn't able to stay."

"So she's gone?" Justin asked blankly. "She won't be back?"

The clerk shook his head. "She's checked out, sir."

"Do you know where she went?"

"Back to the city, I guess. She said something about needing to leave because she'd booked an earlier flight home to Colorado."

"I see." Justin turned away, aching with disappointment. "Thank you."

He went into the empty bar and had a drink, watching the bright, noisy images on a television in the corner without even seeing them. Finally he left the hotel and wandered out into the gathering darkness, hands thrust deep into his pockets as he struggled to wrestle his thoughts into some kind of order.

Madeline had checked out of the hotel soon after their telephone conversation. She'd hurried back to the city to avoid seeing him.

For a moment he felt an urgent desire to get in his car, head back to New Orleans and look for her. She probably wasn't flying out until morning. He could scour the city, go to every hotel until he found her....

But the impulse faded as abruptly as it had come.

There was no point in looking for her. Madeline's actions told him exactly how she felt. She had no desire to see him anymore. In fact, she must really despise him to do something like this.

It was over.

Justin swallowed a sob and got into his car. He sat for a long time with his head bent over the wheel, then looked up as one of Jake Trahan's young officers tapped on the glass. Justin slid the window down.

"You all right, Mr. Delacroix?" the police officer asked

worriedly. "I seen you sittin' here and wondered if maybe you was sick."

"I'm all right." Justin forced himself to smile. "I've got a little headache, that's all."

"I heard Shelby had the flu." The officer continued to examine him with concern. "You better get yourself on home and go to bed. That flu's no fun at all, from what they tell me."

"Good idea. Thanks." Justin closed the window, put his car into gear and headed out of town, fighting a melancholy urge to stop at the little house he'd once shared with Madeline.

Along the bayou road he saw lights glimmering from the cluster of shacks along the edge of the swamp. It appeared Remy was finally back from his trip to New Orleans. Without thinking, Justin turned the wheel and headed for the swamp tour office. He needed another drink, and his brother's quiet company would be a lot less painful than the brooding silence of Riverwood.

He parked near the dock and walked up to the little office, pushed the door open and went inside, then stopped in surprise.

Two people were inside the office, neither of them Remy.

A slim, dark-haired girl in a pink dress sat perched on the desk with her back to the door, facing a young man who lounged casually in the chair, his feet up on the desk. Both of them were laughing.

The laughter stopped abruptly when Justin entered the shack. The young man swiveled and dropped his feet to the floor, then stood up, looking abashed.

"Hello, Mr. Delacroix," he said. "We were just finishing up some work."

Justin recognized the man as Bernard Leroux, a handsome, straightforward fellow he'd known casually for years. And the girl was Claudia Landry, her pretty young face flushed with embarrassment.

"Hi, Mr. Delacroix." She slid hastily from the desk and went to stand next to Bernard, who put a protective hand on her arm. "I had some paperwork to do and Bernard stopped by to keep me company."

Justin forced himself to smile. "You folks don't have to explain anything to me," he said. "I was just looking for Remy."

"Him and Kendall were here right after dinner," Claudia said. "They just got back and they're spending the evening at home."

"I see. Sorry to have bothered you."

Justin looked at the two of them, standing so close together, obviously comfortable in each other's presence. Their companionship and the memory of that warm, happy laughter made him feel even more lonely.

"Mr. Delacroix—" Claudia looked up at him, her face gentle with concern "—is something the matter?"

He shook his head and moved reluctantly toward the door. "No, I'm fine. I guess I'll say good-night if Remy's not around. Could you tell him I was here?"

"Sure," Claudia said, still looking troubled. "I'll tell him."

Justin wandered outside, hesitated a moment in the darkness, then squared his shoulders and went back in. The young people looked up at him, startled.

"It seems," Justin said awkwardly, "that I've done both of you a disservice, but I've been particularly unfair to Claudia."

"What kind of disservice?" Bernard asked, leaning against the filing cabinet with a coffee mug in his hand.

"I gather the whole town thinks I'm having an affair with Claudia."

"I know they do." Claudia's eyes glittered with tears and a flush crept up her cheeks.

"This is an awful town for gossip," Bernard said after an awkward silence. "Claudia's brother thought the same thing. He came over to her houseboat yesterday and said a lot of things he shouldn't have."

Justin looked up at the man's hard face and the knotted muscles in his upper arm, and had a fairly good idea of how the meeting with Claudia's brother had turned out.

"I didn't know that. I'm sorry, Claudia," he said. "It seems I've caused you a lot of trouble, too."

"That's not true," Claudia said loyally. "You helped me a whole bunch. Nobody else ever cared about doing anything for me, Mr. Delacroix, and I'll always appreciate your kindness."

"Thanks, Claudia." He gave her a bleak smile. "But I think we should do something about this particular rumor. I'm tired of the secrets and lies in this town. They've cost me far too much already."

"What can we do?" Bernard asked.

Justin hesitated. "Well, it hasn't been my habit in the past to involve myself in people's lives, so this isn't easy for me."

He glanced at Claudia, who watched him tensely.

"But," he added, "I've gone this far with my meddling, haven't I? Not much point in stopping now."

"No point at all," Bernard agreed.

"So first," Justin said, "I guess I'd like to know if you two are as fond of each other as you appear to be."

Claudia flushed scarlet and looked down at her feet, but Bernard met Justin's eyes with a steady look. "I'm very fond of Claudia," he said quietly.

Justin nodded, impressed by the man's directness. "Then I think we should nip this particular bit of gossip in the bud. And I know exactly how we should do it."

"How?" Claudia asked timidly.

"We should go out to Rick's for a nice meal and enjoy ourselves. You two can sit together, cuddle up, act like a pair of young people out with a middle-aged friend they find mildly entertaining. We'll make sure everybody sees us."

Bernard nodded with perfect understanding. "In their faces," he said. "Pretty tough to gossip about something that's right out there."

Justin thought about his own disastrous evening. "And I haven't had dinner yet," he said, trying to smile. "I'm hungry. So let's grab a burger, kids."

THE PLAN WAS EVEN MORE successful than Justin had hoped. By midnight, practically everybody in Bayou Beltane knew that Bernard Leroux and Claudia Landry were a couple, and a very attractive one at that. The same people had realized that Justin Delacroix appeared to be a good friend to the two young people, possibly even a sponsor of Bernard's new tour business.

And anybody who tried to suggest that Justin had something going on with the girl was treated with withering contempt, as one hopelessly behind the times.

Satisfied with the success, Justin took leave of his friends on the moonlit street outside the café, wondering if these two young people even realized how much in love they were. One day the realization would hit them with full force, he thought sadly, and they'd never be the same again.

He gave them a final goodbye, then climbed into his car, started the motor and headed for Riverwood.

The big house was silent and mostly dark in the autumn night. A dim light burned up in Charles's room and another glimmered from the far wing, through Shelby's closed draperies. Justin parked in the garage and trudged up onto veranda, then changed his mind and headed back down the stairs and around the side of the house to knock on his daughter's French door.

She came to open it, wearing fluffy slippers and a bathrobe over pyjamas.

"For goodness' sake," she said in surprise. "What are you doing, skulking around out there in the dark?"

He stepped into Shelby's parlor and gave her a brief hug. "I just got home and wanted to see how you were feeling."

"I'm fine, a whole lot better today. In fact, I do believe I'm going to survive."

Justin smiled at his daughter. Her face had regained some of its old sparkle, and her nose was no longer bright red.

"Well, honey, I'm real glad to hear that," he said.

Shelby gave him a thoughtful glance. "Are you all right?"

"I'm fine." He started across the room to the other door. "Is your grandfather in bed already?"

"I suppose so. I felt well enough to do a bit of cleaning in the kitchen after dinner, and he came down for a cup of hot chocolate about nine o'clock. He said he was going to read in bed."

"Sounds like a good idea. I guess I'll mix myself a drink, then do the same."

"Did you have a chance to see Mama again before she left?" Shelby asked.

Justin paused with his hand on the doorknob. "No, I was only able to talk with her on the phone for a minute. I've been in the city all day."

"That's too bad. She called this afternoon, said she'd finished up her business in town and booked an early flight back to Colorado."

"Do you happen to know why she left so soon?" he asked, keeping his face averted. "I thought she was staying till Wednesday."

"I guess she just missed her friends and her job. She seems really happy in Aspen, doesn't she?"

"Yes," Justin murmured, his heart aching. "She seems happy." He turned to look at his daughter. "Shelby..."

"Yes, Daddy?"

"How are things with you and Travis? Do you talk to him at all?"

Shelby looked at her father in surprise. "Yes, he calls sometimes. But it's just impossible. We're far too different, Travis and I. We'll never make a happy couple."

"Do you love him?"

Her face turned bright pink. "My goodness, what a question! You've never asked me something like that in all my life."

"I'm asking now," he said quietly. "Do you love this man, Shelby?"

She turned away, staring at the window. "I guess I do," she said at last, her voice barely audible. "Yes, I love Travis. Sometimes, you know, I miss that man so much I can hardly—" Her voice broke and she stopped abruptly.

"Then tell him so," Justin said. "Don't let pride or stubbornness rob you of your chance at happiness, sweetheart. Tell him how you feel, and make sure he understands."

She stared at him, her eyes wide and unfathomable. Justin paused, wondering if he should say something more. Instead, he smiled awkwardly and opened the door.

"Well, good night, honey," he said. "Have a good sleep."

He left her standing there and closed the door gently behind him, then walked through darkened hallways toward the main part of the big house.

MADELINE ARRIVED back in Aspen on Tuesday night, worn out from the journey and the turmoil of her own emotions. But even total exhaustion didn't help her to pass a restful night. She woke the following morning feeling more tired than when she'd gone to bed, and had to force herself to get up and have a shower.

She dried her hair, put on a housecoat and wandered downstairs to have a cup of coffee and a piece of dry toast, so drained and weary that she couldn't even bring herself to call the gallery and see how Tate was getting along without her.

Fortunately, she'd booked off the whole week, so she could spend a few days relaxing at home, trying to recover from that shattering visit to Louisiana.

To her surprise, Madeline had no interest in the gallery at all. Usually after being away she could hardly restrain herself from rushing down to see what had happened in her absence. She always wanted to check the studio, look at her paintings and ask Tate if any of the artwork had sold.

But this morning all that seemed meaningless, somehow. Life in Aspen had lost its sparkle.

Madeline sat in her breakfast nook, staring up at the mountains against the blue arch of sky, and wondered if perhaps it was time to move on.

The images of Louisiana were still strong in her mind—shimmering vistas of lake and swamp, the lushness of vegetation, the sleepy, flower-scented air.... Even the Boudreaux women's weathered shack, eerie and withdrawn in its sinister shrouds of fog, had a kind of allure that wasn't found anywhere else.

In Louisiana, Madeline felt young again. She could sense a richness and excitement there, a warm harmony that wasn't part of any other place. Ever since she'd landed in Aspen and walked off the plane, she'd been feeling lonely and out of place, even homesick.

She'd chalked it up to travel weariness, but this morning the feeling was stronger, even though she was at home and surrounded by all the things she most loved. Because, she realized again, these belongings didn't matter at all, no matter how beautiful they were. It was people who mattered, and all those who were dear to her lived more than a thousand miles away.

One by one, Madeline thought about her grown children, picturing each of them with a fierce surge of yearning. As well, she remembered Aunt Mary and Uncle William sitting placidly together by their fireplace, and Charles out on the shady veranda with the two young spaniels drowsing near his chair.

Madeline began to toy with the edge of her linen place mat, frowning thoughtfully.

Maybe, just maybe, she should consider moving back to Louisiana.

Not Bayou Beltane, she told herself hastily, because Justin would always be there and she couldn't bear to see him again. But perhaps New Orleans would be a good idea. Maybe she could sell Tate her share in Bare Bones and use the funds to open a little gallery somewhere in New Orleans.

The thought was new and exciting, replacing her fatigue with a sudden flood of enthusiasm. For a while she allowed herself to imagine the plan and think how she'd accomplish it. As she did so, it began to progress rapidly from a random idea to a firmly rooted notion.

She got a little engagement calendar from the sideboard and sat down again, studying the dates as she twisted a strand of hair around her fingers. This was Wednesday morning, the third week in October.

Madeline sat erect, staring at the windows in surprise.

Exactly ten days ago, she'd been eating breakfast all alone on her terrace and little Jennifer had wandered over to keep her company. Only ten short days, but it seemed like a year had passed since then.

Suddenly, as if in response to Madeline's thoughts, a

bright flurry whirled across the courtyard. Jennifer herself was running up the walk, wearing pink tights and an orange hooded anorak.

Smiling, Madeline went to answer the door. Jennifer tumbled inside and lay on the floor, drumming her heels and gasping.

"My goodness, what's all this?" Madeline knelt beside the child with a frown of concern. "Are you all right, darling?"

Jennifer struggled erect, still panting. She stripped off her coat, handing it to Madeline. Underneath she wore a long T-shirt patterned with dinosaurs.

"We...saw your light," the child gasped. "Daddy said...you came home early. And I wanted...to tell you first of anybody."

"Tell me what, dear?" Madeline asked.

She realized by now that Jennifer wasn't upset or in pain, just breathlessly excited.

"Guess what?" the little girl said importantly, confirming this impression. She headed for the kitchen, looking with interest at the bowl of fruit. "Can I have some grapes?" she asked over her shoulder.

"You certainly may. Here, we'll put some in a little bowl for you."

Jennifer pressed close to watch this operation. "I like the green ones," she said. "They got no seeds."

"These red ones don't have seeds, either," Madeline said, adding a few to the bowl.

"Really?" Jennifer cast her a skeptical glance.

"Really," Madeline said, bending to hug the child. "They're a special kind."

She handed the bowl to Jennifer, who was perched on one of the kitchen stools, then went to pour herself another cup of coffee. "Now, you must tell me, what's this big news?"

"Daddy's getting married!" Jennifer said through a mouthful of grapes.

Madeline stared at the child, thunderstruck. "Really, darling?"

Jennifer nodded with such fervent energy that her hair bounced. "He's getting married to Kelly. We're going to buy a real house with a yard and everything, and I can have a dog. That's why I'm not in school today. We're all driving into Denver to pick out a big diamond ring and have a party, and Kelly wants me to go, too."

"And you're very, very happy about all this, dear?" Madeline asked gently.

"I love it." Jennifer munched happily on her grapes. "I'll be just like the other kids, with a mom and dad and a house, all in one place. And Kelly's so nice to me. I can't wait."

Madeline smiled and came nearer to stroke the little girl's shining cap of hair. "Then I'm very happy for you, too, my darling. I didn't think your daddy would ever make up his mind to do this."

"You know what?" Jennifer closed her eyes and emitted a small sigh of bliss. "Kelly might even have a baby. Then I'd have a brother or sister. Wouldn't that be awesome, Madeline?"

"That," Madeline agreed solemnly, "would be totally awesome."

"And totally terrifying," a voice said from across the room.

Madeline turned to see Tate lounging in the doorway, hands in the pockets of his jeans, looking at her with a wry smile.

"So it's true?" she asked, going to hug him. "You've finally grown up, my dear?"

"God, no," he protested. "I'll never grow up. That's

why I'm getting Kelly to take care of me. She's agreed to be the grown-up in the family."

"And you're even considering another child?" Madeline asked.

"Kelly wants a baby. In fact, it's a requirement of hers. I find..." Tate grinned at his little daughter. "I find I'm not all that opposed. I was pretty lucky with the first one."

"Tate, this is wonderful, but it's all so sudden," Madeline said.

He shook his head and helped himself to some grapes. "Not really. We've been talking about it for a long time, but we didn't want Jen to know until we were sure. And there are..." His smile faded and began to look awkward. "There are a few complications," he said.

"What?" Madeline asked with quick concern.

"Well...I was hoping maybe I could convince you to sell me your half of the gallery, Madeline. I know we've talked about it once or twice. You've been so great all these years, and God knows I don't want to push you out, but with a whole family to support I'm going to need more revenue, and I thought if we could—"

Madeline laughed and hugged him again, cutting short the stream of nervous chatter. "Done," she whispered, patting his cheek.

"Done?" He drew away and looked down at her. "Just like that?"

"This must all be preordained," Madeline told him, "because I've just been thinking that I'd like to sell you my half of the gallery and move back to Louisiana. Tate, would you like a cup of coffee?"

"Sure. Thanks a lot." He followed her across the room, watching as she ground the beans and filled the kitchen with their rich aroma. "But Maddy, you told me last week you'd rather be torn apart by alligators than go back there."

"Oh, I'm not going back to Bayou Beltane," Madeline

said. "It's far too painful there because of...just because," she finished hastily. "But after I sell you the shop and get rid of this condo, I'll have enough to live comfortably and spend some time looking around. I think I'd like to open a little gallery in the city, perhaps near the Quarter...."

Her voice trailed off and she smiled dreamily.

Tate, too, was grinning. "Hey, you really mean all this, don't you? You're not just saying these things to be nice."

Madeline sobered and gave him a severe glance. "Do I ever do things out of niceness?"

"Only all the time," he said cheerfully.

He looked at Jennifer, who had climbed down from the stool and wandered into the other room to look at the display of china birds in Madeline's curio cabinet.

"Hey—" Tate leaned forward and lowered his voice "—do you want to come to Denver with us today? We're buying wedding rings and all kinds of neat stuff."

"What about the gallery?" Madeline asked.

Tate raised his hands in an expressive shrug. "Closed on account of being in love," he said. "Unless you want to go down and open up for the day, Maddy? Business has been pretty slow all week."

She shook her head. "No, I'm really feeling the need for a nice, peaceful day at home. I had a pretty exhausting trip."

He slapped his forehead and looked at her in concern. "I've been so full of my own plans, I never even asked about you. Was it awful?"

"In some ways. But it was exciting, too. I can't help it, Tate, I just love Louisiana. There's something about the place—"

Jennifer interrupted them, coming back into the kitchen to demand more grapes. Tate gave her a small handful, then knelt to put the orange coat on his daughter and zip it up.

"We have to go, kiddo," he said, kissing her cheek. "Kelly's waiting for us."

"Give Kelly my love," Madeline said. "Tell her I'm so happy for all of you."

She stood in the doorway and watched them leave, her eyes warm with tears when she saw the unrestrained joy in Jennifer's little body and heard the happy ripple of her laughter.

But when they vanished into their own condo, Madeline's excitement drained away and she felt lonely and chilled. She went back inside, sat at the kitchen table and tried to cheer herself up by thinking about all the momentous things that were about to happen in her life. She opened the calendar again, frowning in concentration.

The phone rang. Still distracted, looking at the calendar in her hand, Madeline went across the kitchen to answer.

"Madeline?" It was a man's voice, sounding shy and awkward.

Madeline hesitated. "Yes," she said at last. "This is she."

"Well, this is Uncle William. I need to talk with you, my dear."

Madeline gripped the phone, her eyes wide with shock, totally unable to reply.

CHAPTER THIRTEEN

"UNCLE WILLIAM?" Madeleine said at last. "Is it really you?"

He laughed. "You sound so astonished, my dear. I'm quite capable of using newfangled machines like telephones, you know."

"But I don't believe you've ever phoned me in all my life."

"Then perhaps it's time I started. Think of all the pleasure I've missed."

She smiled, picturing the old man's smooth, silver head, his gentle face and shy gallantry. "So you're just calling me for the pleasure of hearing my voice?" Madeline said.

William chuckled. "I must admit I have a few other motives. I really wanted to talk to you about Justin."

Madeline braced herself to protest. "Please, Uncle William," she said. "I don't want to—"

"Justin came over here the other morning to talk with me," he said. "The day after you visited us for Sunday dinner."

That would also be the day after she and Justin spent the night together, Madeline thought with a hot rush of yearning.

Suddenly the full import of William's words dawned on her. She felt tense and breathless. "Justin came to talk to you?"

"He told me what you'd said about the secrets in our family, and how smothering and distasteful you found it all. And..." William paused, then cleared his throat and continued. "He told me about one secret in particular that had been troubling you a great deal."

"Oh, Uncle William—" Madeline felt tears gathering in her eyes. "I wish..."

"What do you wish, Madeline?"

I wish I could be with you, she thought. *I wish I could give you a hug right now, you sweet old darling, and let you know how much I love you.*

To her embarrassment she began to cry, weeping softly into the phone.

"It's all right," he said, his voice husky. "It's really quite all right."

"But, Uncle William, it must have been such a dreadful shock for you."

"Not really. In fact, I'd suspected it for many years, Madeline."

"You had?" She stared at the phone, astonished.

He laughed again. "I may be a man of the cloth, but I have eyes in my head. And all my life I heard whispers and confessions behind that screen, more secrets than anyone should have to endure. It wasn't too long before I'd figured out a few of my own."

"But nobody else realized the truth until Desiree showed her deed to the property. And even then they didn't want you or Aunt Mary to know."

"I know. That's what Justin told me."

"I can't believe Justin did that," Madeline said, feeling dazed. "After all the secrets, why would he simply march over there and tell you the truth?"

"Because he loves you," William said. "And if flinging aside a lifetime of secrets is what it takes to win you back, then Justin Delacroix is prepared to do just that."

Madeline stared at the glass case filled with small, exquisitely detailed china birds. Near the front, a replica of a snowy owl gazed back at her, its yellow eyes wide.

Unexpectedly, something began to happen inside Madeline's mind, a brightness that was warm and tentative, as if a tiny window had opened just a few inches to let in the morning sun.

She struggled to put the image aside and concentrate on what William was saying.

"Justin…loves me?"

"He's sick with love for you. Justin's life has come full circle, and I believe he understands that nothing matters to him anymore except gathering you in and holding you close."

"But, Uncle William…what about that girl? The one they were all gossiping about? Why did Justin take her out and buy her clothes, and…" She fell silent, too hurt to go on.

"Because he's a nice man. He did it purely out of the goodness of his heart, to help the girl build some self-confidence."

Madeline tried without success to picture her hard-driving, goal-oriented ex-husband taking time from his busy life to offer a hand to somebody like Claudia Landry out of simple compassion.

"You see, what happened," William continued, "is that the girl was in Remy's bait shack one night crying over a young man. His name is Bernard Leroux."

"Bernard?" Madeline asked blankly, wondering if she was really having this conversation, or if she'd somehow fallen asleep and was dreaming.

"Apparently she'd loved Bernard for years, but she never learned to dress or talk properly. The poor child had a dreadful upbringing, Madeline. I used to fear for her."

She gripped the phone silently, waiting.

"So when Claudia was crying in the bait shack, Justin

came along looking for Remy and found her there instead. He asked what was wrong, then said he could help.''

Madeline forgot herself in her amazement at this. "You're telling me Justin actually involved himself in this girl's personal situation of his own free will? He volunteered to help her?"

She tried to visualize a young girl drowning in tears over a boyfriend, and Madeline's self-absorbed, busy ex-husband stopping to listen, expressing sympathy and concern....

There had to be more to the story. It simply wasn't credible.

"He helped Claudia learn the things she didn't know. He gave her hand-me-down clothes from your daughters, took her out to get a haircut and bought her new things from Emily Colbert's dress shop."

"And that night when I saw the two of them at the Bayou Inn?" Madeline asked.

"That was just part of his plan. Justin said she needed to learn how to eat in nice places and use the right fork and so on so she could build some confidence. Apparently it worked."

"What do you mean, Uncle William?"

"Well, the young man in question has certainly noticed Claudia now. In fact, he seems thoroughly smitten."

Madeline struggled to understand, to make sense of what she was hearing.

Inside her mind the window opened a little wider, on an unfamiliar, sunny landscape that troubled and confused her with its brightness.

After a brief silence William started talking again, sounding increasingly shy. "Justin has confided in me quite a lot in recent days, Madeline. He's told me how desperately he loves you. As I've said, I fear for his emotional well-being."

"He actually said that?" Madeline swayed on the chair and leaned back, taking a deep breath to steady herself. "Uncle William..." She wound the cord tightly around her fingers. "Listen, I think you're wonderful to call and tell me about this. But I need to be absolutely sure that you've understood the situation properly. He...Justin really, truly said those things about me?"

"Yes, and more. He feels he was selfish and ruined his marriage, and no other woman could ever make him happy. He feels that even if he doesn't win you back, he still has to make the changes in his life that would cause him to be worthy of you. In fact," William added with a dry chuckle, "he's already beginning. Things are happening here that would amaze you."

"If that's true, he must have...Justin must have changed a very great deal since I was married to him," Madeline said, still feeling dazed. "You know, I can hardly picture any of this."

"I think perhaps Justin has reached a place in his life where he's become more reflective," William said. "You might find it extremely interesting to talk with him, my dear."

"Does he know you're calling me this morning?" Madeline asked.

"Oh, dear no!" the old man said hastily. "Normally I'd be reluctant to involve myself in another's love affair. But I was very moved when Justin told me you were indignant on my behalf. So Mary and I talked it over, and we decided perhaps I should call you."

"Does Aunt Mary know about...Desiree?" Madeline asked shyly.

"Everybody knows," William said. "No more secrets, my dear. Justin won't allow it."

Madeline stared at the window, thinking about Aunt

Mary's gentle, bony face and her fierce commitment to the happiness of this family.

"Well, that's all I have to tell you," William was saying. "We just wanted you to know the truth. Justin is a changed man, Madeline, and he adores you."

"Oh, William..." She began to cry again, tears rolling quietly down her cheeks.

William murmured his goodbyes and hung up. Madeline stared at the dainty white owl, trying to get her whirling thoughts under control.

But she couldn't focus on any of the things in her pretty living room, or the splendor beyond her windows. All she could see was that brilliant light inside her mind, flooding the whole world with a warm glow of wondrous, incredible happiness.

BY THE WEEKEND, Justin's life was regaining some semblance of order. Aimee, the housemaid, came back from her holiday and attacked the dirty kitchen, muttering eloquently under her breath as she worked. Odelle and Woodrow arrived soon afterward, and things began to happen in earnest.

A huge laundry was done, and sheets and pillowcases fluttered on the clothesline behind the house. Food appeared in the fridge again, meals were prepared on time and the hallway tiles were scrubbed until they shone.

But it was still too much work for Odelle to oversee. Justin knew he had to start pondering the necessity of hiring somebody to function as housekeeping supervisor, since none of his daughters seemed interested.

Shelby recovered and went back to work on Friday, looking as competent and cheerful as ever, though Justin sometimes detected a sad, faraway look in her eyes.

On Saturday evening, while Charles was upstairs after dinner, Justin tried to talk to his daughter about the old legal case, the diaries and journals and her dogged search for the truth. But she refused to discuss it.

"Forget it," she said. "There's no problem. Everything's fine."

"But I'm worried about you, honey, and so is your mother. We're afraid you might be stirring up things you don't understand."

"Oh, pooh," Shelby said loftily. "That's all a lot of silliness. Don't trouble your pretty little head about it."

And she was gone with an impertinent grin, whirling out of the house for some kind of date with Joanna, who bloomed with her advancing pregnancy, looking more beautiful all the time.

Charles came downstairs and went with them, planning to be dropped off for a dinner in town with friends. Justin had agreed to drive into Bayou Beltane later in the evening and pick his father up.

He stood on the veranda watching the three of them drive away, then went back inside and wandered around the empty house for a while, looking for something to do. The place was cleaner, but no less bleak and lonely.

At last he found a book in the library and settled to read. But the silence grew more and more oppressive as darkness gathered beyond the windows. All the clocks in the house seemed to tick even more loudly than usual, and those rows of family portraits on the walls stared down at him with the unwinking disapproval that always made him uncomfortable.

At last he got up, tossed the book aside and found his jacket. He went outside and took the dogs for a walk along the path in the woods, then came back, put them in the yard and stared up at the house. It loomed darkly against the night sky, too lonesome to endure. He couldn't stand to go back inside.

Justin stood with his hands resting on the fence, consid-

ering. He had to drive into town and pick Charles up around
ten o'clock, which was—he consulted his watch—about
ninety minutes from now. Restlessly he walked over to the
garage, got into his car and started it up, deciding to go to
town early.

He'd have a coffee at Rick's, maybe find somebody to
talk to. Anything was better than sitting in that empty house
waiting for the long hours and days of his life to pass.

On the way into town he looked at the houses along the
bayou road, all dressed up and decorated for Halloween.
Leering jack-o'-lanterns shone on most of the front porches,
and scarecrows fluttered in the yards, lit by a half moon
that drifted among banks of ragged, silver clouds.

A night to be young in, Justin thought with a stab of
loneliness.

When they were teenagers, he and Madeline used to love
Halloween. She would design costumes for both of them,
outfits so imaginative and artistic that nobody in the county
could recognize them as they slipped from place to place
like bandits, laughing together at the sheer fun of being
young and in love.

Later she did the same thing for the children, but Justin
had been too busy in those days to notice. It was usually
Remy who took his small nieces and nephew out trick-or-
treating, while Madeline stayed home with Charles and
Claire, distributing pralines and popcorn balls from the
foyer of the big house.

So much fun, Justin thought sadly. All the pleasure and
excitement of raising small children, and he'd missed out
on almost everything. What had he been chasing after in
those days? What vital dreams had he been trying so hard
to fulfil?

He couldn't even remember.

A lively crowd was gathered around one of the back
tables at Rick's. Remy and Kendall were there, along with

Jake, Beau and Holly, Drew, and a couple of people Justin didn't recognize.

He pulled out a chair next to Drew and sat down.

"Hey, Justin," Drew muttered over his glass of whiskey. "How's it going?"

Justin looked at his young cousin in concern. He'd always liked Drew, and had the feeling there was probably a fine man in there somewhere if he could ever be removed from his father's influence.

Lately, though, Justin was getting worried. There was an air of sad recklessness about Drew these days, as if he'd given up and was hell-bent on a path of self-destruction.

Justin would have liked to take his cousin aside and talk with him, but Drew was a proud, touchy man, not easy to approach. Besides, they'd never dealt much with personal issues in the Delacroix clan.

Not face-to-face, at least. And certainly not between the two warring sides of the clan…

"How've you been, Drew?" Justin asked, ordering a pint of pale ale.

"Same old, same old," Drew muttered, staring into his whiskey glass. He turned so his face was averted from the rest of the crowd, and concentrated on Justin. "Tell me, did you ever…"

Suddenly Drew fell silent and stared at the door. Justin turned, following his gaze, and saw a tall, attractive young woman standing in the entry. She was slim and erect, with a wide, firm mouth, a springy mass of red hair and a quiet, no-nonsense look about her.

Drew muttered a curse under his breath and set the glass down. "Well," he said, pushing on the table to heave himself upright, "there goes the neighborhood. I'm outta here. See you, Justin."

Justin watched in surprise as Drew headed out the other door, studiously avoiding the new arrival.

"Beau, who's that woman in the doorway?" he asked his son in an undertone.

"Katherine Beaufort. She's new to town. Drew doesn't seem to like her very much."

"Why not?" Justin asked, studying the woman's face as she approached their table and sat next to Kendall. "She seems very attractive. Sort of like a young Katharine Hepburn."

Beau shrugged and gripped his beer mug in his bandaged hands. "Well, you know Drew. He gets these notions and nothing can shake him." He settled back in the chair, smiling at his father. "So how've you been? I heard Mama was in town but we missed her."

Justin's heart began to ache again. He tried to smile. "She felt real bad about that, son." He gestured at the bandages. "And about your accident. She was anxious to see all of you."

"Mama should have told us she was coming. I can't imagine why she didn't. The girls are all sick about not getting to see her."

Justin drained the last of his ale. "I guess her visit was sort of an impulsive thing. She had some business in town, so she just packed up and came, but she had to get back soon."

"I'd love to have seen her," Beau said wistfully. "I think Holly and I should fly out there soon. Maybe we can go skiing before Christmas."

"That would be nice," Justin said neutrally. "I know she'd be happy to have you visit."

"Is she coming back to the bayou anytime soon?" Beau asked.

"No, son." Justin's pain rose and spread, almost choking him. "I really don't think your mother will be back here."

He got up and pushed his chair in, muttered something

to the rest of the group and left the noisy café, conscious of Beau watching him with a worried look.

Outside, Justin got into the car, drummed his fingertips on the steering wheel for a few seconds, then turned almost against his will and headed down the narrow side avenues to the little house on Magnolia Street.

He parked under a street lamp circled by fluttering moths, got out and locked his car, then started walking slowly along the sidewalk, on a cracked surface washed with cool moonlight.

The night was mild, but a breeze tugged at his shoulders, chilling him a little. Justin plunged his hands deep into his jacket pockets and stood outside the tiny house he'd once shared with his young wife, all those years ago.

Nobody was around and the draperies and shutters were pulled tight, blocking out the world. But in Justin's mind, the place swarmed with ghosts.

He could hear the cries and shouts of children, the happy gurgle of baby laughter and the sweetness of Madeline's voice as she sang a French lullaby to one of the twins.

She seemed so close that he could almost feel her slim, silken body in his arms. His beautiful wife nestled close and ran her fingers through his hair, whispering the kind of sweet nonsense that nobody but Madeline had ever said to him.

My knight, she whispered, laughing. *My brave shining knight, out slaying all those fearsome dragons to keep thy loved ones safe. I dub thee Sir Justin, and I adore thee, my noble lord....*

And I adore thee, my lady, Justin whispered in memory, playing the game with her, loving her so much that his boyish heart could hardly contain the emotion. *Thou art the fairest of ten thousand maidens, fairer than the sun!*

Then I give myself to thee, my lord, with all my joy....

She moved away in the moonlight, watching his face

solemnly as she stripped off her silk robe and stood naked before him, so beautiful that his throat went dry and tight with longing.

Madeline, my darling... He reached for her body, lovely and alluring in its slender nakedness.

But she was only a phantom. He stood alone on the silvered pavement surrounded by jack-o'-lanterns and scarecrows, with nothing but a dispassionate moon overhead to witness his misery.

LATE ON SATURDAY afternoon, Madeline arrived in New Orleans and raced through the airport terminal to reach the car rental counter before it closed for the day.

This trip had been an impulse, and none of it was very well planned. In fact, her entire life had been in a strange, chaotic whirl since Wednesday morning when, in the space of an hour, Tate had made his announcement, Madeline had decided to sell the gallery and Uncle William had phoned with his astounding news.

Madeline still hadn't called anyone in Bayou Beltane, not even Justin. All she knew of his feelings was the story Uncle William had told her.

What if the old man was mistaken? Madeline would certainly look like a fool if she acted on the assumption that Justin still cared for her. Because even if he wasn't involved with Claudia, that night in his bedroom might have been a random sexual impulse, or worse, a man's clumsy attempt at kindness toward the aging woman who'd once been his wife....

No, she wanted to come back unannounced to the bayou one more time and see for herself what was going on.

But tonight as she drove across the Twin Span, her heart pounding with excitement, she had a completely different feeling about Louisiana. She didn't have to lie to herself anymore, or pretend that she was a different kind of person now and didn't love the place.

It was so amazingly beautiful. The sunset on the lake, the mellow warmth of the evening air, a sense of peaceful timelessness that was infinitely relaxing...

Madeline sighed and gave herself up to the pleasure of the drive, trying not to think about Justin and the uncertain, awkward encounter that would soon be happening between them.

She checked into the Bayou Inn, greeting the surprised desk clerk with a smile, and was given the same room she'd had before. Coming back to the familiar place was a welcome relief, almost like a homecoming.

Finally, unpacked and alone in the room, Madeline stood in front of the gold-framed mirror and looked at herself gravely.

"What are you doing?" she whispered aloud. "What in God's name are you doing? Get sensible, woman! Remember all your careful plans."

But her eyes shone with excitement, her cheeks were pink and she looked like a lovestruck teenager. Not much visible sign of common sense in that reflection, Madeline thought wryly.

She dressed for dinner, remembering that it was Saturday night again, exactly a week since her first dinner at the hotel.

What would she do if, once again, she encountered Justin by chance in the dining room? Could she be as cool and withdrawn as she'd been the last time? Or would she give in to her impulses, fling herself on him and throw her arms around his neck, kissing him shamelessly?

"Surely not," Madeline murmured severely.

But looking at that glowing face in the mirror, she really wasn't sure.

She dressed in a long skirt of fine ivory wool and a matching tunic, with a copper necklace and earrings, then descended the stairway to the lobby. When she entered the dining room, holding her breath, she was almost light-headed with anticipation.

There was no sign of Justin, however, and no other faces that she knew. Madeline ordered a light meal and forced herself to eat slowly.

Then she went back up to her room, sat on the bed and looked at the telephone. She got up and paced around, pausing to gaze out the window at the massed shrubbery in the courtyard, starred with tiny lights.

Finally she took a deep breath, sat at the desk and dialed the number of the main house at Riverwood.

"Hello," Justin's voice said.

"Justin," she said nervously. "I know you're probably not expecting to hear from me, but I just wanted to ask if we could—"

"We're not here at the moment," Justin interrupted, his voice calm and neutral. "Please leave a message for Shelby, Charles or Justin at the sound of the beep, and we'll get back to you as soon as we can."

Madeline clutched the receiver, feeling both disappointment and relief. She hung up hastily before the beep could sound and began to wander around the room again, sick with restlessness. At last she went to the closet, opened the door and looked inside.

She selected a pair of dark slacks, a black shirt and long belted cardigan, then changed her clothes and went downstairs.

"I'm going out for a walk," she told the young desk clerk, who seemed like an old friend by now. "If anybody should call..."

She hesitated, feeling ridiculous. Who was going to call? Nobody but Tate even knew she was here.

"I'll be back in an hour or so," she said at last, and headed for the door.

The night air was mild and fragrant. On the breeze, a scent of cool lake water mingled with the smoky tang of autumn, and moonlight bathed the quiet streets and yards in silver.

Madeline hesitated for a moment, then wrapped the sweater more tightly around her body, tied the belt and set off at a brisk pace. Without even being fully aware of what she was doing, she found her steps turning toward the older part of town, about a mile from the hotel, where she and Justin had once lived in the little cottage on Magnolia Street.

The neighborhood began to seem more familiar as she walked. Old landmarks sprang up at her one by one, filled with memories.

The broken curb she'd stumbled over when she was pregnant with the twins, cutting her knee. When she got home, Justin had knelt in front of her and kissed the bleeding, bruised skin, then bandaged it with clumsy tenderness.

And the little park where they used to bring the babies on sunny weekend afternoons, leaving them playing on blankets spread on the grass while she and Justin lay next to them, wrapped in each other's arms, making plans for the future.

Tears blurred her eyes and she hesitated.

Maybe this wasn't a good idea, going to look at their first house. The old feelings were already clouding her judgment, making her forget all the years and heartbreak that had intervened, and she needed to have a clear head when she talked with Justin. She couldn't afford this kind of sentiment.

Madeline considered turning and heading back to the hotel, but something made her keep on, walking through streets that were more and more alive with memories of youth and love.

At last she came to the corner of Magnolia, with its faded sign. She looked up at the old lettering for a long time, then started slowly along the sidewalk, remembering each house she passed.

Old Mrs. Cushman had lived here on the corner, and brought fresh-baked corn bread to Madeline after the twins were born because she said it helped a nursing mother to make more milk.

And the Merciers had lived in the next house, a young couple with four children under the age of six. Poor little Clara Mercier had always been so tired, even more exhausted than Madeline was in those days.

A succession of renters had occupied the next two houses, people they'd never really gotten to know. At last she reached the edge of the fence line marking their cottage yard.

Everything looked different and yet, somehow, exactly the same. Madeline could even see the moonlight glittering on the trumpet vine she'd planted so long ago.

Over the years a lot of different people must have cared for that vine, tending and pruning it. For some reason the thought made her deeply sad.

She stood at the edge of a row of honeysuckles and peered around the shrubbery at the house, then stiffened suddenly in alarm.

Just down the street a man lounged at the base of a pole that supported a hanging basket of ferns and flowers. He was also studying the house.

Madeline's clothes were dark and she was in deep shadow. The man hadn't yet seen her, though she was only twenty or thirty feet away from him. The sidewalk, too was dark except for the pools of light around a lamppos at each corner, and the street was deserted.

Madeline felt a stab of fear and an urge to turn and slip off, heading back the way she'd come before the man no ticed her.

But there was a familiar air about him, something tha made her stop and take a closer look. He was tall and broad-shouldered, wearing casual slacks and a leathe jacket, and he was staring at the little cottage with a strange concentrated expression.

A car turned down the avenue behind Madeline and he lifted his head, glancing briefly toward her. She gasped in shock and huddled back into the shadows, covering he mouth with her hand.

The man was Justin.

He continued to look down the street, obviously no aware of her presence, then turned toward the cottage again In the car's headlights, Madeline saw the misery and lone liness on his face, and it broke her heart.

He lifted a hand to brush at his eyes, shoulders quivering under the soft leather of his jacket. Impulsively she came out of the shadows, walked over and slipped her hand into his.

He stared down at her in stunned amazement, his eyes widening.

Madeline felt a lump in her throat and turned away, stil holding his hand, to gaze at the little cottage. "They've painted the house, haven't they?" she said. "It's not as pretty as it used to be."

"Madeline," he whispered. "Where did you come from? Am I dreaming?"

"But the trumpet vine is still there," she added, as if he hadn't spoken. Tears burned in her eyes and began to trickle down her cheeks. "You know, thirty years ago when I planted it, I was thinking about you. I thought I loved you more than any woman ever loved a man in the history of the world."

He gripped her hand and stared down at her, clearly unable to speak.

"I've learned a lot since then," Madeline continued, not looking at him. "I'm not as naive as I used to be, and I know a lot more about love. But I still…"

Her voice caught and she paused for a moment, then turned and faced him.

"I still love you with all my heart," she said. "I've never loved any other man, and I never will."

"Madeline…" His look of shock and amazement was changing to dazed happiness. "Madeline," he breathed, "do you really mean it? What's happened to bring you back?"

"We'll talk about all that later," she murmured, smiling through her tears. "But right now I think you'd better give me a hug, because I'm starting to lose my nerve and feel really silly."

"Oh, my darling."

He gathered her into his arms and held her with infinite tenderness, then bent to kiss her. His lips were warm in the gathering chill of evening, and sweet as honey.

"I love you," he whispered, his voice husky. "Madeline, I love you so much."

She nestled against him, lost in happiness. "I feel like I've come home," she murmured. "As if I've been out wandering around in the cold for years, and now I've come home."

"So do I," he said simply.

They kissed for a long time, then drew apart, smiled at each other and stood together with their arms entwined, looking at the little cottage where they'd first shared their love.

EPILOGUE

MADELINE WAS DREAMING again, one of those misty sun-washed dreams about the children when they were little, playing in the yard at Riverwood. But this time there was no sadness in the dream, just a warm feeling of love and happiness. Justin was there, pushing Shelby on a swing. Squealing, she soared higher and higher, her small legs kicking with delight.

"Mama," she called, "look at me! Look at me, watch me, I'm flying. Mama, are you there? Mama!"

Madeline blinked and opened her eyes. Shelby bent over, touching her shoulder, flanked by Charly and Beau. Marie stood behind them, smiling radiantly.

She sat up and rubbed her back. She'd been sleeping in an ugly green vinyl armchair, covered by Justin's topcoat. She smoothed the gabardine fabric with her fingers, wondering where he was.

Gradually, realization dawned and she stared at her children. "Is it...don't tell me after waiting all those hours, I've slept through everything?" she asked in dismay.

"You were so tired." Charly bent to kiss her mother's cheek. "Daddy told us to let you sleep for a while. It's been less than an hour."

"And Jax...is she all right?"

Distraught, Madeline looked around the hospital waiting room, searching frantically under the chair for her shoes.

"Jax is fine." Marie moved closer, her gentle face alight

with happiness. "Jax is just fine, and Matt's looking after her now. Come with us, Mama."

Her daughters led Madeline into a washroom where she splashed water on her face, freshened her makeup and adjusted her clothes. Then they took her down a long hallway to a room banked with windows.

Still feeling lost in a dream, Madeline stood numbly while a cap, gown and mask were fitted on her. A nurse took her into the nursery where a tall man, similarly attired, sat in a rocking chair with a pink bundle in his arms.

Only when he looked up and his eyes crinkled above the mask did she recognize the man as Justin. Madeline felt a warm flow of love and tenderness, so intense that she swayed on her feet and felt a little dizzy.

"Look, darling," he whispered.

Holding her breath, Madeline moved closer to him and peered down at the soft bundle in his arms.

From her cocoon of blankets, the baby stared back, wide-eyed and thoughtful, though she was less than an hour old. She pursed her lips and brushed at her face with an awkward pink fist, then sneezed.

"Oh, she's so precious," Madeline breathed, pressing against Justin's shoulder, her heart breaking with love as she gazed for the first time at Jax's newborn daughter. "The sweet little darling."

"Mary Madeline Delacroix Taggart," Justin said, getting up and gesturing for Madeline to sit in the chair. "Our first grandchild, sweetheart."

Madeline lifted her arms for Justin to give her the baby. He knelt beside the chair, putting his arms around both of them.

Tears ran down Madeline's cheeks, and he reached tenderly to brush them away. Madeline smiled at him. "I've loved you a great deal in my life, Justin Delacroix," she told her husband softly, "but never more than at this moment."

He kissed her and leaned forward with her to smile at the baby, and Madeline felt that her heart was going to burst with happiness.

"I've come home," she whispered, cuddling and rocking the baby. "At last I've come home."

DELTA JUSTICE

continues with

LEGACY OF SECRETS

by Judith Arnold

Adoptee Katherine Beaufort was a woman with a
mission. Where had she come from? What were
her roots? And why did Philip Delacroix's name
keep appearing in her great aunt's diary?

Available in July

Here's a preview!

DELTA JUSTICE

LEGACY OF SECRETS

"MY ENTIRE LIFE has been built on lies," Drew whispered.

"No. You mustn't think that."

"I believed Aunt Mary was a saint. I believed I could somehow win my father's love. I believed that, no matter that his marriage had failed, he had loved my mother in his own way, and he'd felt some sort of a commitment to his family. I believed I knew who I was—"

"I know who you are," she said, squeezing his hand as if that would make him more willing to accept her words. "You're a strong, brave man. You've been dealt blow after blow, and you're still standing. Nothing can destroy you, Drew. Not your father. Certainly not this." She let go of him and reached for the diary.

Before she could touch it, he caught her hand and closed his fingers tightly around it, as if to protect her from a hazard. For a long moment, he stared at their linked hands, his fingers twining through hers. Then he lifted his gaze to her face. "When I met you, Katherine, I hated you. You were asking all the questions I was too cowardly to ask of myself."

"I can ask them because the answers didn't pose a threat to me," she pointed out.

He moved his thumb gently against her wrist. "I also hated you because..." He inhaled sharply. His eyes no longer looked lost as they searched her face.

"Because why?"

"I wanted you."

Her gaze locked with his. She couldn't have pulled her hand from his if her life depended on it.

"I've always gotten what I wanted—except when it was something that truly mattered. Those were the times I never got what I wanted."

"I want you, too," she heard herself admit. She wasn't sure where her voice came from, why her confession of yearning had now broken free. She couldn't remember having thought the words before she spoke them. They just emerged, the truth she had been seeking all along. It wasn't about her aunt's lineage, it wasn't about an adoption or a murder trial. It was about *this*, her own lineage, the spark of innate passion her mother had endowed to her, her own bloodline burning in her veins. The flare of desire that wasn't right but couldn't be wrong.

His gaze still holding hers, he rose to his feet and pulled her out of her chair. Minutes seemed to stretch into hours, seconds into eternities as he brought his arms around her, as he urged her body against his, as he lowered his mouth to hers. And then time became meaningless. The world stopped spinning. Life and night and Katherine's consciousness condensed into heat, texture, sensation.

He kissed her gently, then fiercely. He caressed her mouth, then took it boldly, filling it with his tongue, thrusting and retreating and thrusting again until she no longer remembered how to breathe and no longer cared.

She was her mother's daughter. Not caring. Obeying her body and ignoring her brain, acting impulsively, wanting something so much she didn't give a damn about the consequences.

The only consequence that worried her was that she'd failed to protect her heart. Somehow, she had let herself fall in love with Drew. And he was definitely not the right man to love.

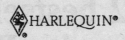

HARLEQUIN®

Not The Same Old Story!

HARLEQUIN PRESENTS®

Exciting, glamorous romance stories that take readers around the world.

Harlequin Romance®

Sparkling, fresh and tender love stories that bring you pure romance.

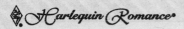
HARLEQUIN® Temptation.

Bold and adventurous—Temptation is strong women, bad boys, great sex!

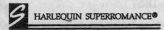
HARLEQUIN SUPERROMANCE®

Provocative and realistic stories that celebrate life and love.

HARLEQUIN® AMERICAN ROMANCE®

Contemporary fairy tales—where anything is possible and where dreams come true.

HARLEQUIN® INTRIGUE®

Heart-stopping, suspenseful adventures that combine the best of romance and mystery.

LOVE & LAUGHTER™

Humorous and romantic stories that capture the lighter side of love.

Take 2 bestselling love stories FREE

Plus get a FREE surprise gift!

Special Limited-Time Offer

Mail to Harlequin Reader Service®

3010 Walden Avenue
P.O. Box 1867
Buffalo, N.Y. 14240-1867

YES! Please send me 2 free Harlequin Intrigue® novels and my free surprise gift. Then send me 4 brand-new novels every month. Bill me at the low price of $3.34 each plus 25¢ delivery and applicable sales tax, if any.* That's the complete price, and a saving of over 10% off the cover prices—quite a bargain! I understand that accepting the books and gift places me under no obligation ever to buy any books. I can always return a shipment and cancel at any time. Even if I never buy another book from Harlequin, the 2 free books and the surprise gift are mine to keep forever.

181 HEN CH7J

Name	(PLEASE PRINT)	
Address	Apt. No.	
City	State	Zip

This offer is limited to one order per household and not valid to present Harlequin Intrigue® subscribers. *Terms and prices are subject to change without notice.
Sales tax applicable in N.Y.

UINT-98   ©1990 Harlequin Enterprises Limited

MEN at WORK

All work and no play? Not these men!

April 1998
KNIGHT SPARKS by Mary Lynn Baxter

Sexy lawman Rance Knight made a career of arresting the bad guys. Somehow, though, he thought policewoman Carly Mitchum was framed. Once they'd uncovered the truth, could Rance let Carly go...or would he make a citizen's arrest?

May 1998
HOODWINKED by Diana Palmer

CEO Jake Edwards donned coveralls and went undercover as a mechanic to find the saboteur in his company. Nothing—or no one—would distract him, not even beautiful secretary Maureen Harris. Jake had to catch the thief—*and* the woman who'd stolen his heart!

June 1998
DEFYING GRAVITY by Rachel Lee

Tim O'Shaughnessy and his business partner, Liz Pennington, had always been close—but never *this* close. As the danger of their assignment escalated, so did their passion. When the job was over, could they ever go back to business as usual?

MEN AT WORK™

Available at your favorite retail outlet!

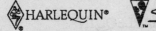 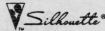

DEBBIE MACOMBER

invites you to the

HEART OF TEXAS

Join Debbie Macomber as she brings you the lives
and loves of the folks in the ranching community
of Promise, Texas.

If you loved Midnight Sons—don't miss
Heart of Texas! A brand-new six-book series
from Debbie Macomber.

Available in February 1998
at your favorite retail store.

Heart of Texas by Debbie Macomber

Lonesome Cowboy	February '98
Texas Two-Step	March '98
Caroline's Child	April '98
Dr. Texas	May '98
Nell's Cowboy	June '98
Lone Star Baby	July '98

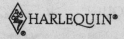

HARLEQUIN®

HPHRT1

Looking For More Romance?

Visit Romance.net

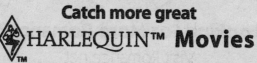

HARLEQUIN ULTIMATE GUIDES™

A series of how-to books for today's woman.

Act now to order some of these extremely helpful guides just for you!

Whatever the situation, Harlequin Ultimate Guides™ has all the answers!

#80507	HOW TO TALK TO A NAKED MAN	$4.99 U.S. ☐ $5.50 CAN. ☐
#80508	I CAN FIX THAT	$5.99 U.S. ☐ $6.99 CAN. ☐
#80510	WHAT YOUR TRAVEL AGENT KNOWS THAT YOU DON'T	$5.99 U.S. ☐ $6.99 CAN. ☐
#80511	RISING TO THE OCCASION More Than Manners: Real Life Etiquette for Today's Woman	$5.99 U.S. ☐ $6.99 CAN. ☐
#80513	WHAT GREAT CHEFS KNOW THAT YOU DON'T	$5.99 U.S. ☐ $6.99 CAN. ☐
#80514	WHAT SAVVY INVESTORS KNOW THAT YOU DON'T	$5.99 U.S. ☐ $6.99 CAN. ☐
#80509	GET WHAT YOU WANT OUT OF LIFE—AND KEEP IT!	$5.99 U.S. ☐ $6.99 CAN. ☐

(quantities may be limited on some titles)

TOTAL AMOUNT	$
POSTAGE & HANDLING	$
($1.00 for one book, 50¢ for each additional)	
APPLICABLE TAXES*	$ _____
TOTAL PAYABLE	$ _____

(check or money order—please do not send cash)

To order, complete this form and send it, along with a check or money order for the total above, payable to Harlequin Ultimate Guides, to: **In the U.S.:** 3010 Walden Avenue, P.O. Box 9047, Buffalo, NY 14269-9047; **In Canada:** P.O. Box 613, Fort Erie, Ontario, L2A 5X3.

Name: _____

Address: _____ City: _____

State/Prov.: _____ Zip/Postal Code: _____

*New York residents remit applicable sales taxes.
Canadian residents remit applicable GST and provincial taxes.

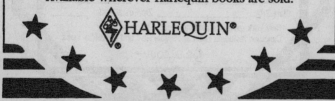